Praise for the novels of
DON CALLANDER . . .

Don't miss any of the ''Mancer'' novels . . .

PYROMANCER
AQUAMANCER
GEOMANCER
AEROMANCER

And don't miss **Marbleheart**

Continuing the adventures of Douglas and Myrn Bright-glade, of Flarman and Augurian, and Marbleheart Sea Otter

D1570342

Ace Books by Don Callander

DRAGON
TEMPEST

DON
CALLANDER

ACE BOOKS, NEW YORK

This book is an Ace original edition,
and has never been previously published.

DRAGON TEMPEST

An Ace Book / published by arrangement with
the author

PRINTING HISTORY
Ace edition / September 1998

The Penguin Putnam Inc. World Wide Web site address is
http://www.penguinputnam.com

Check out the Ace Science Fiction/Fantasy
newsletter, and much more, at Club PPI!

ISBN: 0-441-00555-1

ACE®
Ace Books are published by The Berkley Publishing Group, a member
of Penguin Putnam Inc.,
200 Madison Avenue, New York, NY 10016.
ACE and the "A" design are trademarks
belonging to Charter Communications, Inc.

PRINTED IN THE UNITED STATES OF AMERICA

10   9   8   7   6   5   4   3   2   1

I guess the only fair way to do this book dedication business is to honor my loved ones, one by one. I've already saluted my wife, my three sons, my daughter, and my oldest grandson.

I have a stepdaughter, a stepson-in-law, two daughters-in-law, a stepdaughter-in-law, three stepgranddaughters, two stepgreatgranddaughters, two granddaughters, and a brand-new grandson to go!

It's sort of hard to keep up!

But now it's time to say how much I've appreciated having my brother, Douglas Nash Callander, as friend, advisor, and tireless promoter.

He deserves my love, my thanks, and his very own book!

Don Callander
Orange City, Florida
September, 1997

DRAGON
TEMPEST

✦ 1 ✦
Shopping Trip

RETRUANCE Constable folded his great black, leathery wings against his green-and-gold sides and plunged from the canyon rim, dropping like a stone and snapping his pinions full out at the last possible moment.

Thereby, he avoided a terrible crash into the new-laid tiles of Hidden Lake House's roof.

The Clemsson boys shrieked in terrified delight as the red roof rushed up at them, only to be snatched away a scant moment before disaster. The fifty-foot Dragon jetted a roaring blast of violet fire, did a slow wing-over roll, and skimmed out across the calm surface of Hidden Lake.

Gregor and Thomas leaned far out over the Dragon's scaly brow to wave excitedly at their own reflections in the water, flashing along under the hurtling beast.

"Do it again, *please*!" shouted young Thomas Clemsson, recklessly forsaking his firm hold on Retruance's forward left ear. "Oh, *please*, Uncle Retruance ... dive *again*!"

The Dragon grinned broadly to himself and chuckled five small clouds of hot pink smoke in a neat row before he flapped back toward the brilliant mid-morning sun above the beautiful canyon carved deep into the flanks of the Snow Mountains of western Carolna.

"I think I hear your mama calling, however," he told his passengers regretfully. "See? Down on the upper terrace, there."

Gregor, Clem's nine-year-old, groaned aloud.

"*I* know what she wants. Time for book lessons!"

"Plenty of time to risk your very lives later, then," Retruance assured the boys as he coasted down to land, light as a butterfly, on the edge of the new slate-paved terrace before the Librarian's new house. "Lessons are *almost* as important as death-defying nosedives, I guess."

"Almost!" shouted Thomas, who was seven.

"But not quite!" added his older brother.

Mornie of Broken Land and distant Morningside, maid-in-waiting, best friend, and close companion of Princess Alix Amanda Trusslo-Whitehead, gathered her boys in her arms as they slid from the Dragon's head, smiling her thanks to the vast beast.

"Do you think I could ever be a Dragon Companion someday?" asked Gregor of his mother.

"Yes! I want to be one, too," echoed his young brother.

"You'll have to ask Retruance," Mornie said, shaking her head. "I'm just a regular, normal, everyday sort of mother who doesn't know a thing about Dragon-lore."

"Only if you make yourselves fit for the honor," Retruance said earnestly. "No Dragon wants an uneducated dunce for a partner! Go attack your books for a while like intelligent, brave young gentlemen. I'll find time to take you swimming at the far end of the lake this afternoon— if the weather remains good."

The boys dashed off to their studies.

"You promised, and they'll hold you to it," Mornie warned the Dragon. "You mustn't promise them things you can't be sure you'll deliver, Retruance."

"I promised, and a Dragon's promise is something you can take to the bank, as Tom always says," Retruance told her, nodding his huge head solemnly. "Do you know where he is, by the way? Tom, I mean."

Mornie gestured toward the house.

"In the Great Hall, I think. Manda will be there, too . . . she's compiled a great, long shopping list!"

''Oh, no,'' sighed the green-and-gold beast. ''Lists mean work to be done.''

''There's still a heap of things to do,'' Mornie agreed, unconsciously mimicking her Woodsman husband. ''Lists help keep 'em straight.''

She went after her lively sons to make sure they didn't wreck the improvised schoolroom in the gazebo over-looking the mirror-smooth lake.

Retruance fondly watched her go, then circled the house on foot.

Hidden Lake House had been designed and was being built by the Constable Dragons and Sir Thomas Whitehead, Librarian of Overhall Castle and Sweetwater Towers. Tom was an honest-to-goodness Human from Iowa and the District of Columbia, on Earth . . . wherever *that* might be. He'd been, by way of a strange spell, plopped into the Elfin Kingdom of Carolna, right at a time to do its people the most good.

Tom had been befriended at once by the great green-and-gold Dragon, Retruance Constable. With his new friend he'd driven a band of Mercenary Knights from Overhall Castle, by dint of good old Human common sense when all the spells and magickings of the Elves of Carolna had failed.

ELVES and Humans, Tom had found, were not all that dif-ferent. While he had to admit there was a lot of magic in their world, the Elves tended to rely on it rather too much, to the point where they often were helpless in matters that could be solved much more easily, cheaply, and more sen-sibly by the use of good old Iowa-style common sense.

Actually, Tom realized, his knack for common sense was as strange to the Elves as magic was to him!

The adventure of the retaking of Overhall earned Tom a reputation as a stout fellow and a permanent position on the staff and in the heart of Royal Historian Murdan, Lord of Overhall.

And if that wasn't enough, he'd led a party into the far northwest corner of Carolna to rescue Murdan's daughter from kidnappers, extricated Retruance from the middle of a hollow mountain, and conducted a public relations campaign for Beatrix, the new Queen of Carolna whose political enemies were trying to cast her into disfavor with the King's subjects.

He also rescued the delightful Princess Royal Alix Amanda Trusslo from the King's archenemy, Lord Peter of Gantrell, and wrecked Lord Peter's selfish plot to take the throne, and drove him into exile.

On top of it all, he'd won the heart and the hand of Princess Alix Amanda ... Manda ... and earned from a grateful king and kingdom this vast Achievement on which to build their home.

"Not to mention," reminisced the Dragon to himself as he entered the Great Hall of Manda's and Tom's pleasant, tall-windowed, and warmly welcoming Canyon House, "recovering Manda's baby half-brother Prince Ednol from a wickedly enchanted Dragon ... my *very own papa*! And he helped Murdan defeat the snow-dwelling Rellings when they invaded the Kingdom!"

The Elfin people of Carolna called him "Tom the Rescuer." But Tom preferred his original title: Librarian. He spent much time organizing, cataloging, and preserving important books and historic documents for both Murdan and King Eduard Ten, his wife's father.

"When he found time to build this beautiful house, even *I* can't imagine!" thought Retruance, shaking his head in wonder. "Humans are certainly a remarkable sort!"

The remarkable Human just then was sitting on an overturned packing crate, deep in conversation with his father-in-law, the King of Carolna. Eduard and his wife and twin children were visiting.

"It's in the back of my mind, always," Tom was saying. "It had to be some sort of magic, I guess. And . . ."

"And you fear one day you'll be snatched back to . . . what did you call it? That underground place?"

"The Metro," Tom nodded.

"In Washing . . . Washton . . . ?"

"Washington, the capital of the United States of America. Like Lexor's your capital, here in Carolna, you see."

"Only much bigger and busier, you once told me," the king chuckled, only half believing the story. "Do you *want* to go home?"

Tom leaned against the wall behind them, stroking his chin in thought.

"In some ways . . . perhaps. I guess it's only natural to miss your home of almost thirty years. But, on the other hand . . . no! I want to stay here in Carolna, with Manda and Retruance and you. Especially now! I've never been happier, nor felt as useful, Sir!"

"I . . . I think I understand," murmured Eduard.

"But I still wonder why. Why was I brought here? By whom? Is his purpose finished? It worries me. To think I might be . . . well, sent back. I arrived suddenly. Will I leave the same sudden way?"

"Oh, my boy! There's so much you've done nobody else could have done. You've done so many really important things!"

"Married your elder daughter, for example," said Manda, coming just then into the Great Hall. "What do you do, menfolk? Brag to each other of your past accomplishments?"

She plunked herself down on Tom's crate a trifle awkwardly, due to her thickened condition of pregnancy. "If that's all you two have to do, I'd rather you considered this."

She displayed a long, closely written document that started with: "Brocade coverlets for twelve guest beds, not to exceed four vols' value each, but of the very best workmanship . . ."

"A shopping list!" laughed Tom, giving his wife a quick hug. "That's probably much more important than my worries."

"No doubt about that!" The king laughed in delight. "The answers to your questions, young Tom, will come in time. Some of the best Elvish minds in the country are working on it."

"I appreciate that, sir," murmured the Librarian. "Now, what's on this sixteen-page list, sweetheart?"

"We're ready, you agree, to order furniture?" his Princess-wife began. "I, for one, enjoy roughing it as much as anyone, except maybe Clem, but we *do* need a big, comfortable bed and a few pieces of furniture for our own suite above stairs, not to mention some sturdy bookshelves. Don't you think so, Tom?"

"No argument from me."

He caught sight of the Dragon in the doorway. "Come on in, Retruance! Manda's going to send us shopping."

"Of course I am!" cried Manda, pausing to pat the Dragon fondly on the nose. "Was that screaming I heard a while ago?"

"Just the boys enjoying a flying good time," Retruance replied. "An errand? Where to?"

"Lexor," Manda said, showing him her list. "We need beds and bureaus and wardrobes . . ."

"Wardrobes!" cried Tom. "But I designed this house with walk-in closets! They're the latest thing at home."

"And very, very convenient, husband, but a bedroom looks entirely bare without an impressive wardrobe or two.

New ideas are all very well, but old customs demand certain confections to nostalgia.''

"Yes, they do, and the word is 'concessions,' " replied her husband, grinning at his Dragon and his King. "Go on."

"*Concessions*, then. We'll need a sturdy banquet table, a dozen or two chairs . . ." Manda said, ticking off items from her list. "Four sideboards, three serving boards, twenty silver candelabras . . ."

"Can we afford all this?" Tom wondered, somewhat bemused by the numbers . . . and expense . . . of these bare necessities.

"Easily!" Princess Manda exclaimed. "We haven't even begun to tap our savings, and the wedding gifts were mostly cash. See? I've carefully described each item for you and written the names of the merchants who took my orders last fall. They all promised to have these things ready to ship as soon as the house was ready. Which is just about now!"

Tom and Eduard glanced through her list and added a few husband-type items but, all in all, they decided it was carefully and clearly drawn.

"It would've taken anyone else two years just to think of all this," the King, her father, praised Manda. "You're fortunate to have her as your wife, Tom."

Mornie entered the Great Hall. She bobbed a curtsey, out of long habit, to the King and waved her dustpan at the Dragon, as if it were an everyday thing to find a fifty-foot Dragon in the parlor.

"Mornie, m'love!" Manda said. "I've just given Tom our list. He's not yet given me any trouble about it."

"Nor should he," sniffed Mornie. "I've only one thing to ask for myself, Sir."

"Anything for you, bright sunbeam," said Tom gallantly. "What is it, tell?"

"Go at once . . . and take my poor Clem with you! He's at the loosest of ends, trying much too hard to be helpful with things he doesn't know or care about, poor thing. He needs to get out and stretch his legs."

"I intended to ask him along for help and company, anyway," Tom said, laughing aloud. "I know just how he feels. Building a manor may be work for men . . ."

". . . and Dragons," murmured Retruance quickly.

". . . and Dragons, yes, but making the insides warm and welcoming and sweet-smelling and comfortable is best done by ladies. When do you want us to leave, Manda?"

"Travel with us, of course," said Eduard. "We leave tomorrow morning."

Clematis of Broken Land, Mornie's Woodsman husband, came in, escorting Queen Beatrix and her twin children. Their close family circle was almost complete.

"For all this planning and building, we're careful to keep the beauty and the peace of this wonderful place," Manda was saying. "I've loved it since we stumbled on it while looking for a lost Retruance."

"A terrible trial at the time," the Dragon confided to the seven-year-old twins, "but I can't recall a moment's rest as good since. Will you fly, Majesty, or go on horseback on this journey?"

"Fly, of course!" cried Eduard. "I don't want to take a month to cover the distance home, if I can help it."

"Too long apart from Manda if I were to ride," Tom agreed.

He took Manda's list and folded it carefully, placing it in his jacket pocket.

"I go to Lexor on a shopping spree," he told Clem. "You'll come along?"

"As a free yeoman, sir, I resent being told I *must* do a thing," sniffed the sturdy Woodsman.

"It's not *I* who orders you about, touchy Woodsman,"

cried Tom in mock alarm. "It's your own wife! She says you're driving her to distraction trying to hang curtains and paint window trim."

"Oh? Well, that's different." Clem chuckled. "A wife's orders are exempt from natural law, I guess."

Mornie gave him a hug, saying, "I'll come help you pack. There're a few things I need from Lexor, myself. We're quite out of . . ."

Her voice trailed off as the couple left the Great Hall heading for the stairs to the living quarters.

"I'll be ready to go at dawn, Companion," Retruance promised. "This afternoon I must give certain young woods-imps a swimming lesson."

"I'll join you," Tom decided. "It'll take the place of a bath, which I badly need."

"Let's make it a farewell picnic supper," the Queen suggested. "I haven't had time to swim in the lake, myself."

"Nor I," Manda and her father said as one.

"But should you, now?" her stepmother added, looking worried.

"I'm only five months along, yet. I can still do just about anything I want. Except fly off to Lexor, perhaps. My duty lies here at Hidden Lake Canyon. And my heart of hearts, too, if I'm honest about it."

She had such a happy glow about her these days that Tom bent to kiss her, and she threw her arms eagerly about his neck and kissed him back passionately.

THE green-and-gold Dragon had hardly come to a full stop in the lower courtyard when the heavy door of Overhall's Foretower was thrown wide. A sturdy, rather portly Elf of middle years with a short, sandy beard, dressed in a dark blue tunic, wearing a sort of skullcap of blue and white and clutching a long-stemmed clay pipe, trotted down the steps to greet them.

"*Hoy!* Majesty! Highness! Here's my long-overdue Librarian. Welcome back to Overhall, Woodsman. Retruance, you know to make yourself to home. So good to see you all! How's Manda? The baby's not arrived ahead of time, has he?"

"No, much too early," said Tom, embracing his employer affectionately. Despite the Lord of Overhall's sometimes acid tongue and irascible temper, Tom was extremely fond of him.

The King and Queen and Clem each shook the Historian's hand warmly and reported on their own families as Murdan, hoisting high on his shoulders the little Prince Royal and the Princess, herded them inside, out of the increasing rain.

Except for Retruance, who went steaming off to say hello to his many Overhall friends.

"The next most important question of the day, I guess," said Murdan once he'd seated the twins before brimming mugs of fresh milk, "is whether the Constable Dragons have had any luck finding the foul Plume."

"We've had no word from Arbitrance," Tom replied. "Your Dragon is down in Isthmusi even now, following up on leads, as he calls 'em. Furbetrance and Retruance were in the field until a few weeks ago, of course. Nothing to report."

"Most strange! Those Isthmusians usually know everything going on in their forests and mountains," Murdan muttered unhappily.

Clem nodded. "The Lofters talk to each other with big drums. Some sort of code."

The renegade Plume had once been Murdan's Accountant, but he'd proved to be a spy within the Historian's household in the pay of Lord Peter of Gantrell. When found out, he'd escaped from Overhall's Aftertower and disappeared.

Tom described Manda's shopping list in some detail.

"When you reach Lexor, look up my merchant factor. Named Grindley," Murdan suggested. "Handles all my purchasing and banking there in the east. Good man. Won't take overly much in commission, like some of them effete eastern money-grubbers. Worth every penny he steals, Grindley is."

"I'll need his kind of help," Tom admitted.

"Grindley will see to it the others don't add too much in the way of handling and shipping charges. And speaking of shipping, I presume you won't expect to carry all this cargo, furniture and stuff, home by Dragon."

"No, even with all the Constables together the cargo would be too much to do that," Tom agreed. "Besides, there are better uses for Dragon power. No, I must charter river barges to carry the goods at least as far as Desert Landing. We'll haul it overland from there."

"Desert Landing? That's one I haven't heard of before," Eduard said.

"It's on the north bank of the Cristol, due south of Hidden Lake Canyon, sire," Clem explained. "I built a sturdy dock there, and some warehouses and things. River traffic now stops on its way up and down. A profitable sideline for Tom's Achievement."

The King nodded his approval.

The discussion ranged back and forth until Murdan's housekeeper, Mrs. Grumble, rang the bell calling everyone to dinner in the Hall.

"Just in time!" cried Clem. "My good wife tried to starve us with a mere handful of roast beef sandwiches for lunch . . . and that was eons ago."

Down the River

WHILE the heavily laden barges sailed up the long, narrow Lakeheart Lake three weeks later, Tom and Clem rode ahead by the north shore road. Retruance stayed with the fleet to patrol the route and keep an eye out for problems in transit.

Everything went smoothly with the lakemen's expert handling, and by the end of the fifth week the valuable cargo had arrived at Lakehead and been transferred to a long line of sturdy, ox-drawn wagons for the short leg over the low continental divide to the Head of Navigation on the Cristol River.

"If you ever need steady work," a captain told the Dragon, "I guarantee you gainful employment as Watch-Dragon over our lake shipping. The shock of finding pirates so close to home recently has loosened purse strings among us frugal owners. We're a tightfisted lot, as a rule."

"If you ever need me, I'm at your service for no charge," Retruance promised. "I won't tolerate piracy on Lakeheart or anywhere. Now or ever!"

They had been met by a worried group of barge-owners and river merchants when they'd arrived at the Head of Navigation to supervise the next-to-last transshipment of Manda's purchases.

"There's new banditry," a spokesman told them. "Tolliban, here, lost a cargo just a week a-gone. Crew marooned on a muddy island and his barge stove in proper."

"Pirates on the river, now!" exclaimed Retruance, sending aloft a cloud of angry red smoke.

"How can we help?" Tom asked.

"Young Findles of Aquanelle will lead what we calls a *posse*. He knows the bandits' haunts in the swamps to the south, he says," the riverman told them. "He hopes to track down these filthy robbers. We've agreed to help. We won't have enough left here to guard your barges properly, Sir Thomas, but . . ."

"I understand. Well, Retruance? Will you assist the rivermen and Findles? Clem and I will guard the barges going down to Desert Landing."

"The sight, sound, and . . . er . . . smell of Dragon," put in the riverman eagerly, "would be more than enough to frighten the culprits off our river for good!"

"Two of us should be enough to guard our boats, I reckon," said Clem. "How long is the trip to Desert Landing, can anyone say?"

"Four days, easy sailing with the current," the rivermen's leader told him.

"I'll rejoin you at Desert Landing, then," Retruance promised.

SEVEN long, broad-beamed, flat-bottomed river boats were loaded to scant inches below their scantlings. Clem and Tom stowed their packs in the tiny, stuffy cabin of the lead barge but spread their sleeping bags on its roof. The midsummer weather was hot but clear.

Nights were starlight-bright. The fleet captain declared it safe to continue until well after midnight each night, stopping for a few hours in the darkest hours to rest, feed and water the tow horses, and allow the crewmen and passengers to stretch their legs ashore.

Riverside towns were few, tiny, and sleepy in the heat, although everywhere there were signs of new building and newly cleared farmlands on both riverbanks.

"People down from the north or out from the east," a stationkeeper told Tom at their second night's stop. "The

King's trying to organize a patrolling of the river, too. Here, we're growing like weeds.''

"You find the times fortunate, then?" asked Tom.

"Thanks to you, Librarian, and our good Lord Murdan, who's an enlightened master, active and always willing to listen. People have confidence in you, him, and in Eduard Ten.''

"The reports of piracy don't worry you too much?" Clem wanted to know.

"Worry me? Yes, Woodsman, but we can take care of bandits and brigands. Nip any criminals in the bud, so to speak. A fire-breathing Dragon helps considerable,'' added the stationmaster with a loud laugh.

AT the midpoint of their river voyage the convoy spent the night at a new town called, according to a large new sign painted on the barge station wall, *Whitehead*.

"After a certain famous Dragon Companion,'' the Woodsman called when they saw it. "Fame precedes ye, Librarian.''

"Twit me about it and I'll officially rename Desert Landing 'Clemstown,' '' Tom growled.

But he was secretly pleased by the honor.

"What's wrong with having a town named on ye?" Clem asked. "I think 'Clemstown' sounds just about perfect. Better'n 'Desert Landing,' says I!''

"Done! Tit for tat! If we can have a Whitehead, we must have a Clemstown.''

They inspected Whitehead . . . a large riverside warehouse, a big and bustling tavern still smelling of fresh-sawn lumber, a busy ferry to allow river crossings, and a rambling inn for all travelers with clean stables for the landsmen's mounts.

A very pretty little girl of seven or eight years in a yellow bonnet over a single long auburn braid ran up to Tom and flung her arms about his waist, almost tumbling the Librarian into the river in his surprise.

"Katie! Katie?" her mother called, rushing up to steady Tom and admonish the laughing child. "No way to greet a Knight and a Dragon Companion, girl!"

"Katydid!" cried Tom.

He knelt on the dock to hug and kiss the lively little girl from the southland. Katie and her family were old friends.

"She can see!" he exclaimed to the child's mother.

"Yes! Oh, yes! The physician-magician Lord Murdan sent us quite cured her terrible darkness. She's been catching up with her looking, ever since."

Clem grinned broadly, shook Katie's father Martin warmly by the hand, and bowed gallantly to Phoebe and Katie.

"We come up just to see you, when we heard you was a-coming down river," explained the farmer. "Plus we had a double wagonload of melons and onions to sell."

"We'd've come, anyway," insisted Phoebe, giving her practical husband a wifely poke in the ribs. "You're our benefactor."

Tom blushed and took Katie by the hand as they walked toward the station to get out of the noontime sun.

"Do you like what you're seeing?" he asked the little girl.

"Oh, so very, *very* much!" Katie cried, skipping merrily along the dock in pure delight. "This is the first time ever I've seen a real river. And the beautiful, graceful boats! And the first sight I've had of you, Sir Thomas! You're almost as handsome as Papa!"

"Just call me Tom, please. We'll always be on a first-name basis, you and I," Tom said with joyous tears in his eyes. "Have you ever seen ice cream?"

"No! What is it? I scream? How wonderful it sounds! What is it like, Tom?"

"Like nothing you've ever seen or tasted. I hear they've some for sale, here in Whitehead."

And they went off to discover if the middle-Carolna version of ice cream came at all close to what Tom remembered from the Iowa of his own childhood.

ALL four inhabitants of Desert Landing formed a waving and cheering throng on the brand-new dock as the flatboat fleet approached.

"Hail and hello!" they shouted. "Welcome, Librarian! Make yourself to home, Woodsman! Hooray for our brave liege lord!"

"You know," said Tom, shaking everyone's hand once he was ashore, "I believe this's the very first official welcome to my Achievement I've ever been given."

"We hoped it would be," laughed the young man named Vernal Knox. "Ye'll recall my goodwife? Sally? The man with the red hair is Denton Hammer. His betrothed is Berm Delver, there."

Tom said, remembering, "You and your pretty Sally came from Ramhold, didn't you?"

"Master Talber sends his greetings and wishes you well," said pretty Sally with another breathless bob.

"And you, Denton, came all the way from Sprend?"

"Yes, my liege. I'm a blacksmith's son and a master blacksmith, myself. My girl, here, is from Ffallmar Farm. Curtsey to the Lord Librarian, Berm."

With a nervous giggle the sturdy farm lass spread her skirts wide and bent her knees gracefully.

"I don't require bows and curtseys," cried Tom, delighted with his first freehold tenants. "But a kiss would be quite proper as a greeting."

The ladies complied with laughter and giggles by turn, and the men stood back grinning as broadly as their ruddy cheeks could manage.

"Come in out of the hot sun," cried Sally.

"Yes, we're doing you no favor making you and the bargemen stand around getting even more sunburned," agreed Vern. "This week *I* am Lord Mayor of Desert Landing, so come on to our house. The ladies will prepare lunch for everyone, and there's a shipment just arrived two days ago of excellent Overhall beer, sent down by Lord Murdan's brewer for our clients. Am I right in the word? Clients?"

"Mayor *this* week?" asked Clem.

"We take turns," Vern explained. "Monday next, Dent takes over the job."

"Just as well," coughed the flustered young smith. "I'm no good at makin' speeches."

Clem exclaimed over the sturdy yet graceful construction of the three station buildings that made up the new river port.

"I'm the carpenter, sirs," Vern said. "Lord Murdan sent me to help on your house at Hidden Lake, but I arrived too late to do much there."

"The craftsmanship is splendid!" Clem told him.

"Where did you get the timbers, I wonder?" Tom wanted to know.

"Towed as a raft up from the sea, they was," explained the carpenter-mayor proudly. "Dent and I had to rip the logs to planks and beams by hand, but that let us take special care you wouldn't get from a sawmill crew."

While they enjoyed a hearty lunch of savory fried chicken, potato salad, and cucumbers in vinegar—joined by the seven three-man crews of the flatboats—Tom related their recent adventure, especially the Dragon's pursuit of the river pirates, to everyone's wonder and great relief. The subject reminded Tom of the lady pirates on Lakeheart Lake.

"Lady pirates, by my soul! 'Tis quite unnatural!" sniffed

Mistress Berm. "At Ffallmar Farm we were gently reared to be ladies. Piracy's best left to menfolk."

Everyone laughed long and loud at her words, and the farm girl blushed furiously.

"What would the world be like if all us girls insisted on doing man-things?" she demanded.

"Hungry!" cried one of the bargemen.

"And *lonesome*!" added one of the captains.

Said another, "We're the very first boats unloading cargo here, you say? But didn't I hear there's a new name for this place, Librarian?"

"I almost forgot!"

Tom rapped on the tabletop to still the crowd. "This town is hereby and hereafter to be known as Clemstown. No longer will it be known as Desert Landing."

The boatmen and the four residents of the new town cheered, clapped hands, and called for another round of robust Overhall beer.

"Can he *do* that?" Tom heard Berm whisper to her betrothed. "Change names of places . . . just like that?"

"It's his place," Dent told her, glancing sideways at Tom to be sure he agreed.

"It's to honor a very good, true, and loyal friend," explained the Librarian. "Besides, new maps haven't been drafted yet to show this stretch of the Cristol. It shouldn't bother anyone to change its name."

Sally laughingly soothed her friend Berm, who, she said, was the sort who liked all things unchanging and immutable, things like place names and families.

"But you, yourself, are about to make a name change, Miss Berm," Tom reminded her. "You'll become a wife, shortly."

"Oh, yes, sir, but that sort of change is natural, like the changes of summer to winter or the phases of the moon, so my mother says. Very becoming."

"Becoming . . . but not yet come to pass," sighed the young blacksmith, pulling a wry face. "We can't marry, for there's no magistrate near."

"My fault," Tom apologized. "I overlooked that need entirely! As soon as I can get a commission from the King, Manda and I shall appoint a royal magistrate here. He'll be busy, what with the river traffic and a fast-growing town, property matters, marriages, and maybe occasional law-breakers to try."

"That'll take much too long for me!" wailed Berm, matching her fiancé's long face.

"Not at all," Clem interrupted. "For didn't I hear some-where that a ship's captain may be, under our good King Eduard's laws, empowered to perform such important serv-ices as funerals and weddings?"

"So they are!" cried Tom, who had read it not too long before in one of the great vellum law books in the King's own library. "And here we have not one but *five* captains."

"Oh!" cried Dent, jumping up and catching his be-trothed in his arms. "Can it truly be?"

The five flatboat captains assured him it was all very proper and legal. They drew lots to see who should actually perform the rites, and by dinnertime the bride and groom were ensconced in the cottage their carpenter-mayor had already built for them, but which they had till that moment not occupied, as was only proper.

Mistress Hammer, when she had been Berm of Ffallmar, had been quite firm about observing proper and traditional ways.

As for getting Manda's household furnishings across a hun-dred miles of empty desert to Hidden Lake Canyon, man-power was abundantly available. The flatboat captains had already agreed to lend Tom as many crewmen as he would need.

"The boys are eager to see your new place," one of the captains confided. "In fact, they're saying we captains should be the ones to stay behind with our boats."

"I'll leave that to you, however," decided Tom.

"Willing hands are not the problem, howsoever," Clem pointed out. "How will we tote all this stuff overland to Hidden Lake Canyon? There're no wagons nor pack animals within two hundred miles!"

Tom had thought long and hard about this problem.

"I've a plan," he told Clem. "While the bargemen unload onto the dock . . . very carefully! . . . I believe I can arrange overland transport."

His plan involved going alone into the desert north of the river. Clem insisted he go along.

"Don't care much for dry country," he said stoutly, "but I know enough to treat it with caution due."

"You're on! We'll borrow two of the station's horses, and leave at dawn tomorrow."

"And where will we go?" wondered the Woodsman, who felt something of a fish out of water, there being no woods nor forests anywhere within sight.

"North a ways" was all Tom would tell him.

ANYONE flying over Hiding Land would be excused for thinking of it as featureless and flat. But immediately after leaving Clemstown the next morning, the two riders climbed over a series of low, rocky ridges and, having passed though a low gap, soon lost sight of the river.

"I planned for Retruance to help on this," Tom commented. "He may catch us up yet."

"It's some question if we'll save any time going on without him."

"But if we always fly over this part of my Achievement," Tom reasoned, "we'll never find out what it's really like."

"Hot, dusty, sandy, and very, *very* dry," Clem insisted sourly.

He preferred the oak forests, piney groves, deep blue lakes, and rushing streams of his own Broken Land, far to the north.

"MISTRESS . . . er . . . *Princess*, that is," said the carpenter, shuffling his feet in the grass.

"What word, Master Worthy? Problem with the new lumber? Without my husband, sir, I'm not one to ask about building materials."

Manda grinned up at the gangly young man with saws and hammers and awls and measuring tapes draped about his person.

"No, ma'am. There's someone coming up the valley . . . ah, the . . . ah . . . the canyon, as you calls it. Just within sight, there."

"We'll make him welcome, then," decided Manda, standing and brushing off her apron. She'd been planting young petunia plants in even circles about the front entrance of the new house, alternating red and blue and white. "Anyone you recognize?"

"No, ma'am," replied Worthy. "It'll be some minutes a-fore he gets here. I thought . . . well, you might like to hide, perhaps?"

"Hide? Why so, for goodness sake?" the princess laughed. "But I might like to wash my hands and change my frock. In that you were right, Worthy. I'll do it at once."

She reappeared at the front door of her new home twenty minutes later, just in time to greet a dark, small, rather scruffy-looking individual dressed in dusty tan pantaloons and a faded blue shirt. It surprised Manda that the poor man was barefoot.

"Welcome to Hidden Lake House, traveler," she greeted

him politely. "You're our very first visitor. Come inside and rest in the shade. We'll get you a drink, if you'd like. Thank you for coming!"

The stranger nodded several times but only said softly, "My thanks, Princess. Inside? Yes, well, thank you I'm sure."

Manda led the man into the sitting room opposite the Great Hall, found him a camp chair, and called to Mornie to bring a cool drink for their guest.

"I recognize you from your husband's description," said he, gulping eagerly at the glass. "He told me . . . well, I recognize you, is all I can say. Thank you!"

"My great pleasure, sir. What is your name, may I ask?"

"Ah, well, as to that . . . call me Byron, Your Highness. I bring you a message from your husband, the able Librarian."

"From Tom! Wonderful! A message from Tom and probably Clem, also?" Manda said, calling out to her friend as the Woodsman's wife entered the sitting room with a plate of sugar cookies.

"Ah, well, yes, yes," said the man named Byron.

He opened the top button of his grimy shirt and pulled forth a folded piece of rough yellow paper. He shook it and hit it on the palm of his other hand, dislodging a shower of dry sand.

"I beg your pardon, ma'am," he cried, blushing furiously. "Your clean floor!"

"Has had a lot worse things spilled on it than a little sand since we started building," Manda assured him. "Is the letter from Tom?"

"Er, yes . . . Princess."

He handed Manda the paper and waited as she opened it and read the contents.

"Tom asks us to come down to the river to meet them,"

Manda said excitedly to Mornie. "They've arrived there with the goods from Lexor. The menfolk need help arranging them for transport north."

"Will you . . . *should* you . . . go, however?" Mornie asked, glancing at the letter over her friend's shoulder. "We can leave in the morning."

"It's . . . ah . . . only mid-morning," said Byron softly. "If we were to go, say by Dragon . . . we could . . ."

"Yes, Furbetrance can take us in no time at all and considerably in comfort and safety, too," Manda said with a nod. "Come with me and bring the boys, Mornie. They'll enjoy an outing, also, I'd think."

Mornie went off to pack some clothing and find the Clemsson boys, who were playing at being carpenters, building a cabin on the lakeshore from bits and pieces of scrap lumber.

Manda quickly arranged a lunch, saying they could stop on the way to eat a picnic in the desert. She made the man Byron comfortable in the parlor, after he'd refused the offer of a hot bath and clean clothes.

"No, no, mistress! I'll be fine. Take care of that sort of thing once I get home, you see."

He waited silently and patiently until Manda, Mornie, Gregor, and young Thomas were prepared to travel. The party went out onto the terrace overlooking the lake to wait for their transportation.

Furbetrance Constable arrived in a flurry of powerful wings from the sky above the canyon, snorting pleasant pink and green smoke rings as he came. The stranger cringed and tried to hide behind a line of shrubs.

"Have no fear, Master Byron," cried Gregor heartily. "Uncle Furbie is our good friend and a very fast flyer, too!'

"Well, yes . . . I expected . . . well, it's a-right, now. Startled, I was, you know. One doesn't see a . . . a . . . Dragon that size very often, does one?"

He chuckled nervously and remained jumpy until Furbetrance lowered his huge head and invited the party to board and settle in the saddle between his ears.

"We're off . . . to where?" he snorted jovially, for he was getting bored with the unexciting life in Hidden Lake Canyon, if truth be told.

"Oh, down the canyon," ordered Manda. "And then Master Byron'll tell us which way to go. South, I should imagine. We're to meet Tom and Clem at Desert Landing."

"Sooner the better!" cried the Dragon, and with a tremendous bound he shot into the air, clapping his black wings in a thunderous stroke that sent him into the bright sky over the lake.

"*Oh*, my! Oh, *dear*!" squealed Byron, and he locked both hands to the trailing edge of the Dragon's after lefthand ear.

✦ 3 ✦
Ox Wallow

BY noon the young men had well learned that Hiding Land was no featureless desert. The ground rose sharply on each side as they rode up a series of shallow, dry watercourses. When the fierce sun reached the top of its arc, Clem selected a rocky overhang to one side in which to rest themselves and their horses in the narrow band of shade.

"*Some* shade, at least," he said.

Tom nodded, content to let the experienced outdoorsman call the tune here in the wilderness.

Clem decided against a fire. There was no wood to burn, at any rate. He arranged a saddle blanket on some soft sand for a place to sit and eat cold sliced chicken sandwiches prepared for them by Sally Knox. They drank from their canteens and shared their water with the horses.

"We're used to better pasturing," grumbled Tom's chestnut mare, shaking her head. "I agree with you, furtrapper. Give me woodlands and riverbanks, any day!"

"We can do it, however," Clem's dappled grey gelding hastened to add. "Horses are exceedingly useful in a desert."

"In more ways than just to carry us along swiftly," Tom agreed soothingly. "For example, I've been told you can trust a horse to sniff out water."

"Hadn't thought about that," said the mare, giving the gelding a scornful glance. "In fact, I think one might find water . . . or at least wet sand . . . in the middle of this very draw; over *there*, if one cared to dig a bit for it."

Intrigued by her claim, Clem got a short-handled spade

from his saddlebag and started to dig in the loose, dry gravel in the middle of the riverbed.

"You and Findles claim there's water under this stuff," he said to Tom when he paused to take a breather several minutes later. "But *how far* under?"

"That's one of the things I hope to learn," Tom answered with a grin. "How deep are you already?"

"A couple of feet only," answered the Woodsman. "I'm hitting ever coarser gravel."

After twenty minutes of hard shoveling he was chest-deep in the dry stream bed. Tom stayed in the shade but the horses wandered over to inspect the deepening hole.

"It's getting a bit damp at the bottom, isn't it?" asked the gelding.

"I *told* you I smelled water!" insisted the mare. "Keep digging, Woodsman!"

Tom came to look and, sure enough, the pebbles through which Clem now was delving were darkly wet.

"Hard work in this heat," puffed Clem. "Care to try for a while?"

Tom took the shovel and attacked the hard-packed gravel for several minutes, forming a basin-shaped depression at the bottom of the hole.

"You were right!" cried Clem, who'd retreated to the shade to watch. "There *is* water down under all this dry stuff."

"Not very much." Tom studied the bottom dampness critically. "Maybe a quarter inch."

"It'd serve to keep us alive, if sorely pressed," insisted the chestnut mare. "Let me taste it."

Tom soaked his bandanna in the damp and squeezed a few drops onto the mare's tongue.

She rolled them about for a moment, like a wine connoisseur savoring a new vintage, then swallowed and nodded her head.

"It's water, all right," she announced. "A bit off in taste, however. Minerals, I guess."

Clem came to examine the slowly filling puddle at the bottom of his hole, and cupped his hands to taste it.

"*Phew!*" he gasped, making a wry face. "Tastes worse than seawater!"

"There're a lot of salts and minerals here, near the surface," Tom conceded. "But perhaps if we dug deeper . . ."

"If that's what you want," Clem sighed. "We should've brought more than just one shovel."

"We've at least proved water's not really a problem. It's nice to know we can dig for it, if our canteens go dry."

Clem admitted he felt a bit better about crossing the wasteland. The horses perked up considerably, too.

They waited an hour longer, watching the brackish water filter into the bottom of Clem's hole, and napping in the shade. Finally the sun slid down the sky, widening the strip of shade along the west wall of the dry riverbed.

THERE was no road; not even a trace.

To keep a fairly straight course, Clem used a certain high peak of the Snows on the northern horizon as a guide. Occasionally they were forced by broken ground or deep cross-ravines to detour to one side or the other.

"These little valleys prove that it does rain here on occasion," he muttered. "Maybe once every twenty years!"

"It certainly hasn't rained recently. Not since I've known Hiding Land," Tom agreed. "If there were reliable sources of water on the surface, I think we'd see more greenery. Even a cactus needs *some* water."

They hadn't seen signs of lizards or snakes or even insects in the wasteland, let alone plants.

It came as a surprise when in late afternoon they topped a low ridge and looked down into still another shallow valley, but one in which grew a dozen dusty palm trees around a skimpy plot of coarse grass.

"Oasis!" cried Tom.

"Trees and grass! Water!" snorted the dappled gelding. The horses picked up their lagging pace at the sight.

"Ugh!" said the gelding when they reined in under the palms. "Muddy!"

"Picky, picky!" chided the mare, sniffing the shallow pool under the trees. "You're certainly devoid of any spirit of adventure, old boy!"

The gelding gave her a withering glance but said nothing.

"We'll camp here," Tom told Clem. "A hot dinner would be welcome. It gets pretty chilly at night out here."

"I'll take care of dinner, if dried palm fronds'll make a halfway decent blaze," Clem volunteered.

He began to strip brown fronds drooping from the trees while Tom cleared the scum of greenish-brown algae from the surface of the pond. Underneath, the water was somewhat clearer. He could see a pebbled bottom through which clear water was seeping up from beneath.

"Tastes a lot better than that well you dug," decided the mare after trying it. "And it rises faster, too."

"But not fast enough nor far enough," Clem said to Tom. "Not enough to allow a farmer to plant crops here, as you hoped."

"Don't give up just yet," Tom said cheerfully. "Findles and I figure there's enough water deep under this sand to irrigate thousands and thousands of acres, if we can bring it to the surface."

While Clem fried bacon and made pancakes for their supper, Tom examined the pool and the surrounding oasis. To his disappointment, the trees were not coconut palms.

"Looks like some sort of hoofprints, here," he called to Clem.

The cook put down his frying pan and walked stiffly over to where Tom was pointing at the wet sand.

"Hard to be sure, but yes, I'd say those are hoofprints," he said after a long look.

The mare came to look, sniffed about a bit, and said, "Not horses, however. Oxen, maybe, or some such cloven-hoofed desert beast."

"Of course, if there're any wild beasts in this desert, they'd come to the closest oasis to drink," said Tom. "Don't you agree, Woodsman?"

"No doubt about it. We must keep our eyes open tonight . . . or at least our ears. I wouldn't want to be trampled by a herd of whatever made these tracks. Heavy brutes they must be, to sink that far into the sand."

"They'll probably keep away," Tom said thoughtfully. "They'll be more afraid of us than we could be of them."

"Don't bet on the thinking of wild things," Clem growled. "It'll depend on just how thirsty they be."

CLEM woke to find the moon had risen, a pale crescent that cast a surprising amount of light on the desert floor but left shadows as black as pitch. He sat up quietly, seeing the horses standing facing the pond.

"Visitors," breathed the gelding, catching Clem's eye.

"Wild oxen," the mare confirmed. "Explains the hoof-prints."

The Woodsman squirmed on his stomach to a vantage where he could look across the pond in the middle of the grove.

A dozen great, black forms drank at the shallow pool. Moonlight glinted on heavy, wide-curving horns, and he could hear the beasts snuffling and snorting to each other as they drank.

"Over to the right," the mare whispered, touching his shoulder with her nose. "Something . . ."

In the deepest shadows under the skimpy palms the Woodsman's night-sharp eyes caught a glimpse of a sleek body, crouched low, watching the oxen drink.

"Lion," Clem whispered to Tom, who was beside him now. "I don't think either it or the oxen have spotted us, yet."

"They must have seen or smelled the fire."

"But water is more important to the oxen . . . and the oxen more important to the lion," whispered the mare. "If we leave them alone, they'll leave us alone."

"I *do* hope you're right," quavered the gelding nervously.

"Still, I'd like to . . ." Tom began, then fell silent.

Clem glanced at him, guessing his intention.

"Careful! Let 'em drink their fill first," he cautioned.

"I was thinking more of the lion."

"Even more reason to be careful."

The oxen roiled the muddy water for a quarter of an hour while the travelers and the lion watched silently. The strong, not unpleasant scent of the oxen wafted down a light desert breeze, reminding Tom of the farmyard of the great Gantrell manor house in Overtide, where he'd gone by night to rescue Manda and the Historian.

At last the oxen began to withdraw, carefully avoiding both the lion on one side of the pool, and the men and horses near the low embers of the campfire.

For a long time the lion simply lay, watching the heavy beasts depart into the open desert. At length he rose, sniffed the air, and looked directly at Clem, Tom, and the horses.

"I'm going to enjoy a nice, long drink now," they heard him say in a conversational rumble. "Stay clear!"

"We shall, sir lion," Tom replied in the same tone. "If you'd care to, we'd like to chat for a few moments . . . after you've had your drink."

The lion sniffed, not answering Tom's polite invitation.

His attitude was, clearly, ''First things first . . . and then we'll see!''

''If you don't mind,'' muttered the mare uneasily, ''we'll back off a ways. Cats upset my friend here.''

''Don't wander far,'' Tom told her over his shoulder. ''And move slowly. You know how cats are about a retreating target.''

''I wish you hadn't said 'target,' '' choked the gelding.

The horses slowly ambled to the far side of the campfire and there stood motionless, watching and listening as the crouching lion slaked his thirst.

''WHO are you, then?'' the lion asked suddenly, raising his magnificent head from the pond and turning toward them.

''I am Thomas Librarian, Liege of Hidden Lake Canyon and Hiding Land,'' Tom said boldly.

''Liege?'' yawned the big cat, stretching lazily. ''Yes, I'd heard of your coming. Plan to conquer the desert now, do you?''

''Perhaps,'' Tom answered, rising slowly to a sitting position. ''It's one of the things I wanted to speak with you about.''

The big cat daintily waded through the middle of the pond, shook his feet one at a time to dry them, and ambled up to where the young men sat waiting.

''I'm Thomas of Overhall and Hidden Lake Canyon,'' Tom repeated, less formally. ''This is my friend Clematis Herronsson, a Woodsman of Broken Land.''

''Well! A Woodsman in the desert?'' exclaimed the lion, somewhat sarcastically. ''You're far from home, aren't you, forester?''

''Home is wherever I happen to be,'' Clem replied calmly. ''In the desert, in the mountains, in the tall trees, or beside the river. I've met your kinsmen up north, many times.''

"And hunted them, I suppose?" demanded the great cat, sitting on his haunches perhaps three yards away but keeping well away from the fire, Tom noticed.

"Never! My profession then was furtrapping," Clem explained. "I also hunted the flag-tailed forest deer for meat and leather, and ducks and geese in season. And trapped the furbearers, of course. Now, however, I serve Tom, here, as friend and guide."

"I am called Felis Rex," announced the lion proudly. "Men call me Nightstalker."

"Pleased to meet you, Sir Nightstalker," Tom said. "Come closer. We intend no harm to you or anyone in this place the King has given to me to guard and improve for the good of all."

Nightstalker considered this for a moment, rose and walked carefully to within a yard, and resumed his seat. He regarded the two young men calmly, although they noticed his tail twitched restlessly.

"Well met, then," he said at last. "Tell me why you're here."

"Several reasons," Tom answered at once. "To meet those who live here, for one. To learn the ways and lays of this land. I've a plan to bring underground water to the surface and allow men to plant crops and raise livestock for their use and trade. It'll be my responsibility to make this a safe place for them. In return, they'll grant me a portion of their gain. I'll make my home in Hidden Lake Canyon, so that I may live with my young wife in health and safety and raise my children in peace."

"I'm not sure I like the idea of Men farming our desert," said Nightstalker, implicitly recognizing Tom's claim. "My experience with Men is not the best."

"The Hiders?" Tom guessed.

"That's what they sometimes call themselves. *Vermin*, I call 'em!" snarled the cat.

"I imagine they're not the best of neighbors," Tom agreed. "It's my plan and hope to capture them or drive them away. They're said to be petty criminals and outcasts running from our King's justice. Or maybe to offer some of them a safe place and a new start, here on my Achievement, if they agree to behave and work hard."

"Big plans!" exclaimed the lion, shaking his thick mane vigorously. "Can you do it?"

"It'd be much easier if I had as partner a lion known as Nightstalker," Tom answered softly.

The beast considered these words in silence for so long a time that Clem felt a shiver of fear slide down his spine.

"Nothing to fear, Woodsman," chuckled the cat, as if he could read Clem's thoughts. "We've already determined that we three are fellow travelers in the desert, and perhaps friends."

"Thank you, sir lion," Clem breathed in relief.

He lifted his hand from his belt knife, where it had rested since the lion had approached. "Sorry to seem unfriendly and all."

"Think nothing of it. I've no respect for anyone unwilling to defend himself and his mates," purred the great lion.

He laughed deep in his chest.

"This desert is more than big enough for both farming *and* hunting," Tom argued. "I guarantee my people, when they come, will leave you in peace, if you'll agree to leave them the same."

"Agreed!"

"We'll sit down and discuss details later, when I've solved my other problem," continued the Librarian. "Meanwhile, think of the advantages of settlement to you. Water easily available. Game feeding on new croplands. Such things as that."

"I've already thought of those," admitted Nightstalker. He slumped comfortably to his stomach, resting on his

outstretched forelegs, looking haughty and wise ... and
surprisingly like a tawny housecat.

Like a library entrance statue, Tom thought.

"If you need a recommendation," he said after a pause,
"you should speak to Julia the Jaguar."

"Julia and I are not exactly friends," the lion snorted
gruffly. "Although she and my next-to-last wife were well
acquainted. I heard Julia has accepted your coming and
trusts you and your lady. And I know you are a Dragon
Companion, Thomas of Hidden Lake Canyon. That's the
best recommendation anyone can offer against distrust."

"Thank you, Nightstalker," Tom said sincerely. "And I
know Retruance Constable will also thank you, when he
comes."

"That's settled to my satisfaction," the great cat purred.
"As for the Woodsman, I understand his kind well and will
agree to trust him, also, if you say I should."

"I'll speak for myself," Clem said sharply. "I say I will
be your friend, Nightstalker."

"In that case," the lion decided with a pleased nod,
"you both can call me Rex. More friendly, don't you
think?"

"Exactly, and you must call me Tom ... and him
Clem."

The lion rose and lay down closer to them, now completely at ease.

Tom saw that Clem was now at ease, also. He offered
the beast a bite of breakfast, and the lion accepted gra-
ciously. Clem went to stir up the fire and began grilling
thick slices of Ffallmar Farm smoked ham in his big iron
skillet, allowing the Librarian and the lion to speak together.

"What's this problem you spoke of?" the lion asked at
once

"I've brought five flatboats down the river loaded with

furnishings, materials, and equipment for my Hidden Lake House. A tremendous weight of things, all of which my wife says she must have to make a comfortable home.''

''I understand,'' sighed Rex. ''I've had a few wives of my own.''

''The goods are on the river bank at the new town, Clemstown, south of here.''

''Clemstown, eh? The Woodsman should be flattered.''

''So I am,'' called Clem from the fire, grinning at their new friend.

''I need some muscle, some beasts capable of carrying heavy loads long distances in this desert, to bring our cargo home,'' Tom continued.

''These oxen are a wretchedly dumb and eternally stubborn lot,'' Rex said, considering. ''But they *are* strong and very durable. Tough as tree roots. I think we could persuade them to fetch and carry for you. They're very conservative, politically, which will make it easier for us. They must know by now you're their liege, too.''

Clem called them to break their fast; he began to portion out fried ham steaks and a great mess of scrambled eggs to the lion and the Librarian.

''Delicious!'' exclaimed the beast in some surprise. ''You're an excellent cook, Clem.''

''Plenty of experience,'' Clem told him modestly.

''Now, I can scare up as many of these stupid oxen as you'll need,'' continued Rex after his first three vast mouthfuls of ham and eggs. ''They'll need close watching. Tend to wander off in search of water and grass at all times of the day and night. Stampede at the drop of a pebble.''

''I'll have eight or ten bargemen to help,'' Tom assured him, ''and provide armed guard, in case we attract the attention of those Hiders.''

''The Hiders, yes,'' Rex muttered, licking his chops thoughtfully. ''They could be a problem.''

"How do you mean?" Clem asked.

"They've already noted your arrival," the lion told him. "I saw their scouts skulking about, watching you ride up, last evening."

"Damnation!" swore Clem, who thought he should have noticed. "How many?"

"Two paws . . . er, eight or ten," Rex estimated.

"Will they attack us, do you think?" Tom wanted to know.

"*If* they can be sure they outnumber you and outweapon you, only," replied the cat. "They're a cowardly lot. And sometimes foolish and often cruel. I stay clear of them, not being partial to Elf-meat, myself. They shoot arrows at any poor thing that comes within range. Generally speaking, they're lousy shots."

"What do they find to eat out here?" Clem wondered.

"Anything that moves slowly enough to catch. Tortoises, lizards, harmless snakes. Occasionally lost oxen calves, if they're lucky. Prickly pears and other such awful vegetables, tubers, dates in season. Sometimes they'll go down to the Cristol to catch fish but they greatly fear the river boatmen."

"Well, they're outlaws," Clem pointed out. "They do well to avoid the rivermen, who go heavily armed for fear such men might raid their cargoes."

"I doubt they'd have the courage," snorted the lion. "Bunch of mewling cubs!"

TOM considered the information Rex had given while they cleared the breakfast dishes and poured sand on the fire. The lion snoozed in the shade of one of the palms.

"Rex," called Tom, climbing to his feet. "Clem and I will return to Clemstown. How soon can you bring the oxen there? We'll need at least a hundred, I should think, if we want to bring all the cargo in one caravan."

"A hundred! Well, you'd better give me three days. Once I've got the first bunch—old Greenhide's herd, the ones you saw here last night—on their way, it'll be easier to convince others to follow."

"We'll have dry bedding and fresh river-grass hay for them and, of course, lots of sweet water when they arrive. Anything else?"

"No, not as far as dumb oxen are concerned. How you load them is your problem. I wouldn't know about such things."

"Leave it to the river boatmen," Clem put in. "They're handy with lines and knots."

"I'll snoop about to see what the sniveling Hiders are up to," Rex murmured thoughtfully. "Most likely they won't raid if they see so many people involved. But, just to be sure . . ."

"Farewell, then," said Tom. "Will we see you at Clemstown?"

"Ordinarily I wouldn't come within five miles of any Elf-town, but I've got a cat's curiosity about this new place of yours, Woodsman!"

By the time they'd hoisted themselves into their saddles, the lion was gone, his tawny coat blending perfectly into the shades of the sand.

Silent Canyon

A man on horseback could cover the distance across the desert from Clemstown to Hidden Lake Canyon in three days. A man afoot would expect, if all went well, to arrive after eight.

Fifty well-laden oxen and ten river sailors unaccustomed to driving them, led by a lion, a Librarian, and a Woodsman, took a fortnight.

Their biggest problem, other than keeping the oxen moving in the right direction at a steady pace, was that individual oxen quickly forgot what they were supposed to be doing and slipped unnoticed behind an outcrop or up a side draw, tempted by a clump of grass or a trickle of water.

The boatmen, who considered it all a very great lark, were constantly dashing back and forth, trying to make sure none of the oxen disappeared with valuable cargo when nobody was looking.

Tom tallied the great herd each evening and again each morning before they started out on the trail.

"Five missing!" he cried in dismay. "Manda's crewel draperies! My parquetry for the upstairs hall!"

"I can take a few men and go back for them," Clem offered.

He was getting bored with herding oxen, anyway, and would welcome the challenge.

"No . . . well, yes; maybe," Tom sighed. "We can't afford to lose those oxen, let alone their cargo. I promised Greenhide we'd keep them all together."

"The Hiders are cowards," Rex Nightstalker insisted. He came each morning to breakfast with Tom and Clem.

"Five well-armed and mounted men? They'd not stop running until they got to Mantura Bay!"

"You're assuming the stragglers will be slain?" Tom
asked the lion.

"Of course! Hiders're back there following us, I assure
you. I'd better go along with the Woodsman. Without a
forest to hide under, he might get lost . . . or ambushed."

Clem ignored the lion's teasing. "Hiders are bound to
be petrified of such a fierce beast as you."

"Be careful!" Tom called after them. "We can always
buy more crewel draperies. Friends are harder to replace."

He signaled the petty officer in charge of the party of
land-bound boatmen to start the herd. With much yelping,
shouting of orders, and sharp *whacks* of rope ends on bo-
vine backsides (which, fortunately, the huge, very strong,
and usually placid beasts took as encouraging pats) the
long, wriggly line of Manda's household goods began to
move, slowly but smoothly, as the oxen herd followed
Greenhide's leadership.

THROUGH the long, hot day Tom rode, keeping an eye
turned back for signs of Clem and his crew. It wasn't until
he was wearily counting the milling herd at the evening
stop at a good waterhole that Rex trotted out of the dust
and dusk.

"Ooof," sighed the lion, dropping to his stomach in the
sand. "I've never been so hot, dry, bone-weary, and leg-
sore in my life, Dragon Companion."

"I know! I've decided to stay a full extra day here to let
everybody rest and take a much-needed bath. Tell me what
you've found."

The searchers had found three missing oxen and were
bringing them up as quickly as they could, helped by the
scent of water, which urged the thirsty oxen on.

"There're still two missing?" Tom asked. "I'm sorry,

Rex. You and the rest have done a wonderful job, and I do appreciate it.''

"No offense taken, Librarian. Our Clem decided to bring up the ones we did find. Better three oxen to hand, he said, than five lost among the dunes.''

"Wise decision, if sort of disappointing,'' Tom grumbled. "Ah, well. Manda may have to do without her crewel draperies for a time.''

Rex went to drink before the entire oasis pool was muddied by the thirsty oxen. Greenhide, the patriarch of the oxen, was pleased to hear the train would stay a full day at this oasis, where there was plenty of water, a fair amount of shade, and lots of coarse green grass to crop. He went off to make sure everyone was properly unloaded, had a chance to roll in some dust nearby, and was bedded down, knowing they would welcome the respite.

After sunset the crew gathered to eat supper and complain cheerfully about their aches and pains. Tom doctored scrapes, bumps, and minor cuts suffered on the long day's ride.

"Give me a flatboat in a flood, *any* day!'' complained the Chief Bos'n. "I was born on a farm, you know, but I've never had to chivvy Papa's cattle more than a mile or so, thank goodness! Confirms me good sense to go on the river, I tell you, Sir Tom.''

Clem and his band arrived with the three oxen stragglers. It was a close thing who was dirtier, more tired, and thirstier, the searchers or the animals.

"The other two?'' Clem reported. "Hiders snapped 'em up. We found a place where they butchered and gobbled them entire. All but bones and hoofs. Even took the horns with them.''

"How do they travel? Horseback?'' asked Tom, resigned to losing the oxen and the drapery.

"Little horses. Wild ponies, I think. I've seen their like

on the prairies around Ramhold, at times. Just about strong enough to carry a full-grown man.''

"We're staying here for another day."

"You'll want me to go back?"

"No, stay and rest. Maybe now they've got some meat and some valuable loot, the Hiders'll drop behind. I mean, how many oxen can they eat . . . or drive to a market somewhere? They can't go to Clemstown.''

"Big Denton'd hammer the lot of them, if they did," chuckled Clem. "Any grub left?"

Tom went to tell Greenhide of the deaths of two of his followers.

"Don't fret about it, Librarian," advised the enormous bull ox. "Hiders are always catching up thoughtless stragglers. They brought it on themselves. Should have kept with the herd as they were bid. They'll serve as an instructive example for the others."

"I'm relieved you feel that way, but I'm sorry, anyway. I really must do something to clear this land of these outlaws!''

He was considering calling Retruance to him—Dragon Companions and their mounts shared a wonderful ability to call each other over long distances—when the Dragon solved the problem by gliding silently down into the trail camp.

"*Hoy!*" he called softly, curving his long neck about to study the quiet herd and the sleeping rivermen. "What a mess!''

"You should have seen it before we got organized," Tom chuckled, relieved to see his huge friend. "Good of you not to come booming in spouting fire and steam the way you usually do. Oxen are awful quick to panic at the least excuse. They almost bolted at the sight of a three-foot sand lizard yesterday."

"I'll lay low, then," said Retruance, flattening himself

on the sand beside the fire. "How're things going?"

Tom was explaining about the Hiders when Clem came over to greet Retruance.

Said Tom, "Tell Retruance where you last saw sign of Hiders, will you? I want to go after them riding a fifty-foot, flaming, smoking Dragon. Scare the pants off 'em!"

"No need for you to go," said Retruance, noticing how weary both men were. "Stick around here for a few hours. Leave the thief-chasing to me. I've become an expert."

Forgetting his promise to move quietly, he clapped his leathery wings up, then down, and shot into the night sky.

The herd came as close as ever it would to stampeding off in six different directions, but, with the experience of three days and nights of driving them, the river sailors managed to spring from their blankets, scramble aboard their horses, and turn the frightened oxen back to the oasis.

In an hour or so they were milling about near the waterhole, exchanging wild tales of the terrible menace they had single-handedly averted.

So were the oxen.

By midnight everybody'd forgotten the scare and plumped down to enjoy the cool that came with the desert night.

Tom at last managed to get under his dusty blanket, hungry because he hadn't had time to eat much supper, but feeling more confident than he had since the beginning of the trek, now that Retruance was on hand.

THEY waited for the Dragon to return all the next day. With the rest of the trail crew, Tom bathed, shaved, and ate sitting down for the first time since leaving Clemstown.

The oxen crowded into the shade of wide-spreading, feathery-leafed mimosas, quite content now that they had eaten and drunk their fill. Tom ordered his sailors to sort them out, count them again, and check the condition of their packs.

Retruance had not returned by nightfall.

Tom and Clem discussed whether to stay put for another day or go on without waiting for him.

"We'll move on," decided the Librarian at last. "The water here is turning to bitter-tasting mud, and there's not much grass left. We can't ask the oxen to stay longer."

"Old Retruance can take care of hisself," the Woodsman maintained. "Get some sleep. I'll tell the Bos'n to get 'em going at dawn, shall I?"

Tom slept like a man drugged for the second night in a row, and when he awoke with the first impact of sun's heat, he found Retruance snoozing peacefully under one of the mimosas nearby.

"Next stop, Hidden Lake Canyon," Tom laughed. "Old friend, follow along behind us and keep the stragglers up with the herd, will you?"

"We won't see any more Hiders this trip," Retruance promised him.

"Whatever did you do with them?" Clem asked.

"Oh, rounded 'em up and ran them down to Clemstown . . . great name for a town, by the way! Ten filthy, greasy, bloody brigands, all told. Without weapons or ponies they weren't very hard for Master Vern to handle. The mayor-blacksmith forged them all onto a single, heavy chain. That'll hold 'em for the next boat going up to the Head of Navigation. The Magistrate of Lakehead'll know what to do with 'em."

" 'But ain't there a bunch more Hiders in Hiding Land?" asked Clem.

"So they tell me. Nobody really knows. Thirty times as many as these again, at least. But scattered about, they tell me. It's a big desert."

"Soon as we deliver Manda's dry goods," Tom decided,

"you and I and Clem will go Hider-hunting. I was going
to offer them amnesty and give them work on our irrigation
project in exchange for land to farm. Maybe I'm being too
liberal about this."

"I'm not at all sure what you mean by 'liberal,' " said
Retruance. "But it's still a good idea. The rest will hear
about what happened to my gang and maybe it'll instill
some fear of the Knight of Hidden Lake Canyon into them.
Make it easier to tame their wild spirits."

"Well, we'll see," Tom murmured.

Five more days to go! Tom let himself, for the first time,
anticipate returning to fair Manda and their beautiful, clean,
cool, sweet-smelling new home.

IN the middle of the fifth day after Retruance rejoined them,
Clem led the herd into steep-sided Hidden Lake Canyon.
The high walls leading down from the snow-capped peaks
above channeled a cool wind around the oxen and the
weary sailors. The herd splashed into the shallow, swift
stream at the bottom of the canyon and paused to drink and
comment excitedly upon the lush meadows they could see
ahead.

Clem waved to Tom to ride forward with him.

"Let them drink and eat their fill," he suggested when
Tom came up. "They've earned it."

Tom nodded and, calling to the Bos'n, gave orders for
the oxen to be brought up to the lake in their own good
time.

He and Clem trotted their mounts up the streamside,
pausing only when they reached the lake outflow to allow
the horses to drink while they themselves once more ad-
mired the magnificent view.

The mirrorlike lake reflected the mid-afternoon sky, the
serrated white peaks of the Snows, and the rising roof line
of Hidden Lake House, as well as the blue-green firs, pines,

cedars, and the lighter lakeside aspens and river oaks.

Tom soaked up the beauty and stillness, but suddenly shifted uneasily in his saddle.

"Is everything all right, do y'think? I feel something . . . lacking, Clem."

The Woodsman sniffed the air, peering at the canyon rim above and the lake waters before them.

"Nothing I can see. Maybe you're imagining things? I . . ."

He stared at the new house near the upper end of the lake. He took a brass-bound spyglass he'd acquired long ago from a sailor in Wall and trained it on the building.

"Nobody's working," he reported.

"Well, the work was just about done."

"But I'd thought to see . . . ah, here's someone coming down the terrace to the landing. I don't see Mornie or Manda or the boys, howsoever."

Tom borrowed the glass and inspected his house carefully.

"There's something . . . empty-looking about the place."

"Well, it hasn't got much in the way of furniture," Clem laughed uneasily. "Here we come with the wardrobes and the buffets and the taboret tables and reading lamps and drapes and all. Well, maybe not the drapes. . . ."

"That must be it!" Tom agreed, snapping the glass closed and handing it back to his friend. "Come on! Let's gallop the rest of the way."

STILL, he felt an unreasoned, uneasy foreboding as they crossed the wide new lawn leading up to the front of Hidden Lake House. If there was *something* wrong, however, it didn't show on the faces of the workers who'd seen the riders approaching. They ran to meet them, waving and calling happily.

"Hey, you men! We're home!" Clem called out.

"Where's Manda?" Tom asked, sliding from his saddle. "Is she well?"

Smiles disappeared in stunned shock.

"Isn't she with *you*, Sir Tom?" Worthy, the lanky foreman of the carpenters, asked.

"Why, no! No! Of course not," replied Tom. "What do you mean?"

The master carpenter grabbed his arm.

"Good merciful heavens! Six, seven days back a messenger came bearing a letter from you. The Princess and Lady Mornie and the little boys were to go down to Desert Landing to meet you!"

"I sent no such message!" Tom moaned, his foreboding suddenly becoming heavy dread.

"She was so happy to go! She called the Dragon Furbetrance, at once," Worth wailed in dismay. "She never doubted it was you sending for her."

"Where's the letter?" demanded Clem.

"Manda would have placed it in her letter case in our bedroom," Tom replied. "Let me go see. Maybe I can find it."

As he turned to enter the house, Tom shouted aloud, "Retruance Constable, come to me. Something's happened to Manda!"

From far down the narrow canyon came the boom of Dragon's wings snapped down to launch the great beast into the still air, followed by the startled bawling of ninety-eight oxen and the cries of the rivermen attending them.

Retruance Constable reached Tom's side as he was about to step through the front door of his empty house.

✦ 5 ✦
Kidnapped!

THE Librarian took a deep breath to still his panic, sat on the third step, and began to read.

> *My dearest wife:*
> *We approach Desert Landing and our thoughts are completely with you, so near and yet still two weeks away. Will you come and meet us? It would bring great pleasure to us both, I am sure. This worthy messenger will show you the way.*
>
> *Your loving husband*
> *Tom.*

"Look here," Tom cried when he'd finished reading the note for the third time. "It's close to my handscript. No wonder she went without question!"

"Did you recognize this messenger?" Clem asked the head carpenter. "What did he look like? Had he any sort of accent?"

Worthy shook his head in anguish.

"I hardly saw him. He was pale . . . yellowish . . . small-ish. He didn't talk much, I remember thinking he was almost silent. Polite. *Very* polite!"

"Manda asked her Dragon to fly her?"

"Yes. Furbetrance was about to go fetch his wife and kits from Obsydian Isle," someone remembered. "He was to bring them all here to visit and help move furniture about."

"Which way did they fly, then?" Clem asked.

"Oh . . . well, down the canyon, of course. After that . . .
I don't know."

The bearded carpenter began to sob, unable to hold back
bitter tears. Clem and Tom reassured him as best they could
and sent the gathered workmen off to get tea for everybody.

Tom sat on the stairs and thought, frowning painfully.

"Furbetrance is with her," he said at last. "That's something."

"But she's getting close to her time," said the Woodsman. "Oh, Tom, I'm so sorry! It's my fault! If I'd stayed
here I might've questioned the messenger. But Manda
would be so happy to be going to meet you!"

Tom patted his best friend on the arm and nodded. "It's
not just Manda. There're Mornie and the boys. Manda's
certainly capable, with the Dragon's help, and Mornie's a
cool head, to keep them all from danger."

There were no servants yet at the house, only plumbers,
carpenters, and stone masons building stables, workshops,
and a barn some distance away.

A young carpenter's apprentice came to them, standing uneasily on one foot and then the other. Tom beckoned him
to come near.

"What is it? Fillet, isn't it?"

"I saw the Dragon leave, sir!" said the lad, who was
little older than Clem's Gregor.

"Did you get a good look at the man who brought the
letter to Princess Manda?" Clem asked.

"No! I mean . . . not up so very close. I weren't here
when he came, y'see."

He seemed to be struggling with something. Tom and
Clem waited patiently.

"Y'see . . ." the apprentice began again. "Old man Worthy told us never to go off."

"I understand." Tom tried to sound encouraging.

"You've *got* to tell us, young Fillet!" urged Clem. "Even if you get a licking for it."

"I know! I know! Just hold a bit," yelped the boy. "I'm a-telling you, ain't I?"

"Tell me straight out," Tom said patiently. "I can't say what your master'll do if you've disobeyed him, but I'll urge him not to give you a licking, if that'll help."

"Well, yes, sir, it surely would," the lad admitted, visibly relieved. "See, I went off with the jaguar to the place where the canyon ends and the desert begins."

"The mouth of the canyon, you mean?"

"Yes, Sir Tom, the mouth. Julia showed me a way along the top of the canyon! Along the rim."

"I can't blame you," sighed the Librarian. "I spend spare moments exploring the canyon, myself."

"That's so!" cried Clem. "I've often done just that."

To give the carpenter's helper his due, he stood up and told the truth even though it was obvious he'd strayed far from his work.

"Mistress Julia took me to where I could see the desert. See *all* Hiding Land, it seemed," Fillet said, fighting back tears. "It was b-b-b-beautiful . . . and t-t-t-terrible! She said there was almost no water and no living things to speak of in all that great emptiness!"

"It's so, as I can attest," said Clem, joining Tom on the bottom step. "Go on, lad."

"Well, we were just turning back because it was getting on to lunchtime. We saw Furbetrance Constable come a-flying fast down the canyon, very low. He was carrying Princess Manda and Lady Mornie and her two little boys, and a skinny little man who looked scared to death . . . like he didn't like very much to fly."

"He was scared?" Clem asked in surprise.

"Aye, sir. They came near us, and then the yellow man told the Dragon to turn to the right."

"Ah! To the right. Westward, then?" the Librarian asked.

"Yes, S-S-S-Sir. And my Lady Manda asked him . . . she thought, she said, the Landing was straight south."

"Did you hear what the little yellow man answered?"

"N-n-no, Sir Tom. Too far away by then. But the Dragon turned right and they went that-a-way."

Clem and Tom exchanged stricken looks.

"Certainly don't sound like Plume," Clem said at last. "Unless he disguised himself. But the Accountant's color is more grey than yellow."

"Did Julia hear the words, also?" Tom asked the lad.

"I s'pose . . . we t-t-talked, wondering where Princess Manda was a-going," sobbed young Fillet, giving away to tears at last. "It was all s-s-s-so . . . so very f-f-f-fast! W-w-we didn't even wave or c-c-call out to them. And Mistress Julia was worried we'd miss lunch."

"I'll go have a talk with Julia," Tom decided.

"Now listen to me, young man," he heard Clem say to the carpenter's boy as he left. "With Julia or alone, you know you shouldn't go that far from the house, especially when you've yet work to do!"

"Yes, Woodsman."

"We'll say no more about it, not even to Worthy, but next time I expect you to use better sense. There *are* dangers in the canyon and on the desert, believe me! When you go, you should go with me."

With a face as serious as a ten-year-old could ever show, Fillet promised and, turning on his heels, ran off to join his fellow workmen for tea and worried chatter.

TOM knew at midday he would find the canyon's resident jaguar dozing on her favorite mossy rock beside the lake where she could watch her swirling school of golden fish. He purposely made loud crackling noises in the dried grasses as he approached so as not to startle the shy feline.

"Ah, Tom!" Julia said, raising her head. "Welcome home."

"Thank you, Julia. Met a friend of yours the other day. In fact he's just down at the other end of the lake, right now."

"I *thought* I smelled he-lion," Julia sniffed, a trifle uneasily. "Gross beasts, he-lions."

"Be nice to Felis Rex Nightstalker, however," Tom said, seating himself on her rock. "He's been a great help to us."

"In that case, I'll be the soul of hospitality."

"He won't be staying long. Julia, you took the youngster Fillet to the lower end of the canyon?"

"The lad wanted to see the rest of our canyon and glimpse the desert. Rim Trail is the best way to see it all, easily, for boys with short legs."

"And did you see my wife and her Dragon leaving?"

"We did. Manda, Mornie, the little Clemssons, and a stranger, all aboard Furbetrance."

"The carpenter's apprentice says he heard the man tell Furbie to fly west, rather than south toward Desert Landing. Did you hear that?"

"Quite clearly, Librarian. It surprised me. Why go the long way?"

"And did you hear what Manda replied?"

"She objected. The stranger told her they should not fly over the center of Hiding Land, to avoid the late afternoon heat. I thought it a rather good reason, myself."

"And?"

"She agreed. The Dragon flew as he was bid. Last I saw, he was still flying due west, gaining altitude."

Tom considered her news until he heard Clem calling to him from the lawn above.

"Well and good, old pussycat," he told Julia, stroking

her neck and shoulders until she purred with pleasure. "Forgive the questions, but we fear that Manda and the others may have been kidnapped by the stranger you saw."

"Oh! *No!* Why . . . I was told he came with a message from you, Tom. Most polite, the masons said he was. *Arrrgh!* If I catch him I'll strip his skin from his bones and feed his brains to my fish!"

SHE was still swearing angrily when Tom rejoined Clem and Retruance at the bottom of the lawn.

"Two courses suggest themselves," Clem said.

They were in the Great Hall, eating a hurried lunch which nobody really wanted. "One is hire ourselves a good wizard and get him to trace them magically."

"It'd take way too much time!" objected Retruance, shaking his huge head sadly. "There isn't a decent wizard I know of this side of Lexor!"

"Agreed! And once we found one, it'd take him days to get here and get the spelling right and hours to set it up and make it work."

"We can't wait," growled Tom. "Let's go after this wretched kidnapper ourselves! We know which way he went. And a Dragon is hard to hide, once we get close."

"We might contact the Crossbeaks," Retruance considered. "No, they're away in the east, this time of year."

The Carolna Crossbeak is a unique bird. It migrates east in the spring and west in the fall, as opposed to north and south as other migratory fowl do. The Crossbeaks had helped Tom find Retruance, once, when he'd been trapped inside a hollow mountain.

"But if Manda can be tracked, *you* can do it," Tom said to Clem, confident in his friend's woods-lore. "Perhaps we should head first for Obsydian Isle. There's just a chance Hetabelle's heard or seen or *felt* something of her husband."

"Better to track them by daylight," Clem suggested. "If we leave now, we might miss signs in the dark."

Tom reluctantly agreed, and shortly Clem left to lead the oxen caravan up to the head of the lake so the rivermen could be housed and fed and started on the task of unloading and stowing the cargo before full darkness.

"Manda would so have loved to have been here to see her goods arrive," Tom told Retruance, who'd almost recovered his usual good spirits.

Tom went to his bed and slept hardly at all.

Normally he would expect Princess Alix Amanda to take good care of herself and even to escape or at least ease her own captivity. But the thought of the unborn child worried Tom most of all. He at last fell into an uneasy sleep and dreamed of helplessly watching Manda and their baby flying—without a Dragon—over open water toward towering, black, roiling, thundering, flashing thunderheads.

RETRUANCE was ready to leave long before the sun struck into the deep canyon.

"Fly low. Watch for signs," Clem instructed the Dragon. "Not too fast, or we'll miss something. Recall how Rosemary dropped pieces of her clothing as markers when Freddie of Brevory carried her off to Wall?"

"I wouldn't be surprised if the ladies managed to leave a trail," Retruance said loyally.

"Perhaps . . . once they realized they were captive," Clem snorted.

Tom gave last instructions to his workmen for the stowage of the new furniture and equipment. He arranged for the riverboat Bos'n and eight of his mates to remain at Hidden Lake until he returned, to guard the premises, although he didn't expect there'd be trouble.

"We'll be quite safe," Worth told him gravely. "Go find our good Princess! *That's* what's important, Sir Tom!"

The jaguar's tail was still thrashing angrily.

"Could I come?" she begged. "I've a few things I'd like to do to that foul . . . !"

"No, my dear, please stay here and watch the house and guard the canyon," Tom said. "That would be more a help, believe me."

"Well . . . if you say so, Librarian. I'll do my duty."

RETRUANCE Constable wafted down the winding canyon like a slowly rolling freight train, banking steeply on one wing or the other to round the sharp curves, the wind of his passage stirring up a cloud of yellow sand and brown dust. When he reached the open desert, however, he spread his wings and flew westward in wide-swinging arcs, back and forth, close to the sand.

In this way the searchers covered a wide strip of empty desert.

But they saw no signs of Dragon, ladies, children, nor their mysterious captor.

"It would take them a bit to realize they were being led astray, I s'pose," Clem thought aloud.

"But when Manda *did* realize, she could easily tell Furbetrance to turn back."

"Not if this yellow Elf held them by force or threat," Retruance called up to them. "Furbetrance'd have to do as he was bid, for fear the wretch might harm the ladies . . . or the boys."

"That makes sense . . . and sends cold chills up my backbone!" Clem admitted angrily.

"As they were captured by a ruse," Retruance continued, "most likely they're to be held for ransom or for other demands. In which case, I think they'll be fairly well treated by this stranger. *Hostage* implies a valued person, I'd say."

"I certainly hope you're right!" Tom cried aloud. "Fly faster, now! They left no signs here that we can see."

• • •

By full night, when visibility was lost, they'd reached a part of Hiding Land which benefited from more frequent rains that managed to climb over the rugged coastal hills to fall sparsely at the desert's edge. Retruance chose a sheltered hillside overlooking a tiny rivulet for their first night's camp.

"Maybe we should just push on," Tom worried.

"No, stick to our first and best plan," the Woodsman yawned. " 'Slow and steady wins a long race,' as the tortoise said to the hare."

The truth of old adages was proved once more when they arrived late the next day at the cavern-home of Furbetrance and Hetabelle, his Lady-Dragon wife, and their five quarter-grown kits, four girls and one lively, twelve-foot boy-Dragon.

Hetabelle was shocked by their news but could add little to their information.

"Furbie was to come for us. We were to spend the autumn days at Hidden Lake House at Princess Manda's invitation, as you know."

"I know," said Tom. "You haven't heard a thing from him, since?"

"Not a word nor wisp of steam," Hetabelle assured him, looking very worried and upset.

Tom turned to Clem and Retruance. "If Manda was carried this way, the coast would be the last place she'd have to find a way to leave a sign."

"So, we cast up and down the coast for—what?—forty miles each way?" said Retruance, dandling one of his young nieces on his tail, much to her delight.

"We must send word to Murdan, also, and the King. Could you send one of your kits to Overhall with a message, Hetabelle? They all know the way."

"Of course! The boy'll be proud to go," the Dragon-mother agreed. "But I don't think it'll be necessary."

She pointed back the way they'd come. They saw what she meant at once. A grey-black Dragon skimmed from the east at blazing speed over the long-shore hills bordering Mantura Bay.

"If I'm not mistaken, that's my father-in-law," Hetabelle announced, "and most likely Murdan himself!"

A Serious Note

ARBITRANCE and Murdan made the black glass cavern on Obsydian Isle chime and drone with the tumult of their arrival.

"Ah! *Ha!*" shouted the Historian. "Here you are, my boy! Bad news!"

"Murdan!" Tom rushed forward. "Bad news? Of Manda? Tell it, please!"

The Historian dismounted stiffly, gave his young friend and employee a sorrowful head-shake, a fatherly embrace, and thrust into his hand a piece of the same coarse paper the kidnapper had used to lure Manda into captivity.

Tom read aloud:

To Carolna's King, Historian, & Librarian:
I hold your Daughter, Princess, and wife. I have se-
creted her away in parts unknown. To redeem her,
the Librarian must come to me, unaccompanied by
any other, excepting Lady Mornie's husband. They
must come to Sharp Point south of Mantura Bay at
dawn on the first of July.
  If you love her, Librarian, be there and be
prompt!

                                    Byron Boldface

Tom, not usually given to strong language, swore bitterly. Clem threw his fists in the air and howled like a black wolf in dead winter.

Murdan looked weary and worried.

"What kind of cold, slimy, wicked, midden-trash scoun-

drel would kidnap a mother-to-be?'' bellowed Retruance,
emitting a great jet of white-hot flame that melted a polished volcanic-glass occasional table into a glowing pool
of bubbling slag. "We must go after them at once! I'll toast
this . . . this . . . this cowardly villain to a pile of nasty,
greasy, smelly, grey ash!"

"At once!" cried Tom, turning to climb into Retruance's
saddle. "C'mon, Clem!"

"Wait! Wait! Wait!" shouted Murdan, waving his hands
wildly. "Pause to consider, Librarian! Woodsman!"

"*Nobody* can do this sort of thing to a friend of mine if
I can prevent it!" rumbled Retruance, preparing to launch
himself and his passengers into the evening sky.

"Wait, I *beg* of you!" shouted the Historian, grabbing
for the Dragon's tail-tip. "A moment to think, please, Librarian!"

Tom slid reluctantly to the ground and Clem followed.
Hetabelle placed a calming claw on her brother-in-law's
shoulder.

"We don't know where to go, in the first place," began
Murdan, as steadily as he could manage. "Nor how far, nor
what we'll need to take. Sit and talk for a few moments,
lads! Let us plan. Give some solid thought."

The two young men and the still-fuming Retruance
slumped in Hetabelle's parlor on seagrass mats, looking
dazed, furious, and frightened.

Hetabelle's kits came close to comfort them. The oldest
Constable, Arbitrance, held up a wickedly sharp golden
claw.

"What's this name I heard? Who sent this wretched message?"

"Someone calling himself *Byron Boldface*," answered
Tom, looking at the ransom note again. "Never heard of
him."

"Are there any clues in this note?" Arbitrance continued.

Tom reread the message out loud and shook his head.

"The first thing I note," said the eldest Dragon, "is he addresses himself not just to you, Tom, but to the Royal Historian and the King as well."

"What do you make of that?" Clem asked.

"Why, that his demand concerns the King and his Kingdom, not just you and me, Librarian!" Murdan guessed.

"A political move, then?" wondered Hetabelle, shushing her children, who were chattering wildly in excitement. "He wants something that King Eduard, alone, can deliver. . . ."

"Certainly, I've little to give in the way of wealth and goods," Tom pointed out. "He sees the Kingdom and the King as having the deepest purse to plunder."

"But we would all give everything we have to recover Manda, Mornie, and the boys safely," Murdan muttered. "And the King would, also, I know."

"He expects to make a great deal of money?" Retruance guessed.

"Or gain some sort of political advantage," added Murdan with a nod. "I agree with Hetabelle. This terrible crime may be intended for more than mere monetary gain. This Boldface wants something *only a King* can give."

"What would that be?" Clem wondered.

"Land," Tom ticked on his fingers. "Titles? Privileges? Power? Influence? Immunity from prosecution?"

"One or all of those," agreed Hetabelle. "Or . . . perhaps . . . the power of the Dragon Companions?"

Tom looked up sharply.

"Power of a . . . what do you mean, mistress?"

The lady Dragon shook her head.

"I'm not quite sure. But not only is Manda a Princess of Carolna, she is also both a Dragon Companion, herself, and the wife of one. And there's Murdan, also a Companion. Dragons and their Companions have tremendous powers."

"We can accept that as part, at least, of the nefarious purposes of this Boldface," Murdan agreed.

"The only way to find out," Retruance rumbled softly, "is for Tom to go to him and listen to what he proposes."

"Alone?" cried Murdan.

"I'll go!" Clem insisted. "According to the note . . ."

"You advise that Tom and Clem meet this Boldface person at Sharp Point?" the Lady Dragon asked Murdan. "Tomorrow *is* the first of July, gentlemen. We have to decide quickly."

"We'll go at once," said Tom. "Where's this Sharp Point, Hetabelle?"

"Southeast, across the bay. At the southern edge of Mantura Bay where the shoreline curves back in upon itself. You can just see it from here."

She led them to the entrance of her black glass cavern and pointed out a low, flat promontory twenty miles away over the evening-dark waters of Mantura Bay.

"We'll be there at dawn," Tom decided. He turned to Clem. "What should we take with us?"

Clem and Hetabelle gathered together clothing, rations, and weapons from the Dragon couple's stores, enough to fit in two backpacks, while Tom talked quietly to the two Dragon males and his employer.

"You'll have to go to the King and inform him, sir," Tom said to the Historian. "On Arbitrance you can make it easily in two days."

"I'll do that," Murdan agreed with a quick nod.

"Do you expect me to stay here and wait for your call?" asked Retruance. "I will follow your orders, Tom, even if it kills me."

Tom thought about this for some moments before replying.

"A Dragon your size is *very* hard to hide," he said at last. "You could shrink yourself to the size of a smallish lizard, as I've seen you do once before."

"True. But shrinking has certain . . . disadvantages . . ." Retruance admitted slowly. "Takes a great deal of fire-power."

"That's true," agreed his father, nodding solemnly. "The longer shrunk, the longer it takes to rebuild the fires in the belly. If anything happened while Retruance was small, it'd take hours to regain full blast. Which is why a Dragon seldom shrinks himself, except for very short periods and for very serious purposes."

"I understand." Tom nodded. "Most people know very little of a Dragon's powers."

"That's also true," Retruance agreed. "They know we can fly and spit fire . . ."

"But not how sharp your eyes and ears are! Nor how quiet you can be when you need? Nor how you can merge with your surroundings and appear part of the rocks or the trees . . . or the sea . . . standing very still or moving very fast?"

"You're right," said Murdan, who had much longer experience with Dragons than Tom. "What of it?"

"I propose Retruance stand back at a distance to watch what becomes of us at Sharp Point tomorrow morning, and take such actions as are suggested by what occurs."

"Follow you, you mean?"

"Take us to the point. Return here to Obsidian Isle. Watch what happens at Sharp Point. If we're carried off . . . follow!"

"No problem with that," Retruance said with a nod. "Fly after you if Boldface carries you two off, keeping well out of sight. Even if by some sort of magic? A Constable Dragon should be able to do that, yes. Especially if one of the captives is his own Companion."

"He may just want to make his demands in person," put in Clem, who had finished packing. "Would be handy to have a Dragon watching closely, to see where *he* goes when he departs."

"I agree," said Retruance with a ponderous nod.

"In the meantime," Hetabelle said firmly, "you'll need a good supper and a while to rest. I've started supper, gentlemen. May we address one other question, while it cooks?"

"Of course, my dear," cried Murdan.

"This bothers me," the lady Dragon said, stirring a huge pot on her range with the pointed tip of her pale blue tail. "The note says nothing about my dear husband. Where is Furbetrance?"

"With Manda. I can't believe he'd leave her in such straits," said Retruance. "He's prisoner, also."

"How do you hold a grown Dragon prisoner?" Clem wondered.

"By dire threats to his Companion," replied Hetabelle. "My husband doesn't dare try anything as long as Byron Boldface holds Manda."

"We'll rescue my brother, too, when the time comes," promised Retruance, giving Hetabelle a reassuring bump ... which is the Dragon equivalent of a hug. "Never worry!"

"I'm not the worrying kind. Here, kits. Go wash your claws and snouts and find towels and soap for our guests. Supper's almost ready for the table."

NEITHER Tom nor Clem—nor Murdan nor the Dragons, for that matter—slept much that night. Just as the sky began to lighten in the east over the blue estuary waters, Retruance took Tom and Clem aboard.

"Be off, then," said Murdan gruffly.

"Yes, Sir!" replied Tom.

He tapped Retruance on the forehead with his right heel—the signal to take off.

The Dragon, at Tom's request, flew swiftly and low to allow his passengers to examine the bay with care. Twenty minutes later, Retruance set them down at the flat, rocky tip of Sharp Point.

"Go back, straightaway," Tom advised his mount, "and watch from Furbetrance's cave. If I need you, I'll call. If I call, come fast!"

"No need to tell me that twice," Retruance rumbled nervously. "Take care, Companion and Woodsman. I'll be as close as is safe, no matter what happens, be quite sure."

And he flung himself up and away, skimmed the bay waters for a moment, then climbed into the predawn sky, headed west and north toward Obsydian Isle.

THE sun had just cleared the horizon when they saw a tall, strangely rigged, two-masted ship round a high rocky islet several sea miles offshore and swing toward them, wing-on-wing to the brisk sea breeze.

The vessel moved quickly toward the low cliff on which the friends waited and, when it was close, swung neatly about into the wind, dropped its sails with a great clatter, and coasted to a stop within inches of the stony shore.

"Magic!" muttered Clem softly. "See that? Not a sailor to be seen! Who's sailing her?"

"Can't tell, yet," Tom answered. "Wait and see."

"Why is waiting always so blasted hard?" Clem complained, dropping his hand to the hilt of his favorite hunting knife at his belt.

The ship gently bumped the ledge of rock at the very tip of Sharp Point. It lay easily there, as if waiting.

"I think we're wanted to board," said Tom when nothing further happened.

They walked down the length of the ship's side to an

opening in her rail amidships, where the sturdy rail was folded back to allow them to board.

Clem followed Tom onto a spotlessly clean deck.

The raised section of rail dropped loudly into place, and the ship at once paid off to starboard, furled sails booming and blossoming, trimmed neatly to catch the rising land breeze. She moved quickly away from the shore into the open bay.

No one appeared to work her; no hands came to haul down on halyards or bend clews. Yet she suddenly was under two great triangular sails and a cloud of smaller canvas, heading on a southwest tack.

The morning breeze strengthened with the warming of the land, and the mysterious vessel ran at an angle to it, leaning away from the wind and sending glittering spray over her port counter as she gathered way.

"Hey! Anybody to home?" Clem hailed.

No answer came, except the rising thrum of taut rigging, creak of spars, deep groan of masts, and the hiss of seawater springing up and away as white mist from the junk's cutwater.

Tom and Clem watched their course for a quarter-hour and saw they would pass well to the south of Obsydian Isle, heading into the open Quietness. Still no one came from below to meet them.

"She's on automatic pilot," Tom decided. "Sails herself, I mean."

"And we're alone out here? Not my cup of tea," Clem cried sourly. "I've never been to sea before, Tom!"

"Nor have I, except for a few hours, and that was in a much smaller vessel. Still, despite all, it's rather pleasant, don't you think?"

"I do *not* think!" the landsman snarled.

When it became obvious the mysterious junk was not

taking them anywhere close by but out to sea, the two young men began cautiously exploring.

Tom led the way aft to the helm, a great, many-spoked wheel trimmed with brightly polished brass. When he touched it, then pushed strongly on its polished wooden spindles, the helm refused to budge.

Clem tugged on several halyards pinned to a semicircular fife rail about the base of the mizzenmast.

"No luck," he reported when the heavy iron belaying pins refused to come loose from their holes. "It's like they was glued."

"Well, we really don't know how to sail her, anyway," Tom reminded him.

"Might be handy to be able to disable her, however," Clem argued. "I could try slicing through some of these here ropes . . ."

"Better not," Tom warned. "At least not yet!"

The Woodsman reluctantly sheathed his knife. "If it comes to that, we could always jump over the side."

Clem glanced unhappily over the rail. The prow was pushing up a bow wave that attested to a very good speed. The surrounding water was a deep-sea blue already.

"Here's her name," the Woodsman pointed. "On the side below me."

Tom came over and spelled out the ship's nameplate, which they were viewing upside down.

"*Pelehoehoe?*" he read. "Doesn't tell us much."

"Well, it seems a sturdy-built, well-kept boat," Clem admitted as they moved forward again.

"A ship is a 'she,'" Tom told him with a grin. "And she is a *ship*, not a *boat*."

"As if it made any difference!" sniffed the Woodsman.

"No more difference than calling a stallion a pony, perhaps, or a weasel an ermine. Each profession has its proper lingo."

Just forward of the mizzen (the aftermost and taller of the two masts) they entered a doorway (a *hatch*, Tom insisted) and found themselves in a long, low room comfortably furnished with easy chairs and sofas, a heavy table, glass-fronted bookcases, and nautical prints and charts hung on the walls.

The table was laid for a meal for two, although no food was in sight. In the center of the table, leaning against a silver candlestick, stood a stiff square of the now-familiar brown paper.

"A note from our kidnapper?" Tom wondered.

It was inscribed to him by name in the same spidery script. He read it aloud to his companion.

Make yourselves at home aboard my Pelehoehoe.
Help yourselves to the supplies in the galley, just
forward of where you find this note.

"We're to fix our own grub, then," Clem snorted. "Some hospitality!"

"There's a bit more." Tom read on.

Your voyage will take you twelve days. Everything
for your comfort and safety is provided. Refrain
from attempting to alter course or interfere with the
working of the sails. Have a pleasant trip!
                                    Byron Boldface.

Clem made a sour grimace but went through the forward door and down a short passage into the ship's kitchen— called a *galley,* according to Tom, who'd read a lot about ships when he was younger—where he busied himself fixing hot soup and cold sandwiches from the food, preserved items, and produce he found stored in the ship's food lockers.

Clem's philosophy was, if at all possible, never undertake an adventure on an empty stomach.

AFTER eating the light lunch in the main cabin and cleaning up the dishes, the two went back on deck.

It was a chance for the landsmen to study the action of slatted sails and the bewildering tangle—or so it seemed at first—of lines, halyards, cables, and buntlines with which the sails were raised, lowered, and trimmed, and the heavy yards from which the sails were hung shifted from side to side, properly to catch the wind.

"Clever," said Clem in grudging judgment. "I hadn't known sailing was so carefully worked out."

"In my home-world," Tom told him, "men sailed such ships across uncharted oceans and around the whole globe and back to their homes again."

"Better them than me," Clem sniffed disapprovingly. "How did they find their way, tell me, once out of the sight of land?"

"No great mystery. Sailors use the stars, the sun, and the moon to find their way, just as I've seen you do in a forest or out on the desert."

"But there I'd have the sight of certain landmarks," Clem insisted. "And you know moss only grows on the shady north sides of trees, and the sun always rises out of the east and sets in the west."

"It's the same thing," Tom insisted. "Without the moss, of course."

They launched into a long discussion of celestial navigation, which Tom had read about but had never practiced. Clem found he, himself, knew a great deal, but had never studied it at all closely.

"Right now, you see? We're on a new course," Tom pointed out.

"So we are!" exclaimed the Woodsman. "It . . . she . . .

turned more southward without my hardly even noticing.''

They went down into the main cabin and studied a hand-drawn chart pinned to the forward bulkhead. It showed the coast of Carolna to the right, the broad Quietness in the vast expanse of the middle, and a clutter of islands and the edge of another continent on the very left-hand edge.

"Here dwell Fierce Monsters and Bloody Savages," Tom read along the left margin.

"Oh, great!" Clem snorted, throwing up his hands in dismay. "The mapmaker didn't even know the names of the places."

"Boldface said he'd taken our ladies to 'unknown parts,' didn't he?"

Clem studied the chart more carefully.

"If the fool chartmaker knew only a little of his art, we seem to be heading in this direction."

He drew a finger from Mantura Bay to the west and south.

"No land that way for a long, long space," he muttered.

"These islands on our course have a name, however," Tom pointed out. "You see?"

"Coral Rings," Clem read aloud after studying the ornately inscribed words for a moment. "And further on . . . a larger island named *Eversmoke*."

"Hmmm! And beyond that, a lot more empty sea. Perhaps we're headed for this Eversmoke Island."

"As good a guess as we'll get," Clem decided. "Wonder if there's any fishing tackle aboard! A mess of fish would be tasty for supper . . . and give us something useful to do."

SOMETHING to do became a problem, for the voyage was uneventful for a week.

There were a few books to read, mostly scholarly treatises on astronomy, navigation, and mathematics, or descriptions of travel in strange, foreign lands. Tom never could decide whether these were fantastic or factual, for he and Clem had never heard of any of the lands described. But they made fascinating reading.

They exercised several times each day, trotting around the spotless deck, then climbing each mast, main and mizzenmast, in turn. The view from the mizzen top would have been spectacular if there'd been anything to see other than a perfect circle of ruffled waves and a few fluffy clouds above.

The air became hot and damp, but the constant wind kept them comfortable. They shed most of their clothes, for comfort's sake. It was easier to keep your purchase on the deck and the tarred ratlines, they quickly found, if they went unshod.

They studied the workings of the ship, carefully watching as she adjusted sails, booms, yards, and running rigging to changes in the direction and force of the wind which, by the third day, had swerved from the northeast to puff harder but less regularly from the southeast and then the south, requiring frequent new sail settings to keep *Pelehoehoe* on course.

When the wind swung around to dead southwest, the ship began a long series of sweeping tacks that sent her back and forth across the face of the wind, slowly inching forward on sharply angled courses.

"It's her way of making headway against an opposing wind," Tom explained. "It's called *beating to windward*."

Clem was impressed by the clever, if labored, method to reach an upwind destination.

"It wouldn't work with a sailing canoe," he decided. "This wind'd blow a light boat—Is that right? A canoe is a *boat*?—sideways, no matter how carefully you set your sail."

"But if your sailing canoe had a deep keelboard, the

water, which stays still, would keep her from drifting sideways," Tom explained. "If you noticed, the small boats on Lakeheart Lake had deep keels under their hulls for just that purpose."

"I noticed, but didn't know the reason," Clem had to admit.

"I've read the theory," Tom said ruefully, "but this is my first sight of the practice."

Tom occupied himself with the ship's small library and, with the Woodsman's help, estimated their progress through the water with the ship's log and a minute-glass, following directions in one of the books on navigation.

"We're averaging about ten miles per hour," Tom calculated. "Pretty good! Two hundred and some miles a day, that would be."

Clem shook his head. "The log thing must drift with the current, if there is one here, which could throw your figures off pretty badly. It only *looks* like we're headed due west, just now, but I have this feeling in me gut we're going more to the south than we think."

"It's called deductive reckoning. Commonly known as *dead reckoning*, for short."

"Not very encouraging, that," Clem said sourly.

Tom estimated their daily positions as slowly closing with the thickly clustered islands shown on the chart as Coral Rings.

BEMUSED by *Pelehoehoe*'s weaving course, ten miles behind and twenty feet under the surface, Retruance Constable glided swiftly along with just the tip of his nose, his sharp eyes, and his four ears above water.

Nothing as large as a Dragon was to be found in this part of the ocean. Even thirty-foot white sharks took one quick, uneasy glance at the Dragon's fifty feet of green-and-gold scales, sharp teeth, emerald claws, and strongly sculling tail, and took themselves off to distant parts of the sea.

Curious whales sang out to him from a distance, but stayed well clear out of sensible caution.

A young mako shark foolishly tried to taste Retruance's armored tail and came away with several rows of teeth missing. Retruance hadn't even noticed his nip.

Clouds of brilliantly striped, curious opahs and tetras swarmed under the Dragon's belly during the middle of the hot days. They'd had lunch and were looking for amusement. The flashing scales attracted them first, and in the wide, deep shadow moving under him they found a perfect place to rest out of the merciless equatorial sun.

"I must look a strange sight," the Dragon chuckled, "trailing a banner of fishes in rainbow colors!"

He raised his head out of the water every hour on the half-hour to check the position of *Pelehoehoe*. Occasionally he fell behind, stopping to graze a particularly luscious bed of crisp kelp or snap up a whole clump of tasty clams as an appetizer, shells and all. Food was no problem; he could go on a hundred times longer without any at all, if need be.

Without benefit of charts or knowledge of the ocean hereabout, he was more lost than even Tom and Clem.

But Dragons have one thing as long as their tails . . . patience.

And a curiosity at least as large.

A week out from Mantura Bay, *Pelehoehoe* was rolling along on a starboard tack, all rigging a-thrum in a hot southern breeze. Tom dozed over a book about the distant western land called Hintoo. Clem was lying on his stomach in a shady spot on the poop deck reading the one and only cookbook in the ship's tiny library.

"What in heaven's name is *foo yung*?" the woodsman called out. "Ever hear of it?"

Tom stirred and sat up, rubbing his eyes and yawning.

"*Foo yung*? Sort of omelet, I think. Why?"

"If we had eggs I could make some for supper. If we had some soy sauce, celery, and pine nuts."

"Always liked oriental food, myself," Tom mused. "But it takes some special ingredients, it's true."

As sudden as the blowing out of a candle, the wind died, and within moments the ship slowed to a stop and began wallowing nervously in a dead calm. All about them the waves smoothed themselves into a glassy and somehow ominous stillness.

"Hello!" cried the Librarian, rushing to the rail. "What's this . . . ?"

With a whooshing roar a great, black form surfaced alongside, and shot a spout of foaming brine high in the air.

"What . . . !" repeated Tom.

Pelehoehoe rocked over on her beam ends and quickly rocked the other way, sliding Clem on his bare backside across the deck and into the binnacle before the great wheel.

"*Ooof!* Hot!" he yelped, leaping to his feet. "What . . . ?"

The beast over the side blinked a small eye at them and waved a huge fluke.

"I just thought I'd warn you shipmates," its owner said. "There're waterspouts in the vicinity!"

"Th . . . thanks!" sputtered Tom. "Which way and how soon, master whale?"

The glossy, black-and-white whale rolled over on its back and grinned sardonically—or so Tom thought, viewing it upside-down—at the voyagers, clapping its tremendous flukes with a loud *smack*.

"No more than a mile and a minute," it called back, righting itself again. "If you'll turn your gaze to the south, you'll see 'em coming. Top speed! Can't you swim out of the way?"

Tom rushed to the port rail and yelped at the sight of a towering column of green and whirling water charging down on them. While it was a half mile away, yet, he could hear its rising roar.

Something, Tom thought wildly, *like a freight train.*

"We can't move without wind," he called to the whale. "Save yourself! We'll just have to ride it out. . . ."

And before he could speak further and before Clem could reach his side, the waterspout leapt high in the air and dropped straight down on *Pelehoehoe* with a rising scream.

"Hang on!" Tom shouted to his friend.

He watched in helpless horror as the vast, whirling waterspout descended . . . sure destruction for the beautiful junk!

✦ 7 ✦
Troubled Waters

TOM was barely aware of several things happening at once.

He managed to fling both arms about the taffrail. He saw Clem dive into a flemished coil of line.

And he saw the great bulk of the whale suddenly fling itself high in the air and heard its piercing squeal above the roar of the waterspout.

As the Librarian blinked and gasped in a sudden flood of cold salt water, the whale spun about like a dancer performing a majestic pirouette, flukes widespread, high in the air, directly in the path of the downrushing waterspout.

"No!" he shouted at the whale. "It'll kill you!"

There was a shuddering crash and a deep gurgle.

The whale's port flipper caught the spout just as it was about to crash into the ship's poop, deflecting the column of water to one side.

Even so, another tremendous, terrible rush of foaming water plunged over the ship's stern. Swirls of spray whirled across her waist and shot from the scuppers.

Tom struggled to rise against the push of water across his back. When at last he managed to stand, he ran to where Clem lay tangled in the coiled rope, spitting and gargling to regain his breath.

"Is he a-right?" he heard a voice near his shoulder.

"Yes, just a bit soaked and knocked breathless," Clem answered for himself. "Been doused in a boat more than once, I have. What was it?"

"A great sea spout," replied the voice. "Forerunner of a bad storm, more'n likely, shipmates."

Tom looked up into the starboard eye of the black-and-white whale, who was leaning anxiously over the taffrail staring at them.

"You . . . you . . . swatted it away, did you?"

"Well, it seemed like a good idea at the time," sniffed the cetacean, grinning broadly. "If you aren't hurt and your ship is sound, it was worth the risk, I'd say."

Tom helped Clem from his tangle of rope.

"Washed away the cookbook!" the Woodsman coughed.

"No matter!" Tom told him.

The whale disappeared, to return a moment later clutching the waterlogged book in its mouth.

"Here's your thingie," it said in a voice rather muffled by the book.

"Thank you!" cried Tom. "Thank you for batting that spout on the snout!"

"*Hi!* What are neighbors for? I've been meaning to come by and say hello for some time, but wasn't sure you'd receive it well. Many people are frightened of us Orcae, 'tis sad but true. Can't imagine why. We're gentle as anything."

"Orcae?" said Tom. "I've read of your species. Killer whales, some call you."

"Well . . . we've somehow gotten a bad reputation. Just because we like a little red meat, now and again. We mammalians should stick together," added the whale. "The sea can be dangerous, if you don't mind your course."

"Again, thank you," Tom told the whale. "Is there anything we can do for you in return?"

"No, no . . . but thanks! Are you western Elves, who teach that a good deed *must* be repaid *at once* and *at all costs*? I've heard of such nonsense. I did it because . . . well, it needed doing, and that's the truth of the matter," explained the vast animal, one of the few living things Tom had ever seen almost as large as a full-grown Dragon. "You'll be safe now for a time, I think. You don't see more than three or four such spouts in a single day.''

Clem coughed but said, ''I add my gratitude, Orca.''

''You're quite welcome! Well, if you can manage, now, I must be on my way. I've a class to teach. The pod's large and lively, this year. I'm the instructor in deep sea diving.''

The vast beast waved his right fluke in a jaunty salute and sank into the calm water. They could see him swimming strongly downward at a steep angle.

''Nice guy,'' said Clem, waving after the whale. ''And came by just in time. We'd've been swamped, it being so unexpected.''

Tom nodded.

''There are a lot of things other than just winds and waves to watch out for at sea, I guess,'' Clem went on, beginning to blot his cookbook dry, page by page.

''We should keep a closer eye out in the future,'' murmured the subdued Librarian. ''That was a close thing, Woodsman!''

''Might as well take a bath. I'm wet anyway,'' Clem decided.

''Yes . . . a good idea,'' murmured Tom. ''I'll get the saltwater soap.''

TWENTY miles astern of *Pelehoehoe*, Retruance Constable missed the whole sudden crisis because he was sculling along easily, humming to himself, watching a flock of frigate birds racing northward.

THE Librarian sat up in the dark in the middle of the night, remembering at the last moment not to rap his head on the overhead.

''What's that noise?'' he wondered aloud.

''I heard it also,'' Clem said from the upper bunk. ''Something . . . like cracking knuckles, isn't it?''

Tom padded barefoot up onto the afterdeck. The night

was cloudless, and the sky filled with brilliant stars. The air was warm and still. *Pelehoehoe* rolled only slightly, becalmed since the appearance of the waterspout.

Clem came to stand beside him at the rail near the helm. The friends searched the dark ocean as the *click-snap* sound continued, even increased severalfold.

"Hello! Ahoy!" shouted Tom.

The clicking stopped abruptly but, after a few seconds, began again.

"In the water over the side," whispered Clem, leaning out over the rail and turning his head back and forth, trying to locate the source of the noise.

"We need a light," decided the Librarian.

He went below and returned with a lantern from the salon. By its gleam the two stared at the water below.

"Good heavens!" hissed the Woodsman. "Crab soup."

As far as the lantern's light reached in the gloom, the still water was filled with wriggling, darting, twisting, sidling green-grey forms . . . thousands upon thousands of crabs. The sound was their wicked-looking, upraised claws, snapping and rattling together.

"Move! Go! *Skedaddle! Get away!*" the crabs began to chant loudly. "*Flee! Depart!*"

The crabs closest to the hull began to bang their claws and scrape their tails on the scantling, raising a terrible racket. Further out, the crustaceans unable to pound on *Pelehoehoe*'s hull began to chant even louder, banging their pinchers together in unison.

"*Hey!*" Tom shouted, to no avail.

"No harm, I guess," Clem said after lowering the lantern closer to the water to examine the noisy swimmers. "Not a particularly pretty sight, however. Wonder what's eating them?"

"*I* might," rumbled a voice from the darkness beyond the lantern's glow.

"Retruance!" cried the young men together.

"A rather hungry Retruance Constable, Dragon of Carolna, say rather," came the Dragon's deepest voice. "Crab
salad! A delicacy."

A single huge crab, easily six feet across from claw-tip
to claw-tip, heaved himself up into the circle of lantern light
beside the hull.

"We'll fight to the death for our home waters!" he
shouted, snapping his huge claws viciously. "You'll not
make salad of *my* people easily, I promise you, foul lizard!"

"Lizard!" snorted Retruance, half in anger but half
amused, too. "We'll see about that."

"Nip him! Bite him! *Grind him up!*" chorused the crabs.
"Drive him away or chop him into bite-sized pieces. *Gob-
ble him down!*"

"Here! *Hey!*" shouted Tom over the rising clamor.
"Who's in charge, there? Listen to me!"

His voice was almost drowned by the din, but after he'd
repeated his shouts louder and over again, using his hands
as a megaphone, the angry clamor subsided.

"We demand you scuttle away!" called the large crab,
staring up balefully at the two men at the rail. "We might
sacrifice hundreds, but our thousands will destroy you, in
the end."

"What purpose?" Tom answered. "What are we doing
that's stirred you up, I'd like to know? Why are you in
such a stew?"

"Bad choice of words, I suspect," shouted Clem over
the uproar that followed.

"I'll . . . *ouch!*" cried Retruance, now just visible at the
edge of the lantern's meager light. "We'll see who can
crunch and munch the best—a Dragon or a bunch of ill-
tempered shellbacks! *Ouch!*"

"Stop this nonsense *at once!*" Tom roared. "We're do-

ing nobody any harm. Yet. We're becalmed and cannot
move if we wanted to . . . and believe me, we *do* want to
move!''

His words quieted the multitude of crabs, who milled
about in a thick-packed throng, muttering and waving their
claws menacingly.

The biggest crab disdainfully spat a stream of water on
the hull.

''A likely tale!'' he sneered. ''We demand . . .''

''We'd move quickly enough if we could,'' Tom explained. ''But it isn't all that easy.''

''*Hah!* You came to raid our nursery. I know your kind!
We're protecting our young. Death before dishonor, say we
all!''

At his words the crabs raised a loud shout and rattled
claws even more loudly than before.

Tom shouted over the tumult. ''Now wait just a darn
minute! We didn't know about your nursery, and we don't
want to cause trouble, but we're *becalmed.* Don't you know
what that means?''

''Crabs don't know the meaning of calm,'' one of the
lesser crabs shouted.

''If we *could* move off, we certainly *would,* at once,''
Tom insisted. ''But we need a wind!''

The biggest crab regarded Tom and Clem imperiously
for a long moment.

''Why do I feel you're telling the truth?'' he wondered.
''It's not our experience that intruders come for anything
other than a good crab feast. We're only protecting our
progeny.''

''I know, and you're prepared to die in the attempt,''
rumbled Retruance from the darkness.

''True words, sea monster,'' cried the biggest crab.

''Then give us time and a little room and we'll move
off, away from your nursery,'' Tom insisted. ''As soon as

a wind comes along, we'll be off and away.''

"Some of my bully boys are ready to climb your sides, high as they are, and they'll make quick and painful work of you soft-shelled types, once they reach your deck,'' the biggest crab threatened. "We demand . . .''

"It does little good demanding the impossible,'' Tom reasoned. "We need wind or current . . .''

"Or a hungry Dragon who loves seafood,'' chimed in Retruance.

"Look, friends . . .'' Tom began.

"Not friends!'' yelled a number of the crabs.

"Well, if not exactly friends, honest opponents, then,'' the Librarian amended. "Look, you crabs, let the Dragon come closer and we'll have him drag us away. Let him through! We'll move off at once, as soon as he comes close enough to catch a cable.''

The crabs consulted in low clicks, nasty cracks, and soft mutters for a time. Some of them wanted to climb the side and attack the men on deck. Others advised caution and staying well out of reach of men and a hungry Dragon.

At last the biggest crab waved his heavy right claw over his head and the rustle of discussion died away.

"We'll take you at your word, drylanders,'' he snapped. "The Dragon may come up to you and accept a towline. He's to draw you off at least a nautical mile. One false move, mind you, and I'll send up the shock troops to nip and snip you 'til you die!''

"Agreed,'' Tom said quickly, nodding his head. "Retruance?''

"I'm coming, Dragon Companion,'' came the beast's low voice. "Have a strong hawser ready to pass over the bow. Stand off, you ill-mannered little snips! Or I promise you'll see a Constable's terrible, hot anger . . . as broiled seafood snacks.''

From the deck the young men watched the solid layer of

crabs begin to draw apart, making a clear lane through which Retruance approached the bow, slowly, carefully, his head swiveling from side to side.

"The hawser, then," Tom said to Clem.

The Woodsman had already selected a thick cable from the tier, and he now made sure it was lashed securely to the base of the mainmast. With Tom's help he passed the cable over the side well forward, dangling its end just over the dark water.

"Got it," Retruance called in a moment. "Clear 'way, you delicious-looking crabs. I'm about to move the ship to the west. 'Way! 'Way!"

The crabs, tiny and large, scurried further sideways, clearing the way for *Pelehoehoe* to move slowly forward as the Dragon took up the slack and began to swim strongly away, the tow clamped in his mouth.

"Well, so long, then, crabs," Tom called. "We leave you as we came. In peace."

"Better than in pieces," someone in the water called.

"It'll be light in an hour, Companion," Tom called to Retruance. "Better not be seen with us by then, in case Boldface is watching."

"Understood," grunted Retruance, his voice muffled by a mouthful of hawser. "She's moving along quite well, now. *Oof!* She weighs a ton!"

"More than one ton, I'm sure," laughed Clem, as much in relief as in triumph. "Haul away, old Constable! Goodness knows how soon we'll get a wind."

THE sky in the east was beginning to show color and light when the Dragon spit out the cable end and allowed the ship to glide smoothly by as he lay still, resting in the water.

"Great job!" Tom called out to him. "Thank you once again, bold Companion."

"Flatterer," Retruance snorted. "I'll be behind you

some miles, as before. You should get a wind shortly. I see ruffled waters, off to the north a ways.''

The voyagers waved and, as *Pelehoehoe* slowly lost way and became becalmed once more, they agreed there was nothing more they could or should do, and retired to their bunks to sleep until the arrival of the promised breeze.

''WERE the crabs an accident?'' Clem wondered after the breakfast dishes had been washed, dried, and stacked in the cupboard. ''Not to mention the waterspout.''

A warm and yet cooling breeze had just sprung up, taking *Pelehoehoe* in charge. She was once more quartering the wind and heading southwestward, humming cheerfully to herself.

''Crabs? We blundered over their nursery beds. An accident.''

''And the waterspout, too? Orca admitted they were common at this time of year. Could this here Boldface've raised them against us?''

''Why in the world should he? He wanted us to come to him. Why should he make it difficult? You'd think he'd do everything he could to hasten us along. Besides, that waterspout could easily have sunk his beautiful junk!''

''Well, maybe. I've known some folks regularly contradict themselves. Like Mornie, some times. Be nice as pie one minute and snappy as a she-turtle the next.''

''Hard to figure women at times, I admit. But . . . well, I think this Boldface would rather hurry our voyage than delay it.''

''So you think these happenings're just . . . bad luck?''

''I see no reason to doubt it. Might as well blame our adventures on someone we *know* has a serious grudge against us.''

''You mean Plume, I suppose.''

"Why not? More likely Plume than Boldface. Perhaps time will tell."

He pushed the idle speculation behind him, changing the subject.

"I've read every book in the library below. How about some rummy? I noticed a pack of cards in the cabin."

"Cards? Well, you'll have to teach me. Never learned to play cards. Mama frowned on such idle wickedness."

"A good way to pass time, however," Tom insisted. "And only as wicked as the players are, I say."

"Rummy, then. Anything to pass the time," the Woodsman conceded. "I wish we'd caught some of them crabs. Retruance says they're delicious with melted butter. If we had any butter."

✦ 8 ✦
Stormy Weather

"THERE'S a funny color to the sky," Clem remarked. "*Gin!* That puts me over a hundred. Game and rubber!"

They were sitting on the main deck in the wide shade of the mainsail after breakfast. It was the thirteenth morning out from Mantura Bay.

Tom gathered the deck of cards to put them away.

He blinked. "How funny?"

"Sort of coppery-green, y'see. I've never seen sky that color before."

Pelehoehoe was wallowing in long, smooth swells, with the merest breath of wind astir to keep her moving on course toward the southwest in a totally empty circle of horizon.

"According to the *Seaman's and Navigator's Manual*," Tom said, pushing the cards aside and drawing the tattered, stained old book closer, " 'yellow sky of a morning be a fearful storm warning' . . . as is a glassy sea like this, for that matter."

"On the good old theory that when things are going well, expect trouble," Clem snorted.

He considered seamen, as a whole, a superstitious lot.

But before they'd finished lunch, a new wind had begun to blow strongly but fitfully from the northwest.

Pelehoehoe lay over on her port side with the force of the first gust, then righted herself, quickly shifting her sails to catch the new wind.

" 'One hand for yourself and t'other for the ship,' " Tom quoted from the *Manual*.

"This here boat can take care of itself," Clem growled.

"I want both hands to hang on with, thank you just the same."

On a fairly even keel once more, *Pelehoehoe* shot forward, her rigging thrumming nervously and the newly trimmed canvas booming. Her passengers watched towering black clouds upwind rolling rapidly toward them.

"I hope ol' what's-his-name built her to ride out a typhoon," said Tom.

The wind increased suddenly, and *Pelehoehoe* thrust her starboard cheek into the onrushing waves, shipping tons of chill, green brine across her foredeck. Clem clutched his friend by the arm to keep from being swept off his feet.

"Maybe we'd better go down to the cabin," he shouted over the hiss of water across the deck and out through the scuppers. "Storm means no good to us poor landsmen."

"I'd rather see it coming," Tom sputtered. "If it gets-*really* bad, we could go below, I guess."

Not to be outbraved by the Librarian, Clem merely shrugged and snatched up a length of rope to lash them both to the wheel.

"What did you call this?" the Woodsman called over the wind's increasing roar. "The storm, I mean?"

"What? Oh . . . a *typhoon*. Tropical storm at sea. Some of 'em, back home, got pretty fierce, I've read. High winds. High waves!"

"We don't have such fearsome things where *I* come from," Clem shouted back.

"No? What about those white blizzards you told me of? No telling up from down, hardly, you said. Or a tornado? The shepherds at Ramhold talked about twisters they'd seen, crossing the open plains at a hundred miles an hour—strong enough to lift a whole house!"

"Oh, well, they're *expected*," Clem scoffed. "Familiar to all, you see. I'd settle for a good old-fashioned Broken Land blizzard right now. Fifteen feet of snow in the door-yard and cold to freeze the brooks and lakes solid to their bottoms.''

"Not me!'' the Librarian shuddered. "If I'm going to be endangered, let it be a warm peril, at least.''

FOR the next six hours they crouched in the stern, lashed to the tiller post, alternately drenched by seawater taken aboard and stung by spray flying through the air. *Pelehoehoe*, with bared poles now, topped one after another towering swell and plunged like a roller-coaster car down the back slope.

The wind soared to breathtaking force, and then rose even higher. Rain came in stinging horizontal sheets, the huge drops lashing their hands and faces like warm sleet. More and more often the ship shuddered from the crashing breakers which struck her bows and geysered spray as high as the fore-topmast crow's nest.

Time and again the ship struggled like a living thing to shed the tons of green seawater surging across her decks. She righted herself with dogged effort each time, preparing for the next plunge, roll, and twisting lift.

"We shoulda gone to the cabin,'' Tom admitted, when he could get his breath after one submersion.

"Too late,'' Clem sputtered in the moment before the next assault. "Hang on . . . !''

BIGGER by more than half than the last, a rogue wave pounded *Pelehoehoe*'s starboard afterquarter, spinning her out of control broadside to the howling wind. Tom looked over his shoulder at the angry, swirling, heaving water and tan-white foam, as the gallant junk rolled almost on her port beam-ends, threatening to capsize.

"Come on, old girl!'' he shouted. "You can take it!''

Pelehoehoe shook like a great dog after a bath and dragged herself around to face the blast once more. Her standing rigging shrieked like a chorus of tortured souls. Her deck under them quivered and bucked . . . and her whipping main-topmast snapped like a dry stick.

An instant after, the whole mast was torn away, swept overboard, not slowed by its dozens of lines, halyards, and stays, which parted with pistol-shot *cracks*.

"Can it get worse?" Tom wondered aloud.

His words were swept away as soon as uttered.

"Yes, it can!" he answered himself.

Pelehoehoe shook her head like a dazed boxer absorbing another terrific blow to the chin.

"Watch out!" he thought he heard Clem shout in his ear.

Looking up, he saw the bare mizzen-topmast lean drunkenly over and slump between them and the cabin, smashing the cabin roof and the lee rail, trailing streamers of wildly lashing line.

The ship gave a terrible shriek and an almost human groan of agony, but somehow managed to right herself once more.

"Good old *Pelehoehoe*!" the Librarian cheered. "Do it again, old girl."

The Woodsman disappeared as a dark new wave charged down the slanting deck to wash over them, tearing away the wheel and the binnacle and flinging everything into the boiling sea.

Tom felt the heavy taffrail give way as he smashed into it. He fought to hold consciousness, aware that he was being carried over the side, clear of the ship, by the tremendous force of the swirling, green wave.

SOMEWHERE in green darkness he heard his inner voice calling urgently for Retruance Constable. He was consumed with a terrible need to inhale but fought it.

His head broke free of the surface for a scant moment.

He took two great gulps of salt spray and air before the boil and moil rolled him under again.

He caught a glimpse of Clem's tattered shirt whipping by in the rushing torrent. Clem wasn't wearing it. Tom struggled out of his own shirt and trousers, which were weighing him down and down.

A deafening, terrible roar filled his head almost to bursting.

A wave caught him up and thrust him forward, his body planing down its green-glass slope, hurtling him before it at breakneck speed like a chip of wood in a millrace. A moment later the curling crest overreached him and smashed him deep into the trough.

He struck hard bottom in a stinging cloud of sand that scoured his eyes and filled his nose and mouth. He stroked with all his strength for the surface, only to be pulled heels over head again under the waves after taking a choking half-gulp of precious air.

He shook his head to clear his eyes of the sharp-edged particles of broken shell and sand. As he rose wearily to the surface once again, he thought, *I'm coming up for the second time, so next I'll go down for the final time!*

His thought was, strangely, neither of panic nor of fear, but merely a matter of detached, academic interest.

Where was Retruance?

He felt something pluck at his undershirt from behind, lifting him clear of the surface. He kept his stinging eyes closed tightly and shook his head once more, trying to spit out the sand between his teeth.

"A moment now," said a muffled voice from the neighborhood of his upper back. "Here's higher ground."

"R-R-Retruance!" Tom choked. "Clem?"

"I see him, Companion!" replied the Dragon calmly. "I'll be right back."

Tom realized he was lying on his stomach in loose, wet,

flowing sand. The roar of rain, wind, and surf went on unabated, tearing insanely at his rags of underclothing, but he was no longer floundering in deep water.

He lifted his head, took a few ragged breaths, and felt driving rain beating the back of his head. Turning toward it, he let it wash the last of the salt and sand from his mouth, nose, and eyes.

He rolled over and when he got his legs under him at last, he scrabbled on hands and knees up a steep slope, leaving the pounding waves behind. At the top of the dune he collapsed on his stomach again, groaned, rolled over, and sat up, coughing on salt water, seaweed, and sand.

Retruance appeared close overhead, flailing the typhoon winds with powerful black wings. As Tom watched in dazed interest, the Dragon landed, spat Clem from his mouth onto the wet sand beside the Librarian, and grinned broadly.

"Rest here for a few minutes, Tom dear, but we really should move further up the strand," he screamed in Tom's ear.

The sodden and dazed Librarian nodded and crawled over to check the Woodsman, turning him on his back and allowing the pelting rain to wash sand from his eyes and mouth, also.

"R-r-right, then," Clem sputtered. "Are you the real Tom . . . or his ghost?"

"Just the real old Tom," coughed the Librarian. "We have to move up away from the sea, now. Can you walk?"

"Crawl, rather," Clem gasped. "You okay?"

"Just about," replied Tom, helping the other to rise to hands and knees.

Terrible storm wind caught at them and threatened to bowl them heads over heels, but they dug their fingers and toes into the heavy, wet sand and stayed half erect.

"Wind's dying down a mite," they heard Retruance say from nearby.

He was also crawling on his belly, sideways, providing them a modicum of lee from the blast.

"There's some sort of tangled mess ahead," the Dragon added, pointing an emerald claw. "That way, m'lads!"

THE wind indeed was moderating, but the pounding of giant surf on the beach continued, making conversation impossible. They reached the tangle, whole palm trunks and fronds piled helter-skelter with great, wilted clumps of brown kelp ripped from the deep seabed. They burrowed under the lee, letting the rain wash the salt from their bodies and slake their raging thirst.

"What . . . what happened to poor old *Pelehoehoe*?" Clem gasped at last.

"No idea," Tom answered. "Torn to pieces or sunk."

"I saw her driven ashore before the wind, just as I caught up with you two," Retruance said.

He was lying in a curve about their makeshift shelter, taking most of the rain and wind easily on his back, wings, and powerful shoulders. "I think she struck hard aground after you dove over the side."

"We were *washed* over the side," Tom insisted.

"Didn't the storm bother you at all?" Clem asked, amazed that the Dragon could still chuckle.

"Oh, it was no great problem as long as I stayed *under* the water," admitted the Dragon. "Once I was above the surface, though, the wind made it extremely difficult to fly and the spume and wrack made it all but impossible to see. But I caught sight of you both in time to pull you ashore."

"Where, I wonder," asked Tom, sitting up at last, "is here?"

"I was hoping *you'd* know," Retruance replied. "I just followed your lead, Companion."

"Well, wait 'til the wind dies down a bit and then we'll look around and see where we are," the Librarian decided.

He spat and snorted, trying to rid his mouth, nose, and throat of the last of the sand. After the terror and confusion of being swept overboard, he found himself on the very edge of exhaustion. He yawned mightily.

"Go ahead. Take a nap," Retruance Constable encouraged them both. "I'll keep an eye on things. It's too early to move from here, anyway."

Tom lay in the chill, wet sand and let his eyelids close. Despite the constant uproar of the breakers a few yards away, he fell asleep immediately.

Beside him, Clem did the same.

The Dragon watched over them fondly. When a torn piece of sail blew by, he snagged it deftly with a sharp claw and, after blowing his hot breath on it for a minute to warm and dry it, covered the two men and tucked them in.

✦ 9 ✦
Castaways

CLEM awoke to look about in relief and wonder.

The sun was already high, hot in a cloudless sky. To the south he saw a line of standing sticks against the horizon, marching in even ranks from left to right. After a moment of puzzlement, he realized they were trees without their leaves.

Between the low sand dune Retruance had chosen for refuge and the line of trees was a pale green lagoon so clear he could see heads of brain coral on the bottom dozens of yards away.

Schools of bright tropical fish, thankful to have escaped the worst of the storm's turmoil, darted about, snapping up bits of whatever it was they liked to eat that had been stirred from below by the waves of the wild day and night just passed.

Beyond the pile of uprooted palm trunks, bits of splintered timber, piled-up sand and seaweed, and the lagoon, a higher bit of land, clothed in a tangle of bright green, rose from a wide beach.

A great many white and grey birds flew in excited circles overhead. At first Clem thought they were screeching about the dead fish and bits of shredded vegetation washed up on the beach. Then he realized they were upset by the sight of Retruance, calmly bathing in a shallow tidal pool, all fifty gold-and-green feet of him.

''*Hoy!*'' the Dragon called, seeing Clem on his feet, if still a trifle unsteady. ''Wake yon lazy Librarian and we'll go find some breakfast.''

''I'm awake,'' Tom groaned, rolling over and rising to

his knees. "Not much in the way of food here, unless you count all those bright-looking fishes."

"Well, let's go see," answered Retruance.

He waded out of the water, much to the consternation of the gulls, terns, ernes, skuas, pelicans, and petrels circling in a raucous cloud overhead.

"It's all right fellas," Retruance bellowed good-naturedly at the noisy birdlife. "I'm fine. So are the boys. Thanks for your interest!"

The birds scattered at his voice, deciding the huge beast was no threat to them or their young. Retruance stopped at the edge of the water to shake himself dry, sending crystal droplets flying every which way.

THE Dragon and his passengers flew slow and low across the wide lagoon toward the rising ground beyond.

"Coconut palms, I bet," Tom shouted. "Put down, Retruance! They'll give us something to eat—and drink, too."

Sure enough, under the frondless palm trunks above the shore lay hundreds of huge brown and green coconuts torn from their trees by the typhoon.

"How the devil do you open one of these things?" asked Clem after he'd picked one up and examined it carefully.

"Start them with your knife," Tom instructed. "I saw it on television, once. Strip the outside fibers off. Puncture the inside shell to drain out the milk."

"This better be worth it," Clem grunted doubtfully.

His sheath knife had somehow survived the wild night. He drew it and began to worry its sharp point into the tough coconut hull.

"Here, let me," offered Retruance. "So these are coconuts? Ones I used to see at country fairs were rather smaller and rounded and sort of hairy."

"That's the inside shell," Tom explained.

"You're right!" The Dragon laughed, genuinely pleased

by this reminder of his youth in distant Carolina. "I punch a hole or two, here and here . . . and we can drink the juice. Right?"

Suiting words to action, he easily stripped away the tough, fibrous copra with his powerful emerald talons, then carefully inserted a single sharp claw in two of the three depressions at one end of each inner nut to release the rich, cool milk.

"I was *thirsty*!" Clem exclaimed with surprise and pleasure after he'd tasted the milk. "Great stuff! I don't s'ppose these trees'd grow at home?"

"The inside's very good too," Retruance told him after draining four more nuts and cracking them to expose the thick white meat.

He handed a quarter of a nut to each of the men, and for a while they spoke very little, enjoying their first food since breakfast two days before.

"OTHER than that," Clem said wiping his mouth on the back of his hand, "there's always plenty of fish. Dragons are good fish-catchers, aren't they, Retruance?"

"The best," the Dragon boasted. "Do you want some now? Or wait 'til lunchtime?"

"Later, I think," said Tom. "Let's look around a bit, first."

Almost as soon as Retruance was airborne again the Dragon said, "I see something of interest, gentlemen."

He swooped down again, off to the west of their landfall. A strange brown and grey shape, smashed and a-tilt and at first almost unrecognizable, lay half buried in sand just out of reach of the waves.

"Poor *Pelehoehoe*!" Tom exclaimed. "Set us down, Retruance. She seems to be in a single piece . . . more or less. There may be food and tools aboard we can salvage."

"Pretty much a total loss, I'm afraid," observed the

Dragon sadly, spreading his wings to brake their descent. "Hull's holed. Keel's cracked. Too bad!"

The storm surge that had washed the junk ashore had been both cruel and kind to her. It had lifted her bodily over an outer reef of solid coral and set her down in soft sand . . . just hard enough to break her back.

"Boost me up," Tom asked Retruance. "I'll see if any of our gear remains."

Clem followed him onto the steep-tilted deck. The scene before them was sad chaos. They were surprised how fond they'd become of the gallant vessel.

Tom waded into the main cabin, still a foot deep in seawater and tons of wet sand. He pushed broken furniture and torn fabric out of the way . . . the cabin was a total shambles. Nothing had survived intact, including the prints on the walls, the books, and the nautical chart.

Clem pushed through to the galley and returned shortly with a wooden crate filled with boxes, bottles, and bags of foodstuffs.

"Every egg's smashed," he reported sadly, for he loved his morning eggs most of all, "but there's several slabs of bacon and half a smoked ham. I found jars of marmalade, too, but there was no bread that wasn't spoilt by salt water. The flour's ruined, but these soda crackers somehow survived everything . . . not even a crumble!"

"And here're our backpacks," Tom said, holding them up. "Our extra clothes are safe and dry."

After they'd laid their salvage out on the half-smashed cabin roof to dry in the sun and be examined with more care, both gratefully changed to clean, dry clothing from the skin out.

"We should seek fresh water, though," said Tom. "For bathing—here's some soap I found—and for cooking and drinking, too."

"Let's pop over to the island, then," suggested the

Dragon, daintily nibbling a clawful of soda crackers spread with marmalade. "Must be water there. All that greenery means fresh water, I should imagine."

A short flight brought them across the lagoon to a storm-littered beach. Beyond, the steep cone in the center of the island was actually a hollow shell of steep cliffs. Within the circle of cliffs lay a sparkling turquoise lake.

"I think it's a volcanic crater," Tom guessed as they landed on its narrow beach. "Is the water fresh?"

"Highly flavored with something," Retruance reported, having snaked out his neck to taste. "Barely palatable."

"I saw several waterfalls on the outer slopes," Clem said. "And streams down to the sea. The lake might be good for a Dragon's bathtub, but running water might be safer for drinking."

They found a shaded glen on the north-facing hillside into which a thin fall dropped from above, cooling the torrid midday air. Lush trees which had somehow escaped the typhoon provided shade, and the stream slaked their thirst.

Clem made a small fire and brewed tea from the galley stock he'd recovered. They showered under the waterfall. While they ate dry ham sandwiches, with crackers serving for bread, the Dragon went aloft and was gone for an hour.

When he returned he brought five large sea bass for supper. Clem took them in charge and dunked them into the pool below the falls to keep until he could clean and fillet them, and broil them over their fire for supper.

"Well, how long must we stay here, anyway?" he asked Tom.

"Not a bit longer than we can help. I'm concerned about Manda and Mornie and the boys. Goodness knows what Byron Boldface will think when his junk doesn't come in."

"He must know of the typhoon," Retruance reasoned. "He can't blame you if you were shipwrecked."

"The problem is, *Pelehoehoe* knew where she was going, but we can only guess," Tom said.

He told the Dragon about their study of the chart in the main cabin.

"Sounds logical, if anything is logical when dealing with a madman who kidnaps women and children," the Dragon sniffed.

"The problem is getting to this Eversmoke Island," said Clem. "If he sees we've brought a Dragon along . . ."

"There's that, of course," Tom sighed. He turned back to Retruance. "What did you see up ahead?"

"Hundreds . . . maybe thousands . . . of little islands. Most of them are barely above the sea, with only a few palm trees and some underbrush."

"The Coral Rings, I suppose," Tom nodded, remembering the lost chart. "Did you go further?"

"There's a big island over the horizon. It's much larger, with sharp peaks giving off smoke or steam. A pleasant place for a Dragon, I'd say. Could that be your Eversmoke?"

"Hope it is!" cried Clem.

"Well, there appear to be people living there, at any rate," said Retruance. "If it's not this Boldface's island, maybe the natives will know of him."

Tom considered. "It'd be foolish to think he wouldn't see us if we flew in at night, I suppose. Could you carry us under the water, say?"

Retruance thought about this for a while but shook his head.

"No, I think not. I do it by staying totally submerged except for my nose, eyes, and ears. You and Clem would have to stay underwater, too, with just your heads out . . . and in this clear water someone looking down from a mountaintop, say, would easily see you, while we were still some miles off."

"How far to this bigger island?" Clem asked.

"Maybe fifty, maybe sixty miles as a Dragon flies. I stayed as far away and as low as I could so as not to be spotted."

"Then," Clem decided, "what we need is a boat. He'll sight *us* coming, but if you stay far behind and underwater as before, he might not notice you, Retruance. If you're careful, that is."

"Most careful," the Dragon promised. "But where do we get a boat? *Pelehoehoe*'s hopelessly wrecked. Including her lifeboats."

Clem stood and laid his hand upon the bole of one of the trees growing beside the stream.

"Build a boat?" Tom asked, guessing his thoughts.

"We can do it, given a few tools. Maybe we can do better with pieces of *Pelehoehoe*. Many of her timbers are still sound, and there're plenty of sails and nails to salvage."

"Let's go look," said Tom.

In a few minutes they were standing on the steeply slanting afterdeck of the wrecked junk, looking at her with a view to building a boat.

THE most important elements were there, once they sorted them out from the ruin of the gallant vessel.

Pelehoehoe's stout timbers and spars would provide the materials, and her heavy carpenter's chest would provide the nails, saws, hammers, and drills, once they found it in the jumble the storm had left everywhere belowdecks.

"HOW do we go about it, then?" Tom asked the Woodsman.

Clem was checking the edge of an ax he'd pulled from the chest, finding it reasonably sharp although already a bit rusty.

"What do *you* suggest, Librarian? I've little knowledge at seagoing ships or large boats, and I gave little heed to river or lake craft I've been aboard. I could do a canoe blindfolded, however."

"Then let's make a canoe."

Clem shook his head in doubt.

"Canoes're so ... well ... *fragile* and ... *tipsy,* if you know what I mean. Recall them big waves? They'd toss a canoe about like a jackstraw. Rip 'er to shreds in no time at all."

"I've read of oceangoing canoes built to sail long distances, at home. Called 'outriggers.' "

Smoothing a patch of sand, Tom sketched the outlines of a long, narrow hull with floats fixed to one side for stability. "Or we can make it, even better, a *double-hulled* boat, a catamaran. Like this ..."

He smoothed away his first sketch and drew in the sand a twin-hulled version.

"Hey!" exclaimed the Woodsman, leaning over his shoulder to watch. "We could do that. Great!"

They began work at once, gathering materials and tools together, lifting things to the flat sand beside the wreck. The Dragon was their crane.

"I see!" cried the Woodsman with growing enthusiasm. "Two long, narrow canoes fastened firmly together with cross-braces. Add a mast and a sail, or perhaps two, so we can catch the wind."

"Not much in the way of luxury accommodations," Tom admitted. "But it should get us there, if there's not another typhoon."

Nightfall caught them before they'd hardly begun. Clem wanted to work by Dragon-light, but at last he was convinced to stop for supper and sleep, to begin again early in the morning.

Retruance carried ashore and flame-dried some mattresses from the junk's bunks for them to sleep upon. The floor of the glen by the waterfall was rough with spreading, twisted roots reaching eagerly for the running water.

"How much time have we got?" Clem asked after they'd eaten sea bass poached in sweet coconut milk.

"Until what? Yes, I see," said Tom sleepily. "Well, the important date is Manda's birthing. That's off yet maybe three or four weeks, with any luck at all, but you always have to allow for early labor, especially with a first child, according to Flabianus."

"I found that to be so," agreed Clem. "Gregor was a full month early, by Flabianus's calculations."

"He may have miscalculated, or Mornie may be the sort to deliver her babes ahead of schedule. I've read a bit about it, you see . . ."

"So, count on . . . what? . . . a scant ten days, at most . . . allowing a few days to return Manda to Carolna by Dragon, to either Hidden Lake House, or to Overhall. That leaves us less than a week to settle this Boldface's hash, rescue the ladies and my boys."

"Allow a couple days just to reach Eversmoke. Allow another week to find Boldface if this island *isn't* Eversmoke. Allow, allow, allow! We haven't all that much time, to answer your first question. How long to build this canoe of yours?"

"Two, three days. It'll mean working in the heat all day, and some at night when it's cooler."

"We'll spread an awning for shade. An old sail will do," Tom suggested. "We can get Retruance to flap his wings for ventilation, if it gets too hot."

"Gladly!" they heard the Dragon call from under the fall, where he was happily showering away the last traces of dried salt and barnacles from his lustrous scales.

•   •   •

Two identical hulls posed the greatest problem.

"We could build each hull up with strakes from *Pele-hoehoe*'s siding," Tom thought aloud. "Heat them with the Dragon's breath? We could force them to curve onto a framework of ribs . . ."

"That'll take way too long!" Clem objected. "Here . . . how about hollowing out a couple of these two-foot beams. Make 'em dugouts, as the Waterfielders do down south where birch bark is scarce."

"That's better, certainly," Tom agreed, examining the heavy beams. "Maybe shape them with axes and then fit the two halves together? I'm afraid my ax-work is far inferior to yours, Clem."

He paused, glancing at the Dragon, who stood over them with wings widespread, shading them from the morning sun, which was already fierce.

"Or we could *burn* them into shape with fire," he mused aloud.

"Heat stones and . . . ?" Clem caught at the thought.

"No! Retruance is an expert at burning things! Come here, Retruance, old Constable! Burn us a groove down the center of this beam, like so . . ."

By dint of several hours' huffing and puffing, clouds of acrid wood smoke, a great deal of salty steam, and some expert ax-wielding by Clem at the end to refine their shapes, graceful twin hulls emerged from the heavy timbers.

"Splendid!" Tom exulted.

Retruance, not a bit wearied by the flaming, easily dragged the finished hulls into the lagoon, where the men carefully checked them for balance and watertight integrity.

"Each would be a nearly perfect single canoe, by itself," Clem congratulated the Dragon. "Beach 'em and let's do the fine work. Retruance, you rest a bit."

They worked until sudden darkness fell, and even after

that, by Dragon-flare and moonlight. They finished at last, long after midnight, weary but well pleased with the night's work.

The catamaran stretched fifteen paces long and, while the individual hulls were only a pace wide or so, with strong cross-braces between them and a flat deck nailed above, the finished canoe was six feet wide amidships.

"We need to rig a rudder, step the mast, hang the sails, and provide some sort of anchor," Tom ticked off the tasks yet to be done. "Shall we stop until dawn? Or . . ."

"Keep working 'til we're done," Clem finished. "We can rest while we sail."

Bone-weary and stumbling in the deep sand, they lashed down the final forestay to support a fifteen-foot spar from *Pelehoehoe*, stepped well forward, as their single mast. A wide triangle of canvas, folded carefully on the new deck, was ready to hoist to the long yardarm.

Retruance had collected and husked two dozen coconuts to stow in the hulls, both as ballast and as a food supply, being careful to balance the load evenly.

"Any reason we can't leave at once?" asked the Woodsman, wiping his brow with a soaking kerchief.

"I vote we take a minute or two to bathe," Tom suggested, "and eat a hearty and hot breakfast before we cast off. We didn't allow for cooking aboard our yacht."

"Fire would be too dangerous. Once afloat, we'll live on the stores from *Pelehoehoe*. And Retruance's cache of coconuts and the butts of water. And fish, of course."

After a reviving shower under the falls above the glen and a mixed grill of ham from the square-rigger's pantry and fresh shrimp from the lagoon, eaten with the last of the ship's crackers, they still returned to the sand spit well before midday.

"Well, so long, *Pelehoehoe*," Clem said, patting her shattered stern in the same manner he'd so often thanked a spent horse. "I hate to leave you like this, but it's necessary, after all."

Tom nodded sad and sleepy agreement.

Retruance towed the canoe south across the lagoon and out into the open sea beyond the southern reef. The three watched anxiously while the new vessel bobbed and dipped to an easy swell, leaning away from the light northeast breeze.

"She'll do just fine!" Tom decided. "Let's go!"

They hugged and patted the nearest available portions of the Dragon and waved to him as he stood in the shallows watching them set the mainsail and the smaller jib, and glide away south, gaining speed at once.

"I'll be no more'n five miles astern of you," Retruance called. "If you need me, just yell."

"Don't worry, we will," yawned his Companion. "See you when we get to Eversmoke."

IT took them some time to master the idiosyncrasies of their jury-built catamaran. Too much sail, even in a light breeze, tended to heel her over and lift one of her slim hulls almost clear of the water. Someone had to watch her heading at all times and make constant corrections with the long steering sweep. Otherwise she tended to sail in swooping curves and eventually ended up broaching to, across the wind.

The oar they'd used for a rudder proved much too heavy for easy steering. Turning—"going about"—called for all their combined strength . . . one man to wrestle the sweep, the other to swing the heavy mainsail boom.

But that first long afternoon served to teach them, and by the next noontide, following a good night's sleep, they were almost at ease in a circle of sea dotted at some distance by dozens upon dozens of the low coral islets.

As they lunched on coconut pieces and cucumber-and-onion pickles from *Pelehoehoe*'s stores, Clem suggested, "We should name her."

"What would you call her?"

Clem considered and chewed.

"Well, I'd call her *Manda* or *Mornie*, but it strikes me she's a bit awkward for that. The lady picked might take offense."

"I doubt either would. She moves with some grace, I think, and quietly, and quickly. Like a cat."

"Well, you did say her kind is called *catamaran*," chuckled the Woodsman.

"How about *Julia*?"

"The lady jaguar'll be positively thrilled when we tell her," Clem laughed. "*Julia* she is!"

Sea Dragon

TOM had brought along *Pelehoehoe*'s minute-glass that he had found unharmed in the wreckage of the junk's cabin. He now spent some time, mornings and evenings when the sun's heat was most tolerable, casting an improvised log into the water at the bow and allowing it to float back with the boat's forward movement.

When it was opposite the stern, Clem, at the helm, would yell "Mark!" and Tom would check the sands in the timing glass to estimate how long it had taken the junk to pass the floating bit of wood. From this he could roughly calculate their speed and distance.

A northwesterly wind blew steadily with only minor variations, now and then, calling for *Julia*'s crew to adjust sails.

"I figure an *average* of five miles an hour," Tom announced the third morning. "Figuring in nautical miles . . . five thousand feet . . ."

"Not exactly a racer," Clem said dryly.

"Still, in two full days we've made at least a hundred miles."

They'd decided to furl the sail that first night and drift before the wind. The water there often shallowed quite suddenly. Some of the atolls were not even awash. In daylight they could spot them by the swirls of white water marking sunken reefs.

But deeper water came before the second night, and they sailed on after sunset.

"At this rate, we'll sight the island Retruance spotted any time now," Clem estimated. "I guess this wind is blowing her smoke away from us. Retruance says Ever-smoke is quite lofty. A grand landmark.''

Tom nodded, shading his eyes against the sun's glare to scan the southeast horizon one more time.

''I'd prefer to approach in daylight, so Boldface can't claim we were sneaking up on him—if he's there.''

Clem began to ease a halyard, lowering the sail while Tom bundled the lower edge about the boom. Their speed was reduced to a rolling crawl, the boat kept moving by the small triangular jib alone.

AFTER sunset they sighted a reddish glow on the southwestern horizon. The volcano!

Retruance's head, or a small part of it, appeared beside *Julia*'s stern. The Dragon was keeping the bulk of the catamaran between himself and the island . . . just in case.

''Ahoy!'' Tom hailed. ''Had a good day?''

''I circled ahead at noontime,'' Retruance spluttered, his mouth barely above the water. ''There are no shoals or reefs until you near the island, then there's a circling barrier of coral. You'll have to drag the boat over that, or find an entrance.''

''There must be an entrance, or *Pelehoehoe* couldn't have come to port there,'' reasoned Tom with a frown.

''I didn't take the risk to look,'' Retruance gurgled. ''Damnation! I'll be happy to get in the air once again. I think my belly scales are beginning to wrinkle from constant salt water soaking.''

''Don't get waterlogged,'' Clem cautioned.

''There's not much I can do to avoid it, as it happens,'' grumbled the huge Dragon. ''Well, we're almost there. Right on course. You should see the mountain itself in the morning.''

Tom peered over the side into the black water.

''I fear someone ashore will spot you, even if you stay

way back. Maybe you should wait to come inshore after dark, tomorrow night.''

''I thought I'd approach the island tonight,'' Retruance countered. ''I'll come ashore from the far side. When old Boldface spots you, he won't be watching his back door too carefully, perhaps.''

Tom agreed to this, and Clem opined the Dragon's plan was sound. Retruance lifted an emerald foreclaw in a parting salute, took a great breath, and sank beneath the waves with hardly a ripple.

RETRUANCE Constable swam deep underwater for as long as he could, then floated on his back near the surface to catch his breath and examine his surroundings, slowly sculling with his tail, figuring his green underside would be less visible in the night than his golden top.

The water under him had quickly become shallower and shallower as he neared the island, although it was still close to twenty fathoms deep here.

He proceeded slowly, wing-stroking so as not to cause a visible ripple on the surface, carefully dodging occasional brain corals and hidden rocks.

By moonrise he'd found an entrance through the reef and passed around the northeast tip of Eversmoke, if this was indeed Eversmoke Island. He swam slowly along the northern coast, examining the land closely. A Dragon's night vision is very good.

The island here was high, and had a rising shoreline without visible beaches. Hundred-foot cliffs, topped with lush jungle growth, dropped directly into the sea. The sea was still quite deep, close inshore: twenty fathoms or more.

It was also very black and almost still. The wind, now blowing steadily from the southeast, shortly was blocked by the island itself as he passed around to the western side.

He rested for a moment by a dark and lonely rock thrusting out of the deep, clinging with his foreclaws to its rough surface.

"While you're at it," rumbled a deep voice, "scratch a bit lower. I tend to collect barnacles between my shoulders where they're hard to reach."

"*Hello!*" Startled, Retruance remembered at the last moment to speak softly. "Sorry! Didn't mean to intrude."

"No apologies necessary," rumbled the voice.

Out of the dark water a long neck and sleek head arose, curving back toward him. A glowing pair of amused eyes blinked at him.

"A land-loving species of Dragon, I see," the sea creature said, chuckling with a sound like distant surf. "Well met, land Dragon! There're all too few creatures of our sort here. I sometimes get lonely."

"Who are you?" Retruance asked, beginning to scratch industriously with his emerald claws at the hard-shelled lumps on the creature's back.

"The name's Flo," replied the stranger. "Short for a long name that starts Florenz Stillacho MacNess."

"A Sea Dragon?" Retruance paused to guess.

"Don't stop! You're doing a splendid job on those pesky barnacles."

"Gladly! May I introduce myself. I am Retruance Constable of Carolna, off to the east and north some distance."

"Never been there, but I've heard of the place. Met a lady Dragon from there, once, ages ago. Name was . . . let me see! It was quite long ago . . . Mehetable? Something like that, was it?"

"Hetabelle?"

"Yes! I remember now. Hetabelle she was! We just had a brief encounter. She was flying low over the sea, looking for an abalone bed. We exchanged pleasantries, and I was able to direct her to a particularly rich abalone colony, not far off."

"Hetabelle's my sister-in-law. Pleased to meet you, Master MacNess! Not so many Dragons around these days that it isn't a great treat to meet a new one."

"There's one more pesky barnacle, a particularly itchy one, just at the point of my left lower hip," the Sea Dragon directed, rolling easily in the water. "There! You've got 'em all. Dratted nuisances."

He righted himself and gestured toward the open sea. "We should perhaps move offshore a bit where there's more light."

"A very good idea," Retruance agreed.

They turned away from the towering cliff's dark shadow on the sea and swam easily, side by side, until they reached the moon-brightened waters beyond.

"We're of a size, I see," said Flo as they swam. "How many of you are there, over in Carolna? I've been thinking of organizing a gathering of Dragon clans, y'see. There hasn't been a Dragon gathering for almost five hundred years. I feel we should get to know each other better and keep in touch!"

"Well, let's see," mused Retruance, swimming easily. "There's my father Arbitrance Constable, and my brother Furbetrance . . ."

"Ah, yes! The fortunate husband to the fair Hetabelle?"

"Right-o! Furbetrance and Hetabelle have a brood of five kits. They're several years old and just learning to fly. Lively little lizards."

"I can imagine! It's been eons since I've had kits around. You must enjoy them."

"As their bachelor uncle I can enjoy 'em without having the worries of rearing 'em," Retruance chuckled.

"I'm a great-great-grandfather, myself, so I know just how you feel. Any more?"

"Other than Hetabelle, only our mother. She lives on a remote island in the southeast Quietness. You haven't run into her, have you? Her name is Bridgette Brightwing Constable.''

''A beautiful name! No, I've yet to travel that far. I will, some day. If you see her, say I may drop down to meet her, especially if my plans go forward for a gathering.''

''Mum'll be quite interested in a gathering. She always said we Dragons were much too standoffish. Still . . . our family *is* close. Oh, and I know of one other Dragon. He's rather a sour apple, if you know what I mean, but not really a bad sort, at all. His name's Hoarling Frostbite. He's an Ice Dragon.''

''Oh, I say! I've never run across that breed, nor ever heard of them. He lives near you Constables, does he?''

''Well . . . to the northeast of Carolna, above the Blue Ocean, last I heard.''

The new friends chatted for a while, well out of earshot of the shore. Retruance exchanged news of the latest Dragon and Elf doings in Carolna for Flo's tales of the South Quietness.

''But here! I'm a terrible host! Let me invite you to my grotto. We can rest better there, have supper, and talk in greater comfort. I can offer you food and drink, of which I've aplenty.''

''I'd be flattered,'' cried Retruance, for Dragons are notoriously secretive about their lairs.

They swam downward at a steep slant until they reached an undersea shelf a hundred feet below the surface. Entering a cleft in the rock, the Sea Dragon followed a tunnel lighted by thousands of twinkling starfish clinging to the ceiling and walls.

The passage curved gently upward at last, and shortly Flo and Retruance broke water in a pool in the middle of the Sea Dragon's vast and sumptuous cavern.

''My wife of many centuries,'' Flo explained after he'd shown his guest to a comfortable seat on a pile of fragrant dried seaweed and provided a tall pipe of Wyvern Ale, "passed on some decades ago. We lived together on the coast of Galorrea, west of here. After her death, I decided to return here for its peace and quiet."

"I've yet to find a mate, myself," admitted Retruance, sipping the heady brew cautiously. "This is delicious! Do you make it yourself?"

"No, I've no talent for such things. I get it from a red griffin who lives on the coast of Prestoli Triges. You don't know it? I must give you a copy of my book, *World Views*. In it I tell of the lands and peoples of the west. Fascinating! Great scenery and wonderful foods."

Flo was a scholar and a traveler. He'd been almost everywhere in the western reaches of the Quietness.

"No idea why I never got to your parts," he said, a trifle sadly. "My leanings have ever been west and south, I fear. Now I know there are so many friendly Dragons like your family that way, I really must travel eastward. My research is charting the great ocean currents, you see. I love the challenge of such intricate puzzles. Ocean currents, especially the Great Equatorial Streams, are magnificent conundrums."

He launched into a description of the systems of slowly moving sea currents that heated or cooled the coasts of the three great continents. Meanwhile he set a wide stone table with all the foods Dragon-folk trot out when they have important guests.

At last the host apologized, "Oh, my, I do run on so! Comes of living too much alone, do you suppose? I should ask what *you* are doing here, Retruance Constable, in a part of the sea so far removed from your own aerie."

"I was about to tell you," Retruance said, delicately touching his lips with a chamois serviette as big as one of *Pelehoehoe*'s mainsails. "I came with my Dragon Companion, a young man named Sir Thomas Whitehead, the

Librarian of Overhall, looking for his kidnapped wife . . .''

"*Oh!* That would be the strange Princess!" cried Flo. "Beautiful young Elf-lady, they say. Delightful, I'm told, despite her relationship to that old fakir Boldface."

Retruance was stunned by his words but managed to nod eagerly.

"You've met her? Princess Manda, I mean."

"I've not actually *met* her, but the island fishermen have spoken in my hearing of her and I've caught glimpses of her and her companions walking on the cliff tops, now and again. I was pondering if I should introduce myself, actually, when you fastened your claws on my back among the dratted barnacles."

"If I tell you what we know and have done," asked Retruance, "might you help us recover the Princess and her friends? They're held against their wills by this nasty Boldface chap. We could use your help and local knowledge."

"I'll do what I can, certainly!" exclaimed the Sea Dragon. "I'm somewhat leery of Boldface, for he's often a bad-tempered, rather strong-willed sort and, I gather, a powerful magician. But . . . *kidnapped*, you say? How very frightful! Tell me all, Master Constable. I'm sure I can help."

BY the time he'd finished his dinner and his tale, Retruance had gained a staunch ally.

That it wasn't all good news didn't surprise him.

"This island Elves call Eversmoke? It's a volcano, of course. But then, so are most of the islands in this reach of the Quietness."

"I assumed as much from my own observations," Retruance told him.

"But Eversmoke's considerably larger than all the rest

put together. And it's disturbingly active—witness the smoking! Hear the grumblings?

"Not only that," the Sea Dragon added, frowning earnestly. "If my calculations are correct, my friend, it's going to blow itself into tiny bits very shortly. I'm already planning to move. These waters are likely to be rather dangerous for a very long time. Even for a Dragon!"

✴ 11 ✴
The Masked Wizard

THE Wizard of Eversmoke Island was dressed in a gorgeous robe of brilliant orange and flame-red hummingbird feathers. He concealed his face with a wildly grotesque wooden mask with fiercely-glaring turquoise eyes, purple seaweed hair, and a wide, gaping, gleaming, nasty mouth exposing daggerlike teeth of mother-of-pearl.

Accustomed as they were to his wild and fierce appearance, the natives of Eversmoke, who called themselves Parvaiti, had never quite learned to approach him with any boldness.

Unlike most of the *tikis* of their legends and folktales, this one was no pushover for pots of poi, lustrous pearls, coconut wine, or even the occasional pretty handmaiden. This *tiki* bluntly stated his demands and threatened to punished any who failed to pay close heed to his wishes and instant obedience to his orders.

"Brothers!" the *tiki*, who called himself Byron Boldface, growled after the usual ritual preamble chants. "Brothers *and* Sisters! Heed my words! Obey me!"

Unlike the older, milder sea-gods, this new one meant business. A few rebellious Parvaiti had been flung screaming off the high cliffs on the far side of the island for refusing willing and instant subservience. The long plunge into the deep, dark water was terrible enough. The swim around to the coral sand beaches on the east coast soon convinced the most recalcitrant to keep their doubts to themselves and a smile on their faces.

And to follow their *tiki*'s orders unquestioningly.

It was so much easier and better for everyone if Boldface's orders were obeyed. Most dealt with planting, weeding, and harvesting of the taro roots, pineapples, rice, and sugarcane growing in the black, fertile soil of the walled terraces climbing up the volcano's lower flanks.

Now Boldface was insisting they rush work on the great war canoes being hacked out and sewn together on the lagoon shore.

"He'd have us build enough canoes to carry the whole village—men, women, and children—over the deepest and most dangerous waters," some of the older, more experienced, menfolk murmured in private.

"*Shush!*" hissed the older women. "Just do what he says. What's the harm, eh? Besides, you're much too old to swim all the way around from Sunset Cliffs."

So the men had spent the long, warm, breezy Eversmoke Island days carefully fashioning first the great junk named *Pelehoehoe* and now these new war-size canoes, while the women chewed, spun, wove, dyed, and sewed together the tough pandanus cloth for the great triangular sails the *tiki* demanded.

For the usually easygoing islanders it was arduous, boring work, even though they made a game of it all and sang and joked and laughed as they labored.

Even the children worked hard fetching and carrying, and plaiting tough fiber cordage for rigging.

Now there were a half dozen of the new craft, finished or nearly so, on the white sand around the harbor. Two more had just been begun.

This morning the *tiki* had something different in mind.

"Brothers and Sisters and children," barked Boldface sternly. "Soon we will be visited by the powerful magician and his frightful assistant, of whom I have already warned you!"

The crowd, kneeling before the wizard's throne, shivered with fear.

"Do not fool yourselves!" cried Boldface. "The men of Parvaiti may be tall and lean and strong and awesome warriors when aroused, but they will be as children before this terrible magican!"

The men looked even more worried, glancing aside at their friends. The women bit their knuckles and moaned softly.

In the old days, their looks seemed to say, we beat off the Araqui raiders who came to steal our daughters. We were victorious. We were even feared. Respected! Now, however, fate sends terrible magicians and bloodthirsty assassins against us. We're as helpless as the smallest baby, afraid to lift a spear or bloody a war club.

"Hear my words!" shrilled Byron Boldface, waving his thin arms. "This terrible wizard will destroy you, one and all, if you resist. I may not be able to save you from the fire to come, very soon.

"Unless . . ."

He paused for dramatic effect, watching carefully through the mask's wide mouth to judge his audience's reactions.

"Unless . . . when they come you greet them with all ceremony, respect, and proper dread. Bow low to them. Offer them the very best food and drink. Beg to know their names and ranks and titles. If one of them says he is called *Librarian*, hail him and tell him you will bring him to me here in my palace on the quaking mountain."

The islanders nodded their understanding and willingness for their fearsome *tiki* to face these dreaded invaders, rather than oppose them with their puny shark-tooth swords and fire-charred bamboo spears.

"Do not *for a moment* think to harm these frightful intruders," intoned their masked demigod, pounding on the dais with his ironwood staff. "Leave them to me!"

"Yes, *tiki*! Yes, Lord and Master! Yes, O Wise and Beneficent Boldface!'' the islanders chanted in reply.

He gestured them away and the crowd quickly withdrew, not daring to speak or comment on this morning's orders until they were well out of earshot of the *tiki*'s bamboo-walled compound on the mountainside.

''Does this have something to do with the young lady and her party the *tiki* brought to our island a month back?'' one of the older men whispered to a companion.

''No telling, Grandfather. But I assume we'll find out soon.''

''If a *tiki*'s fell purposes can ever be fathomed,'' grunted Maorai, one of the islander's younger leaders. ''How long . . .''

He was about to commit sacrilege by questioning their complete subservience to the scrawny little *tiki*, but his companions shushed him fearfully, glancing back over their shoulders at the Bamboo Palace.

''IF I've learned anything,'' Clem growled in frustration, ''it's that you can't expect to know what an ocean will do. With this here wind we can't just run about until we find an opening in yonder reef. *Pelehoehoe* mighta done that . . . but not poor little *Julia*! What's to do, Librarian?''

Tom stood in *Julia*'s prow clutching the forestay with one hand and using the other to shade his eyes. There was no visible break in the swirl of breaking waves and bare rocks which stretched between them and the calm, inviting lagoon beyond.

On the distant shore he saw thin trails of cookfire smokes, under high, steep-pitched palm-frond roofs.

''The wind's holding from the northeast, now,'' he said at last, turning to rejoin Clem at *Julia*'s tiller. ''I guess the only thing to do is run south along the coast. Let's see if we can get around the end of the reef, or stumble on an opening.''

"I can't think of anything better, unless it's to swim," Clem nodded.

He eased the tiller over, and Tom scurried to change the set of the two sails. *Julia* ran happily parallel to the reef's white churn, and Tom stood watch for outlying coral heads or shallows in their course.

The sight of the steep-sided volcanic cone was nothing less than spectacular. As they watched, a great burst of black smoke—ash, perhaps, Tom realized—shot from the summit into the clear morning sky. Glowing lava bombs the size of a man's head sprayed from the caldera and plunged into the greenery on the lower slopes, setting a number of fires.

"There's enough dampness in the undergrowth to keep 'em from doing worse, I guess," said the Woodsman. "Look alive, now, Tom! These'll come too close!"

Hot bits of molten stone, already cooling to black and blue, fell just short of *Julia*'s stern. The travelers felt a wash of heat and salt steam.

Clem put her tiller down and allowed *Julia* to shoot before the wind further out to sea, where the water was calmer.

"*Whew!*" cried Tom, dropping into a seat beside his friend at the tiller. "Should we try the backside of Eversmoke, do you think?"

"You mean take some beating back and forth . . . what you call *tacking*? Well, we'll try. If we stay with *this* course, we'll end up way out to empty sea again."

They worked to bring *Julia* onto a starboard tack, pointing her double stem at the swampy southern tip of the island. As they approached, Tom could see it was not only choked with trees but most of them were standing in the shallow salt water.

"Mangroves, I suspect," he decided, although he'd never seen a mangrove nor a mangrove swamp before, except in pictures. "Land here if we have to, Woodsman, but I'd prefer something drier . . . and less infested with alligators or crocodiles or whatever prefers to live in such swamps."

"I agree completely. We'll steer to miss the tip of the island. Maybe there'll be shelter on the far side. We can paddle, if we have to."

Tom nodded and watched as the swampy southernmost point of Eversmoke Island glided by. Clem twisted the tiller to port and sent *Julia* at a slowing pace into the lee.

By mid-afternoon the breeze had disappeared almost entirely, leaving just enough wind to keep *Julia* moving slowly to the northwest on a very tight tack to windward. As the volcano rose higher and higher above them, the shoreline flats, no longer wetlands, narrowed and were choked thicker and thicker with green tangled undergrowth.

"We'll be blown ashore, if we don't tack soon," Clem estimated. "And look ahead! We're sailing into the cloud coming from the volcano. That's not a good place to go, if we can help it."

Tom, who was taking his turn at the helm, nodded. "We'd better go ashore and climb over the mountain from here. That way we'll avoid the fires and showers of whatever it is flying from the volcano."

"Leave *Julia*?" Clem objected. "Well, as you say . . . it's a better course than sailing blind through that cloud."

Tom twitched the tiller until *Julia* pointed ashore. Fortunately, there was no surf. The sea in the lee of the mountain was a deep, deep blue and calm as a millpond. Occasionally a gust of powdery grey ash blew over them, bringing a wave of heat and the sharp smell of hydrogen sulfide that reminded Clem of rotten eggs and Tom of Yellowstone National Park.

Eventually the catamaran's double keel scraped the bottom a few yards offshore.

"Over we go and wade," Tom decided. "Let's beach her as high as we can."

The water was only a couple of feet deep and warm as blood. The bottom of firm, black sand provided easy footing. The young men pulled the lightened *Julia* across the narrow strip of beach, manhandling her as far from the water as they could.

"Should I call Retruance?" Tom puffed from the last effort. "He can drag her to a safer mooring. I don't know how the tides run here. Not too high, by the looks of the high-water marks, I should think."

"No, we can manage. We may never need old *Julia* again."

Clem took a coil of inch-thick line salvaged from *Pele-hoehoe* and attached it to the mast. Together they tied it as firmly as they could manage to a sturdy-looking tree at the edge of the beach.

"It'll hold, I think," the Woodsman decided, "unless there's another typhoon."

"It'll have to do. Let's go under the trees and see if we can find something to eat. It's been a long time since breakfast, and we're going to have a bit of steep climbing to get to the village we saw."

"Do you think it'll hold off?" Clem asked anxiously, shouldering his pack and setting off after Tom through the jungle. "The volcano, I mean? It seems to've calmed down a bit for the moment."

"We'll have to trust to luck. Let's head for that notch, up there. I think there's a stream coming down here— maybe some fresh water."

"More likely it's something stinking to high heaven," the Woodsman complained. "But even that sounds good; our canteens are almost empty."

•   •   •

UNDER the canopy of the forest it was hotter than ever, close and steamy, and almost silent. Even their footfalls were muffled by a mat of fallen leaves and a deep layer of dust.

They followed the streambed with its trickle of greenish water, much too malodorous to even think of drinking it. The watercourse was, at least, free of undergrowth, which often consisted of three-inch-long thorns with hooked ends.

No living thing inhabited the jungle, from the leafy roof overhead to the sandy soil between the ferns and thorns. No birdsong rang out. There was no scurrying in the sand nor skittering of tiny beasts up the rough tree trunks.

"It should get better," Tom encouraged his companion.

"We shoulda called the Dragon," the Woodsman admitted, wiping at his face with a red-and-yellow bandanna produced from a hip pocket, one of the few things he'd salvaged from the wreck of *Pelehoehoe*. He folded the kerchief carefully and tied it across his forehead to keep sweat from rolling into his eyes.

They lost all sign of the streambed and faced a solid wall of greenery. They took turns slashing a path through the tough vines and thick limbs with Clem's belt knife, slowly clearing the way.

Tom sighed. "We're making something like a mile an hour, I imagine. It'll take us *days* to reach the ridge above."

"And then we'll have to fight our way down the other side," Clem said wearily. "Call the Dragon, I say!"

Tom, who was taking his turn with the knife, stuck it into the bright green loop of a fat vine ahead of him. He turned to face the sea, preparing to issue a call to his Companion.

"Wait a moment!" cried Clem, pointing.

Where Tom had slashed the vine in front of him there had appeared a sudden gush of clear liquid.

"Water!" Clem cried. "Or so it seems! Careful now. It may be . . ."

But when Tom wet his fingers in the streaming liquid, he tasted only pure water with a rather pleasant overtaste of greenness. He cupped his hands, gathering enough to sip, and pronounced it palatable.

Clem gingerly tasted, and before the flow from the slashed plant ceased of its own accord, both men had drunk enough to feel satisfied.

"A pitcher plant?" Clem wondered.

"No. As I recall, a pitcher plant uses a few drops of water to catch insects and then digests them."

"Ugh! Unnatural!" Clem objected.

"Not at all. Very natural. This plant gathers rain, somehow, and stores it. Lots of succulents, cactuses and such, do the same."

They rested for a quarter-hour, filled their canteens from another water vine, and resumed their climb.

"Why not call Retruance, anyway?" the Woodsman asked.

"I'm saving him as a sleeve card," Tom explained. "In case things get much worse than this."

Clem grunted unhappily but made no further objection. A Dragon is a large and useful asset, not to be wasted on minor discomforts like a raging thirst and climbing a steep volcano in tremendous heat and humidity.

At last, after four hours, they gained the ridge which had been their goal and threw themselves onto a patch of rough grass to pant and dab at their wet faces in a cool breeze that blew from the northeast.

Above them Eversmoke had decided not to huff and chuff further for the moment, and the cloud of ejected smoke and ash had disappeared entirely, leaving the sky a fierce electric blue lined with towering black-and-white thunderheads along the northwestern horizon.

"If we stay here and rest for an hour or so," Clem said thoughtfully, "it'll rain. *Hard,* most likely. That will cool things off a bit."

"We'll wait, then. I admit I'm bushed, Woodsman."

A stiffening wind off the ocean charged up the eastern slope, turning the leaves over to show their lighter undersides. It felt good to the weary climbers.

"There's a village down there," Tom called to his friend. "I see the roofs and the shoreline. There are boats and people, too."

"We're more than halfway there, then," Clem said, brightening at the news. "Well, they can wait. Let it rain!"

And as if his words had turned the tap, a roaring downpour fell like a curtain, blotting out all sight and masking all sound other than that of the falling water. They shed their clothing and let the cool rain wash the sweat and dirt from their bodies, and launder their clothes, too, at the same time.

On the lower slopes a moment before the afternoon rain began, a Parvaiti in the pineapple field had glanced up and sighted the strangers on the ridge. He cried out in wonder and a bit of fear, too, pointing at the strangers.

"It's the terrible magician foretold to us by our *tiki*!" he said, and ran to report to Samoy.

"Remember!" warned the elder. "Remember the *tiki*'s orders! Welcome them with friendly words and offer them food and drink. Lead them to the *tiki*'s palace!"

THE whole tribe streamed up the steep path to the ridge on the volcano's southern flank, knowing the way by heart even in the driving storm. When they came to a place where they could make out the strange sight of grown men capering naked in the rain, Samoy called a halt and shouted a greeting.

"Hail! Hail, strangers! Welcome to Eversmoke Island, the home of us Parvaiti."

Tom and Clem, startled by the sudden appearance of a crowd of shouting, smiling, and apparently friendly natives, snatched up their sodden clothing and hurriedly dressed in some embarrassment. A quartet of very pretty, lightly clad girls, laughing and calling, danced gracefully up the last slope and flung about their necks garlands of tiny, sweetly perfumed white, pink, and yellow flowers.

A white-haired elder solemnly raised his arms and gave a welcoming speech while the others rhythmically clapped their hands, all but drowning out his rolling rhetoric.

"Thank you! Thank you," replied Tom, more than a bit mystified as well as flustered. "You're most kind! I am Thomas, Librarian of Carolna. This is my friend Clem . . ."

"Librarian? Wonderful! Come to our village," cried the elder. "My name is Samoy. We shall prepare for you a grand feasting and bring you heady coconut wine to drink after your arduous journey."

"Dinner?" Clem asked, pleased by the thought of food.

"It's our custom, Sir," explained a younger man standing with Samoy. "Please accept our hospitality."

He was introduced as Maorai the Shipwright.

The procession reversed its course and led the strangers down the steep mountainside, singing and capering as they went.

"I see you're building some new craft here," Tom said to the Shipwright as they approached the village in the palm grove. "Beautiful! You must be a great seafaring people."

"Hardly," admitted a pleased Maorai, shaking his head. "We've never built such large canoes before, you must know. We do it . . ."

". . . because we do it," interrupted Samoy hastily. "Because we do it well and hope to sell them."

"Islanders can always use good stout boats," Clem observed.

He'd not missed how the older man had overspoken his young associate. He exchanged a wary glance with Tom.

"Great and revered Librarian!" cried Samoy when they came to the pleasant, shaded common in the center of a circle of twenty or thirty narrow, high-roofed bamboo-and-palm-mat houses. "Sit with us here in the cool shade while our women prepare the very tastiest fish, the plumpest chickens, and the most succulent pigs, all in your honor."

"And perhaps you'll answer a few questions for us?" asked Tom, a trifle impatiently, despite the evident good will of the natives.

"If we can," answered Samoy. "Here! Sit before our council house, here. It won't take long . . . will it, ladies?"

This last was directed to the women. When they heard it, they dashed off and began furiously preparing food over a communal fire some distance away.

"Palm wine!" called Samoy.

When it arrived in polished coconut-shell cups, he rose and proposed a long and windy welcoming toast to their guests' health and fortunes that said practically nothing but sounded good.

"This guy would make a great Session speaker," Clem whispered to Tom.

"Easy! No reason to antagonize."

"Ask 'em about Manda and Mornie," hissed Clem, who was, if anything, less patient than Tom for news of their wives and his children.

"I will," the Librarian promised. When the elder had finished the long toast with a deep bow to them, cup extended, Tom rose quickly to his feet and sipped the powerful, sweet ferment of coconut milk.

"I will respond," he said before Samoy could launch into another windy discourse. "At once!"

Samoy looked rather surprised but sank to his seat and gestured to the others in the circle to listen to their visitor.

"Dear friends!" Tom began, composing his speech mentally only a split second before it left his lips. "Parvaiti! Citizens of Eversmoke Island!"

The crowd fell silent.

Tom hurried on. "It's a great pleasure at last to reach your tall island and sandy shore and greet you, the strong and graceful people of this . . . ah . . . wonderful place."

At that moment there was a low rumble, and the nearby houses and palm trees seemed to flicker and weave in the warm, moist air. To Tom's surprise, the natives paid no attention to the tremor but sat waiting politely for him to continue.

"My friend the Woodsman and I have come a long way by land and sea to meet you—over swift rivers and deep blue lakes, high hills, rich farm fields, and dry deserts, through rugged mountains, and an even greater distance over the almost endless ocean."

His listeners seemed impressed.

"These past several weeks we sailed on the great ship *Pelehoehoe* . . ."

Sharp exclamations of surprise came from the crowd.

". . . but sadly, that splendid vessel was driven on a reef by the recent terrible typhoon . . ."

Cries of "Oh, *no!*" came now from the women and many of the men.

"But my good friend Clem and I survived by very good fortune."

His listeners leaned forward eagerly as he described the fury of the sea storm and the shipwreck on one of the Coral Rings.

"So from the wreckage we built and sailed our *Julia* catamaran in which we at last reached your island safely," Tom concluded.

"We've never heard such a curious tale," Maorai called out over the sudden applause. "You call her a cat . . . cata . . . ?"

"*Catamaran*. First devised long ago by an island people much like you but far, far away. It carried them many days, many weeks, often many months across open sea, far from any land."

"If we should study and perhaps copy your design," said the Shipwright hesitantly, "we'd not be breaking *tabus*, would we, Librarian of Carolna?"

"No, there're no *tabus* attached to building or sailing a catamaran that I'm aware of. Clem and I would be delighted to give you a hand."

"We would be most grateful!" said Samoy.

"Perhaps you'd consider an exchange," said the Librarian, turning to the Sage. "Our help with your new ships a-building here, in exchange for information?"

Samoy both smiled and frowned, obviously torn between an eager reply and sudden caution.

"*Perhaps* we could help you . . ." he began.

"*Our* help is given, quick as offered," Clem pointed out smoothly.

"Yes, and our questions are natural, from concern for our wives and children," Tom added.

"Well, ah . . ."

"What harm?" hissed Maorai to the Sage. "They'll learn soon enough."

"Well, ah, *er* . . ." Samoy had the grace to look embarrassed. "Well, if it's our place to answer, we shall, I assure you, but . . ."

"I think I understand," Tom interrupted him. "Well, let's try a direct question and see if you've an answer for us."

"Fair enough!" cried the Shipwright quickly.

Samoy gave him a withering look but nodded to Tom to continue.

"We came around the curve of the ocean looking for two young women and two little lads. One woman is my wife and the mother of our soon-to-be-born first child. She is named Alix Amanda Trusslo-Whitehead, Princess of Carolna."

The crowd muttered in growing interest, but Tom hastened on.

"The other lady is wife to my friend and champion, Clematis of Broken Land, here. The two boys are his sons, Gregor and Thomas Clemsson."

"Ah!" sighed Samoy. "We have often seen the beautiful young Princess and her entourage, of course."

"Then they *are* here?" Clem asked eagerly. "On this very island?"

"Well, yes," answered the elder, looking rather embarrassed again. "They are the guests of our *tiki* Byron Boldface."

He pointed up the mountainside. The travelers could just make out some sort of structure in a grove of flowering flame-trees on a sharp ridge high on the volcano's eastern flank.

"Guests?" asked Tom. "Or prisoners?"

"Ah, er, *ah*!" Samoy hesitated. "We were told they are *guests*, Sir Librarian. By our lord *tiki*, you see."

"May we meet this Byron Boldface and be reunited with our wives and children, then?" Tom asked sternly.

"Well, of course," sighed the elder. "In fact, our *tiki* has ordered us to bring you to him, when your meal is finished."

"I'm finished," said Clem, dropping his plate-leaf and jumping to his feet.

"And it was excellent," added Tom, more politely. "Thank you all!"

• • •

SAMOY had expected to lead them up the mountain with
an escort of young warriors, but as they set out the entire
village fell in behind them.

"Is my wife in good health?" Tom inquired anxiously
of Samoy. "I'm concerned, as her time is but a few days
off by all calculations."

"As far as we can tell *from a distance*, she is! You must
ask our *tiki*. He sees the lady each day, I imagine, although
I can't be certain. We only see them from afar, these two
young women, about the guest compound. The two lively
little boys," he chuckled for the first time in several long
minutes, "are ever about with their new friends, climbing
over rocks, swimming, riding the surfboards. They seem
most happy . . . at least from a distance."

"It'd better be so," muttered Clem grimly.

Tom gave his companion a warning look, and the
Woodsman swallowed further angry words.

A ten-foot palisade of foot-thick, yellow bamboo posts set
close together enclosed the *tiki*'s palace. Samoy apologet-
ically trotted ahead of the procession to strike a wooden
gong hanging from an arching aerial root of a banyan tree
before the gate.

Almost at once the gate swung wide.

An aged Parvaiti in a colorful sarong and a neat white
jacket of some unknown origin bowed deeply three times
to them.

"Lord Byron Boldface, our great and powerful *tiki*, expects you, gentlemen . . . and, er, ladies," he added, for the
village women were crowding up to the gate in such numbers that it could not be closed on them.

"Lead the way, Fartha," directed Maorai, speaking for
the villagers.

"Well, of course! Fine . . . er . . . this way," coughed the elderly servitor, and he turned on his bare heel and led them across a wide courtyard turfed with soft, fragrant grasses and over a high-arching wooden bridge across a fast-running stream to the front door of the bamboo palace.

Inside, the gatekeeper led them down a wide corridor into a large semicircular room hung with brightly figured pandanus-cloth examples of the native weavers' art. Large unglazed windows overlooked the village, the calm lagoon, and the restless sea beyond the reef.

At the side of the room opposite the entrance was a low dais, and upon this stood a chair sturdily constructed of an intricately carved and highly polished, dark and oily-looking wood.

Late-afternoon light entered the Great Room through high western windows. Through these the visitors glimpsed the smoking peak of Eversmoke.

The volcano, just then, belched a great round puff of yellow-brown smoke laced with dark streaks of ash. The ground beneath their feet trembled for a long three seconds, with a deep, angry rumble.

The islanders swayed easily to the tremor, paying it no particular heed. Caught off guard, Tom and Clem staggered a moment before regaining their balance.

"That happen often?" Clem demanded of Maorai.

"Several times a day," answered the Shipwright with a shrug.

All eyes swiveled sharply to a door in the right-hand wall. Unnoticed during the temblor and roar, a strange figure in a feathered cape and wooden fright mask had appeared there. As Tom watched in startled surprise, the newcomer slowly approached and climbed the dais. He sat upon the throne chair.

"This must be our host," murmured Tom, just a bit sarcastically.

"Bow down! Bow down!" bellowed Samoy, remembering his duties. Everyone bent their knees and fell forward to touch their heads on the woven floor mat. "Revere our all-powerful and fearsome *tiki*! Hail Byron Boldface! Bow your heads!"

"I rather think not," said the Librarian firmly.

He nodded politely to the little man in the heavy, gaudily carved and painted mask instead. Clem bowed stiffly from the waist, ready to listen or fight, whichever seemed most useful.

They silently studied the man in the mask.

When he looked more closely, Tom could see the man under it all was slight of build, rather spindly of legs and arms . . . and more than a little nervous.

"Come forward," the *tiki* said in a stage-quality hollow voice. "Come to the foot of my throne, Mage of Carolna."

"Let's get something straight from the start, sir," Tom said quickly. "I have the honorable title of Knight of the Kingdom of Carolna. I am Royal Librarian to His Majesty King Eduard Ten of Carolna. I am also Librarian to the Royal Historian, Murdan of Overhall. I am lawful and loving consort to Princess Alix Amanda of Carolna . . . *and* I am a Dragon Companion. But I am *not* a magician!"

The man behind the glowering mask seemed taken aback by the stranger's boldness, for he allowed Clem to identify himself as a freeholder of Carolna, husband of Lady Mornie of Morningside, and father of the two young Clemssons.

"I believe you know them?" he ended with a hard glare in his steely blue eyes.

"I know who they are," Byron Boldface admitted . . . a shade too quickly.

"Now that you know who you've brought here by magical means in a manner that, to many, would seem grossly foul and quite unfair," said Tom loudly, "who are *you*, Sir?"

The figure on the throne drew himself up and sat as tall as he could.

"You have been informed of my name," he said, matching Tom's volume. "Samoy . . . !"

"Leave this very nice old man out of this!" snapped Tom, letting his anger show for the first time. "This matter is between *us* and *you*, Byron Boldface, or whatever you choose to call yourself. Where are our wives and children? We demand to see them at once!"

"In my own house! On my own island! You dare to speak thus to . . ."

"A kidnapper!" Clem ground out. "A stealer of little children and innocent women! Someone'll pay for this, believe me!"

Tom nodded in cold anger. "Take us to our wives, at once, *tiki*! It's the only honorable thing to do, first and foremost."

Byron Boldface trembled with anger. Or fear? Tom couldn't decide. The little *tiki* addressed his listening people instead.

"Samoy! Parvaiti, all! Go back down to the village and await my orders there. This business is not for your ears and eyes. Go at once, and quietly."

Although Maorai and some of the young men hesitated, Samoy turned away thankfully and began shooing the crowd from the room with soft words and urgent gestures.

In a minute only Tom, Clem, the elderly butler, and the masked *tiki* remained.

"Close the gate," Boldface ordered his servant. "Await my call outside."

Fartha bowed deeply and trotted from the room. Shortly they heard the heavy bamboo gates bang shut and the bolts shoot across.

"Now," said the masked man. "Consider yourselves prisoners."

"*You* may consider us prisoners, but we'll be the judge of that," said Tom. "We want to see our families. The Princess of Carolna is pregnant, in case you hadn't noticed, and must be cared for."

"The Princess?" asked the man on the throne. "Yes, she's with child, I know. Our midwife sees her daily and assures me she and the unborn child are quite well, swelling quite properly. The Princess is in good health and spirits. I'll take you to her shortly. But first . . . let us talk of *my* demands."

"I assumed you have some demands. Most kidnappers do," Tom said flatly. "How much do you demand for their release, safe and sound, and at once?"

"Not money!" Boldface insisted, sounding very determined. "Sanctuary, rather. For my people!"

"Sanctuary!" Clem cried. "Sanctuary? From what, may I ask?"

"*Death and destruction!* What any man would fear most!" gasped the *tiki* of the Parvaiti with what sounded suspiciously like a sob. "Prisoners, be seated and hear *my* story."

✦ 12 ✦
Tiki's Tale

"I was born in Faldagor on the southwest coast of Hintoo," Byron Boldface began when they'd seated themselves uneasily on low benches in front of his dais, "of poor but honest parents. Father was a herbalist. He and Mother had seven children. I was the third—their eldest son."

Clem squirmed, about to speak, but Tom silenced him with a glance and a shake of his head.

"When I was twelve years of age, as is the custom, I was apprenticed to a certain dervish named Pallardi. He was a wretched, slovenly old magic-dabbler of poor repute and no prospects. He agreed to train and school me in his craft; he would charge no fee for the service. Which is why my poor parents chose him, I suppose.

"I tried very hard to learn what Pallardi tried to teach me, but after eight years, having learned very little except sweeping floors, laundering Pallardi's filthy linen, and keeping him from stumbling drunkenly under the wheels of some high noble's carriage when he staggered from a tavern late every night, I slipped away!"

"No one could blame you for that," said Tom into the pause that followed. "You would be much more comfortable if you would remove that ridiculous wooden mask and hot feathers, sir."

Boldface pretended to be offended, but then he sighed. He reached behind his neck and unfastened a leather strap that held his heavy grotesquery in place.

Under the mask his face was lean, brown, unbearded, deeply lined, sorely pinched, and rather sickly. In contrast to the evil mask, his expression was mild but deeply worried. When he also removed and carefully folded the beautiful feather cloak, he was revealed as thin . . . in fact, quite literally skin and bones.

"Much better," he agreed wearily. "I am fearful of showing these fine, strong, healthy Parvaiti what I really am. They've lived peaceful lives separated from the rest of the world for so many generations. Well, let me go on."

"Please do," the Librarian urged.

"I could find work nowhere, being a starving and runaway apprentice. I came close to death many times there in the crowded, filthy alleys and back streets. In desperation I hid myself aboard a foreign merchant ship that came into the harbor. She was well out to sea before I was discovered.

"The captain proposed to heave me overboard, but I managed to convince him that, though I might be small, I'd work hard for my keep. He turned me over to his crew to train."

The little man wiped his forehead. The feather robes and the mask, Tom realized, had been oppressively hot. The evening air was still and humid.

Tom and Clem waited silently for him to continue.

"I was rated a common seaman for twenty-five years. It wasn't a bad life, although lonely. Sailormen are not my sort, being mostly rough, hard of hand, foul of mouth, and immoral. But I proved my value over and over again to Captain Perad. I think he rather came to like me. Or perhaps I amused him. He taught me navigation and seamanship to while away long days and nights at sea and the ways of seamen and ships and the inconstant winds. At the very least, I ate regular meals.

"Fortunately . . . or perhaps unfortunately . . . our ship never called again at my home port. I never saw my family again. Yes, it was a lonely life."

He turned away for a moment and blew his nose loudly.

"I knew I'd never rise to become even a petty officer,

let alone a proud warrant officer. When my good captain, my protector, suddenly died at sea, his crewmen, out of jealousy, seized me, stripped me of my few belongings, and marooned me on a cold, barren spit of gravel in the far south.

"How bitter I was! But bitterness gave me strength to survive and overcome adversity. I lived alone on that cold, cheerless coast for over seven years, eating bird's eggs, and fishes scooped by hand from tidal pools. It was a cruel, hard, cold life and even more lonely than before.

"In the middle of the seventh year, while wandering on the strand looking for crabs, I saw and picked up a brightly polished piece of stone. Forgotten lessons from my drunken master returned to mind. The bauble was a magic amulet, anciently carved of clear sky-blue mineral, and engraved with strange letters I could barely read.

"I studied this blue stone for the better part of a month, until at last I devised and deciphered its inscription describing its powers and uses. It was a Jewel of Displacement!"

"I'm not familiar with such magicks, myself," admitted Tom. "What could it do?"

"When used properly it allowed its possessor to transport anything or anyone from one place to another in the twinkling of an eye. Most useful! Most valuable!

"I determined to use the Jewel of Displacement to escape the deserted strand. I would set up in business as a Magician specializing in shipping quantities of goods swiftly and safely, moving cargoes from place to place, or perhaps herds of cattle, or even crowds of people.

"I envisioned myself as becoming extremely wealthy.

"I experimented with the blue stone for some weeks to be sure of my mastery, and then attempted my first great transportation. But I learned the blue stone would transport anything, anyone . . . but not its *user*! In the end, I ordered the stone to bring me a sailing dhow. It arrived offshore in a great flash of light, and I left my lonely exile at once, arriving safely three months later on the south coast of Hintoo.

"I felt I was on top of the world at last."

His head drooped sadly.

"Alas, I knew so little of the world's wickedness, cruelty, and depravity."

"What happened?" asked Clem, interested despite himself.

"I went to Rajal, the great imperial capital of Hintoo. There I found that all great magicking in the Empire is rigidly controlled by a Mages' Guild. To join I must either enter the lowest rank and work my way up for forty or fifty years or pay an enormous fee in pure gold for full Guild membership. I had no money, just my blue stone, and I couldn't part with that, for it was to be the foundation of a great fortune."

"So you bootlegged?" guessed Tom.

"I'm not familiar with the term, Librarian, but your meaning is clear. I sought out men who wished transportation but could not or would not pay the exorbitant fees the Mages demanded. Very quietly, I began to accumulate the required Guild entry fee.

"I was in a constant agony! I lived in abject terror that Guild Proctors would discover my petty deals, strip me of my precious blue stone, then have me tried and burned at the stake as an unlicensed practitioner."

"Not a pleasant life, I should imagine," murmured Tom when Boldface paused to consider his memories.

"No, not even for me, who was used to being kicked and spat upon and forced to do the most menial tasks for minuscule pay. I was ever more bitter in my new fortune . . . so I was fair game for a sympathetic ally. I met Ahmedek the Artful."

"Artful?" wondered Clem.

"Yes! He was, and I knew him to be, a minor member of the Mages' Guild. He admitted privately he'd stolen certain Power Tools from a dying Guild Fellow. Then he'd buried the body in the desert to avoid charges of theft and, perhaps, murder. I believed I'd found a fellow sufferer from Guild injustice. We became secret partners."

Boldface rocked mournfully from side to side.

"Eight *years* we worked, side by side, and made a great mountain of gold and another of silver, always keeping a step ahead of the Proctors by dint of bribery and Ahmedek's sly strategies. He taught me minor magickings that he'd learned from his own study before he'd grown impatient with the slowness of his progress and had struck out on his own.

"I . . . foolishly . . . confided to him the secret of the blue stone. He told me to keep it well hidden and work to our common benefit with it. We earned enormous fees by moving whole armies from one end of the empire to another in a twinkling. With my stone we purloined vast treasures from deeply buried, secret hordes. Sometimes on commission. Sometimes on our own initiative.

"Then, one late night near the end of the eighth year of our partnership, Ahmedek came to me with dire news. The Guild Proctors had learned, through an informer he said, of my part in our business. I must flee far and fast, Ahmedek insisted, or face instant arrest, secret trial, and public immolation!

"He claimed he, himself, was safe. His name had not been mentioned in the secret Guild indictment. With me gone, he said, the persecution would wither away."

"Ah! Do I smell a muskrat?" cried Clem.

"A muskrat? A dead monkey, as we say at home," sniffed the scrawny little man. "He proposed that he use my stone to send me to a far place where the Guild Proctors would never think to look. He promised that, after a suitable time, he would send for me and we would resume business as before."

"And that's when you came here?" Tom asked.

"Not quite. Ahmedek the Artful took my blue stone and sent me to a western desert sheikdom far beyond the reach of Emperor or Guild. I had my small magicks to sustain me, and I settled down in relative comfort to await the day when Ahmedek would send for me. Fristiastan is a poor, tiny, unimportant, flyspeck of a place, but my slight powers were appreciated there and licensing requirements were nonexistent. I should have been content!"

"Ahmedek never sent for you," Clem guessed.

Boldface nodded.

"*Years* passed . . . twelve years for my indictment to lapse, Ahmedek had told me, and thereafter I daily expected him to use my stone to return me to his side.

"In my *seventeenth* year of exile I heard from an itinerant crystal-cutter that a certain Magician named Ahmedek had been elected Grand Master of the Mages' Guild in Rajal! His description convinced me this was the same Ahmedek who'd been my partner. Now that he headed the powerful Guild, my old friend would send for me, I was sure. I waited for another three years."

"No word?" asked Clem.

"At last," continued the renegade Mage, nodding, "I wrote to him asking when I could return home. He didn't answer.

"I convinced myself that the letter had been lost between Fristiastan and Rajal. I wrote again and waited yet another year. Finally, in desperation . . . and greed and anger, too, I admit . . . I decided to travel back to Hintoo and confront my former partner. Even if he wouldn't accept me again as partner, I was sure he would arrange a Guild membership for me to assure my continued silence. I even expected him to return my stone!"

"So?" Tom and Clem asked together.

"It took me two long, hard years to reach Rajal. I traveled as a trader in colored inks. I was wracked by doubts and torn by fears. Had Ahmedek *purposely* abandoned me? What would he do when I revealed myself to him? I resolved to be circumspect, to spy out the lay of the land most carefully before I faced my old partner and demanded my stone.

"In Rajal I wheedled some business selling my inks at an enormous discount to the Chief Scribe of the Mages' Guild. He was a gossipy old soul who loved his wine and whose mouth ran like an artesian well, even when he was sober. I learned from him that Ahmedek was hated and distrusted by many in the Guild, having vaulted himself into a position of great power almost equal to that of the Emperor of Hintoo.

"I was desperate! Despite all the stories I'd heard about his cold cruelty and evil temper, I would confront the new Grand Master in his innermost chambers. I was willing to risk his worst . . . even death! Anything he did would be better than the disappointment, the uncertainty, the anger, the fear I lived with, day to day."

"Bold move!" Clem cheered him on.

"I decided to hide in Ahmedek's palace one evening after a drinking bout with the Chief Scribe. I waited until all but the Grand Master's personal servants and bodyguards had left for their homes and barracks.

"I crept into Ahmedek's innermost apartment and hid behind a tapestry. My informant had said Ahmedek came here every night to perform certain rites necessary to nourish and increase his powers.

"At midnight Ahmedek appeared . . . in company with another, whose aura of power shook me to the very core. I never learned his name nor saw his face, but I'm certain he detected me in my hiding place.

"He said nothing about it, however, which surprised me greatly. Instead, he spoke to Ahmedek at length, seeking to persuade my former partner to sell him my blue stone. This surprised me even more, for I was sure no one knew of the stone's existence. Ahmedek was caught in fearful surprise, also. We'd never showed the blue stone, not even to our closest associates and best clients.

"Ahmedek adamantly refused to part with the Jewel. The strange Elf began to recount Ahmedek's career in most unflattering detail, asking, 'What if the Guild Proctors heard even a faint rumor of your evil thievery, your false witnessing, the sworn lies, the foul murders in the night?'

" 'The blue stone must be mine!' the stranger declared.

"Ahmedek became terribly angry and threatened to send the stranger away by using the very blue stone!

"But the other was younger and much quicker than Ahmedek by a long stretch of rope! When Ahmedek reached for the stone in its hiding place, the stranger plucked it from his grasp and spelled Ahmedek elsewhere. I've no idea where! Ahmedek, hearing his fate pronounced, screamed loud enough to make the very walls tremble.

"He was gone in a blinding, silent explosion!

"I could hear the Guild guards rushing to investigate his wild cry and the flash of the explosion. As I stood immobile in icy terror, the stranger paused to think, it seemed, then turned quickly and dragged me from my hiding place.

" 'Ah!' he cried, seeing me cowering there. 'It's time for us both to depart!'

"He stroked the stone again and spoke its powerful words quickly. How he learned the proper spell-words I'll never know.

"I was whisked away in a second flash. What happened later in Hintoo, I've never tried to learn."

"You were sent to this island?" asked Tom, wondering how much longer the strange tale would continue.

"Yes! I found myself here in the swamps at the south end of the island. There'd been a minor eruption. The Parvaiti, as is their usual precaution, had taken to their canoes, paddling far out to sea, fearing the overflowing lava and great flying chunks of half-molten rocks."

"How did you come to be what they call you . . . their *tiki*?"

"A *tiki* is a guardian spirit—sort of a demigod. Only when the eruption died away and the rocks had cooled did the Parvaiti return, which gave me time to disguise myself in these robes and this heavy mask. I found them in a shrine in the jungle. I let them find me on the still-smoking slopes."

He shook his head.

"I was still quite amazed by events. I still am afraid of them, afraid of the mountain, afraid of what I think might happen."

"Another eruption?" asked Clem.

"Much worse," cried Byron Boldface. "Much worse! My early training under old Pallardi included reading stones. He used the craft to divine winning horses in races, except he sold his tips rather than betting on the races himself, for enough to buy his liquor.

"The stones here tell me of coming *total* devastation! Death and fire! Tidal waves, furious white-hot winds, and unimaginable explosions!"

"Warn the Parvaiti and get them into their canoes again," suggested Tom. "Find another, safer place to live?"

"Easier said than accomplished. This touches on the Princess Alix Amanda, the King of Carolna, and his Historian, and you, Thomas Librarian.

"When they found me dressed in the sacred feathers, I didn't dare deny I was their *tiki*, come to life. I'd come, I told them, to save them from total, fiery destruction, but they must do my every least bidding! I at first ordered them to build this palace, then construct a great junk in the Hintoo manner. I would use it to escape the coming catastrophe. They did so, and they called her *Pelehoehoe*."

And he began to weep, not angrily, but disconsolately, heartsick.

"Soon I came to realize I loved these peaceful, happy, friendly people. And that they *need* me! I wanted to save them, as well as myself. And now I've probably ruined it for all and good. *Pelehoehoe* was to be our means of escape! What am I to do? What are *we* to do?"

Tom and Clem exchanged glances. The Librarian laid his hand on the *tiki*'s arm.

"Wait a moment, Byron. Slow down," he said soothingly. "What is . . . was . . . your plan? And how did Manda figure in it, after all?"

"Yes," said Clem, rather disgusted by the Mage's tears. "Drop the other boot, for goodness' sake."

Thinking they would be better off in a more private place—and looking all the while for the hiding place where Boldface had secreted Manda, Mornie, and the boys—they led the weeping *tiki* to another part of his palace, into his sparse private quarters, neat and clean, open to the evening breeze and light across broad lanais and gardens planted with exotic flowers and shrubs.

They found there a bare but bright and colorful sitting room furnished with rattan furniture softened by brightly dyed pillows, mats, and rugs.

Boldface recovered himself enough to answer their questions.

Clem said to him, "You haven't said what your plan was, have you?"

"I . . . I'm rather rattled," admitted Boldface. "I've never been any good at things like this, making plans and pulling strings and getting people to do what I needed them to do.''

"But you *have* done so,'' Tom pointed out. He dropped wearily into one of the chairs. "You seem to be a strong leader. The Parvaiti evidently follow your orders without question.''

"Still . . .'' began Byron. "Well, from the very first it was obvious they didn't grasp what Eversmoke would do to them. When I explained, they didn't really understand. The island has *always* bumped, burped, and growled, they insisted. It never had more than occasional spills of molten lava. When that happens, they explained cheerfully, they'd take to their fishing canoes and flee to the Coral Rings, off to the north, to wait for the eruption to end. Meanwhile they would live by fishing and gathering fruit and coconuts. They believed these times of thunder and smoke were sort of a holiday, a lark!''

He settled down enough to offer them a drink of fruit juice and a plate of coconut macaroons, which Clem found very tasty even though he was rapidly tiring of coconut in any form.

"It's quite evident from all the signs that when the *next* eruption comes—it's a bit hazy *when*, but it may come as early as this autumn's full moon and neap tide—it'll blast the entire island into dust, leaving a seething hole filled with boiling seawater. It's happened before, nearby . . .''

"The Coral Rings!'' Tom exclaimed, understanding at last their strange formation.

"Yes, Librarian. Each of them was once a volcano. Their sizes varied from a few acres to hundreds of miles around, and as tall as a thousand feet above the sea. Most just died down, but a few destroyed themselves in terrible explosions! The evidence is there to see, if one looks closely.

"To save the Parvaiti . . . and myself . . . I knew we had very little time. If only I still had my blue stone . . . but it's gone! I set the natives to building *Pelehoehoe*, to carry everyone to safety.

"But first, I went to the east to capture suitable hostages. In Carolna I settled on Princess Manda. Everyone I met spoke of her, and of you, Librarian! I plotted to bring you here to deal for her release in return for land in Carolna.

"When *Pelehoehoe* failed to return, I set the Parvaiti to building the large seagoing canoes."

"The typhoon changed your plan," Tom guessed.

"Samoy and Maorai and their men at once started a fleet of great war canoes very carefully and beautifully. They don't know how to rush such fine work. Every task has a necessary ritual! I try to rush them, but they say, 'You are a *tiki*, Lord, and a *tiki* knows it takes a long time to build a good, safe, seaworthy war canoe this large and strong. It must be done *just so*, or not at all . . . as you know!' "

"I can understand, I think," Tom mused. "I've known men who brush their teeth that way. Have to do it *just so*, this many strokes for each tooth, even if it means the house'll burn down around them."

"Precisely," agreed Byron, smiling slightly for the first time.

"Before we go to meet my wife," Tom said gravely, "I still don't understand how she and I, and Murdan and my father-in-law, the King, fit into your plans. Or did, before *Pelehoehoe* was wrecked."

"You're right, of course," sighed Byron, the shame and sorrow written on his face plain to read now. "I *desperately* sought a safe refuge for my people. All I could think of was distant Carolna. It would be much more difficult to sail west to Hintoo. Winds and currents would be ever against us. And even if we reached the Empire, we'd be driven away, I feared, or more likely enslaved! Strangers are not welcome in Hintoo.

"So, I took my splendid new ship, which my minor arts

had equipped to sail without a crew or a captain, to your coast. I gathered information about Carolna. The stories of the people I spoke with were filled with descriptions of a wise liege lord named Murdan, a good King named Eduard, and a powerful Knight, much loved by everybody, who'd won the King's eldest daughter to wife.

"I found my way to your Hidden Lake Canyon. I forged a note with your signature, to lure your Princess-wife to come away with me on her very own Dragon. It worked remarkably well!

"I planned to hold her gently but firmly until a grant of land was ceded to the Parvaiti by your King. Then I would apologize profusely and let her go. I've explained all this to the Princess, and I think she understands. And maybe forgives."

"Now to see if her husband can forgive you," muttered Clem through clenched teeth. "Where are the ladies?"

"I'll show you. It isn't far."

HE led them through a side gate, and they climbed by a steeply winding pathway up the mountainside, through rustling bamboo forest and terraced fields of pineapple.

"When I realized *Pelehoehoe* was lost, I hoped we'd have time to build enough war canoes to replace her. That course was obviously quicker, if less sure, than building another junk."

"Your fishing canoes wouldn't be large enough?" Clem asked.

"Not the usual craft my people build for fishing and such. These war canoes, to serve, had to be three or four times larger . . . and much stronger. We can't escape this time by sailing even to the farthest Coral Rings. They'll be swept by great tidal waves when Eversmoke finally destroys itself. I hope the war canoes will serve. If not . . . and the Parvaiti can't escape, I'll perish with them!"

"Perish with them!" Tom exclaimed in disbelief.

"I can't desert them now! They *trust* me, admire me, follow my strange orders! They fear me, I suppose, but they think the world of me. It is, I've found, their very nature to love, rather than to hate. I can't let them know what a p-p-poor excuse for a fool I really am."

"*Was*, perhaps," the Woodsman conceded.

"Ah, now I see!" Tom exclaimed. "You would still need Manda . . ."

"Unexpected and unwanted, we'd be unwelcome, hated immigrants to Carolna! There wasn't time! I settled on a desperate course. I'd take the hostages with us. Your King Eduard must value his daughter enough to cede us a small plot of land somewhere.

"I decided to ask you to come for your wife and deal with my propositon, Sir Thomas. It seemed to me the Carolnans and their King would accept your plea for your young wife. To ask the King or even his half brother, the Historian, to accept defeat would shake the foundations of the Kingdom, already badly shaken by recent events. Or so I thought."

"But, man! Why couldn't you just *ask*?" Tom cried. "I'm positive Carolna would've welcomed you! There's plenty of space for settlers, and we have a long tradition of toleration of strangers."

Byron considered his words carefully.

"Your Eduard seemed so very weak . . . almost a cipher! A mere figurehead! I *couldn't* risk rejection! If we arrived in Carolna, I believed, just as in Hintoo, we'd be turned away or slain or enslaved. That's what I feared would happen, if we set foot unbidden on your soil."

"Didn't you know it very wrong to hold hostage two innocent women and two little children?" Clem demanded.

"I . . . I . . . thought it the *only* way! It was wrong, but what was I to do? There wasn't time!"

Clem began to argue, but Tom patted his friend on the shoulder to quiet his anger.

"Let's find Manda and your family first. I need a bit of time to consider all this, and Manda's got a good head for this sort of thing. Better than either of ours. She knows her father and her countrymen better, too."

Clem sighed, still red with fury, but nodded reluctant agreement.

"I want to hear from our ladies how they've been treated," he growled. "It bears strong on what we decide to do to this here *tiki*."

"No matter what you do to me," Byron said earnestly, "I have to do what I can to save my Parvaiti! They had no part in my scheming."

"I'm already considering that," Tom assured him mildly.

THE *tiki* led them on up the steeply winding path cut into the mountainside, past a series of deep blue pools of steaming water and, at last, to another, smaller bamboo compound.

Shrieks and shouts of defiance met them as they stopped at the closed gate.

"*Great griffins!*" swore Clem, flinging the gate wide, a look of fear and horror marring his usually stolid face. "What's going on here?"

Tom rushed after him into a wide, neatly raked, graveled courtyard. When the Woodsman stopped short with an exclamation of utter amazement, Tom all but bowled him over.

At the far end of the courtyard Gregor Clemsson stood waving a thick club. With her back to them was a very pregnant Manda—Alix Amanda Trusslo Eduardsdotter, Princess of Carolna, wife of Dragon Companion Sir Thomas of Overhall and a Dragon Companion herself—preparing, if somewhat awkwardly, to hurl a missile at the child with all her might.

Behind her crouched prim Mistress Mornie of Morningside, clapping her hands and screaming at the top of her voice: "Burn it in there, Manda baby! Blow 'im away! Strike him! *Strike him!* He can't hit the broad side of a donjon!"

The younger Clemsson, Tom's namesake, screamed and danced back and forth, ready to dash from one elaborately embroidered pillow toward another, some yards away, when he saw the two men standing aghast in the gateway.

"Papa!" he shrieked at the top of his piercing, four-year-old voice, and ran full tilt into the Woodsman's outstretched arms.

"Great grizzly's sake!" Clem growled to the Librarian. "It's that idiotic game you taught 'em."

"Well, who's winning?" Tom gasped, choking with relieved laughter.

"I think it's me!" said his flushed and puffed-up wife, dropping the makeshift baseball and throwing herself recklessly into his arms.

✦ 13 ✦
Where There's Smoke . . .

"WHAT *are* you doing, Manda?" cried Tom when he could get his breath at last. "In your condition . . ."

"She *had* to pitch, Uncle Tom," young Gregor pleaded earnestly. "Mama can't get the ball *near* the plate."

"Some strange ritual of your country, Librarian?" asked a bemused Byron Boldface.

"It's a pastime, a game . . . we call it *baseball*," the Librarian explained quickly. "The lads will tell you of it later, *tiki*."

"It's so *wonderful* to see you!" Manda was saying, drying her tears of joy on his sleeve. "How'd you get here? Have you brought Retruance?"

"He's not far off," her husband replied. "Are you well? The baby?"

"Rolls about like an acrobat," giggled Manda proudly, patting her tummy. "No sign of joining us, just yet. I think Flabianus may have been slightly incorrect in his estimates."

"I hope so, most sincerely," said Tom. "We've still got a bunch of matters to settle before we can go home."

"Yes, old Byron's poor people . . . the volcano and all. Have you seen him? He's told you?"

Tom was surprised for a moment, but then he laughed aloud.

"*Here* is Byron Boldface. May I present you to him, Princess? But you've already met, I think."

Manda laughed. "Well, I've never seen him without the fancy decorations and big teeth. Your real appearance is better by far, *tiki*. I really prefer you unmasked."

Byron blushed deep crimson and stammered his apologies.

"I'VE been thinking about all this business," said Manda, drawing Tom and Byron aside while Clem and his young family chattered a mile a minute about their adventures. "You agree we should help them, in spite of Byron's nasty plan gone awry?"

"If you can forgive him, I suppose I can," her husband sighed, giving her another hug. "And, yes, we *must* help the Parvaiti. But I worry most about your birthing."

"I don't have to be at Lexor or at Hidden Lake Canyon to deliver our child, you know," said Manda with a happy chuckle. "The island midwife's quite expert at such things. She knows all the right things to do and say. She's been doing it for a lifetime."

"Still . . . well, you're right, of course," her husband admitted slowly. "If you feel well . . . if the baby's well . . . that's the important thing."

"Alive and kicking," said his wife. "I want to know how you found us."

"Let's go under the shade of those remarkable ferns or whatever they are," suggested Tom, "and we'll tell you the whole tale from the beginning. Boldface's tale, too, unless he's already told you?"

"I've told them all," said the *tiki*, smiling broadly now.

"And I understand all," Manda insisted. "It has made our stay here much more comfortable. In fact, rather pleasant . . . except for the earthquakes."

Tom stood before them and in his best Librarian manner started at the beginning to weave all the strands together, right down to the present.

"We *must* save the good Parvaiti of Eversmoke Island," Manda insisted again. "My Tom can do it," she added to Boldface. "He's a Human!"

Byron stared at Tom in sudden awe.

"I never suspected!" he cried. "Yes, I see the signs! Well, that gives me greater heart. We'll follow you . . . I and my Parvaiti, too, I assure you, Dragon Companion."

"Speaking of Dragons," Clem interrupted, "where's Furbetrance? You'd better call Retruance from wherever he is, too. It'll take a while for the Parvaiti to get used to them being around. Does their folklore include Dragons, Byron?"

"Come to think of it, yes," said Byron, stroking his chin. "They speak of a mysterious great Sea Dragon, and believe all Dragons are the children of fire mountains like Eversmoke."

"That should be a help," Tom thought aloud.

He left them, going off to walk alone in the pleasant garden, mentally calling his mount as only a Dragon Companion can.

He'd barely returned to the gathering under the tree ferns when the sun was momentarily blocked by a swift-moving shadow. Retruance Constable, flashing emerald green and highly polished gold, looped over the nearest shoulder of Eversmoke and swooped down into the courtyard, blasting bright jets of orange flame and bellowing like a water buffalo stuck in deep mud.

"Hello, Manda! Mornie! Boys! Good to see you all healthy and together again. Your menfolk have been near impossible, I can tell you."

"We all knew you'd come to our rescue," Manda cried, throwing her arms about the Dragon's muzzle, despite wisps of delighted smoke still clinging there. "Welcome, my dear! Your brother will be even more delighted, I'm sure."

"Speaking of my brother, where is he? If we leave at once, we can beat the new typhoon . . ."

"Oh, no! *Another* storm?" cried Manda, her dismay echoed by everyone, even the boys. "How soon, Retruance? Can you tell?"

"My friend Flo, the great Sea Dragon," Retruance explained, blowing a quick string of smoke rings into the hot, still air, "assures me it will begin late tonight and last for two days and nights. Torrents of rain and savage winds. I was about to come warn you when I heard your call, Tom."

Byron called to a servant and sent him plunging down the mountainside trail to warn the villagers of the coming storm and to give them a brief report of what had occurred that evening at the mountainside palace.

"He's listened to everything we've said, of course," he confided to Manda. "It's a part of his job."

"So he's loyal and not an alarmist," frowned the Princess.

"Oh, most loyal. As are all of them, as I'm sure you've seen, Princess."

"It must be long after dinner," Clem was saying. "Why don't we find something—no coconuts, please!—to eat while Tom fills Retruance in on things."

The ladies went off to raid the pantry with the help of three pretty island maids and two husky young men who'd been assigned by the *tiki* to serve them in their captivity.

By the time they'd provided a delicious meal of broiled albacore, cold roast pork, fruit salad, and steamed rice with pine nuts—no coconuts in this meal, at all, to Clem's relief—Tom had brought his Dragon up to the moment.

Retruance silently considered while they ate, seated on fragrant grass mats under the cool ferns. A short rain shower fell, cleansing the air for a while of wayward fumes from the mountain. Several times during dinner they felt brief, sharp movements underfoot, reminding them of the volcano's menace.

"Well, there're several problems involved," the Dragon

said, downing a final gulp of banana beer and smacking his
lips appreciatively.

"So I would say," agreed his Companion.

Ticking items off on his sharp claws, Retruance went on.
"First: the time element. Flo tells me the big bang will
certainly occur around Autumnal Equinox. Perhaps a day
or two earlier or later."

"The Sea Dragon is reputed to be an excellent prophet
of weather," Byron Boldface said quietly. "I suspect he's
also a predictor of other natural occurrences. His estimate
is certainly less *inexact* than mine."

"So," continued Retruance, nodding thanks to the *tiki*,
"we are agreed that there's no time to build another full-
sized junk. And I would say, Woodsman, that *Pelehoehoe*
is beyond repair?"

"Quite certain," Clem agreed. "The keel's split quite in
twain. And we pretty well tore her up to build *Julia*."

"*Julia!*" Tom cried. "We left her beached on the west
coast. We'll have to go for her. She's not big, but she's
seaworthy."

Byron shook his head. "There's no time now to sail her
around to the village lagoon!"

"After the storm, perhaps?" Tom asked. "*If* she sur-
vives. She's too valuable to leave behind!"

"Problem number one is to arrange some means of transport for all of us, Carolnans and Parvaiti alike," Retruance
said firmly, to bring the discussion back to his first point.

"Couldn't you and Furbie carry us to safety . . . I mean,
all of us?" asked Manda.

"Not even with Flo's help," sighed the Dragon. "Not
even with the help of Flo *and* Furbetrance *and* Hetabelle.
Where *is* my baby brother, by the way?"

"Oh, for goodness' sake!" cried Manda, jumping up.
"He in a cave up the hill a bit. He refused to leave us, and

Byron allowed him to find a comfortable place to live. He's far too big for this villa.''

''Dragon Furbetrance Constable was willing to cooperate,'' admitted Byron. ''Especially after I explained our predicament and he was convinced I intended no harm to my . . . *er* . . . guests.''

The Clemsson boys, impatient with all the adult talk, volunteered to take a torch and fetch Furbetrance from his cave. They dashed off as if the climb up a rumbling volcano in pouring rain was nothing to them at all.

''Youth!'' exclaimed Clem with a father's sigh and a proud grin. ''Go on, Retruance.''

''I'm sure you've all thought of these things. Our hope lies in the new war canoes.''

''They're nearly completed,'' reported the *tiki*. ''And they should be enough to carry everybody if we crowd them.''

''Number two problem is where you'll go, once you've the means.''

Tom said thoughtfully, ''I see no problem settling the Parvaiti in Carolna. If they want to learn to become farmers, Manda and I can grant them freeholdings in Hiding Land. They'd be most welcome!''

''Desert farming'd take some getting used to,'' warned Clem. ''Our whole west coast is pretty rugged and rather dry. Not very good for farming, I fear, until Tom brings the water up.''

Manda said, ''They'd rather settle right on the coast somewhere, I'd think. Close to the Quietness.''

''Yes, if we're near the ocean, we could fish,'' Byron said. ''We're excellent sailors and superb fishermen.''

''If there's any objection to settling there,'' said Mornie slowly, ''it'll be the cold winters.''

''Not so severe by *our* standards,'' agreed Tom, recalling the previous winter spent in a tent at Hidden Lake. ''However, heavy snows and freezing temperatures overnight were not uncommon.''

''I imagine they'd get used to it,'' Clem considered. ''They can get warm furs from the trappers at Wall in exchange for their fish.''

''I think,'' Tom said thoughtfully, ''I've a suggestion that'll solve problem number two at a stroke.''

''That's my husband!'' cried Manda, beaming proudly. ''We sit around wishing we had Byron Boldface's Jewel of Displacement while Tom solves problems like sailors play rum ginny!''

''*Gin rummy,*'' her husband laughed. ''I suggest we do *not* move the Parvaiti to Carolna at all. I suggest we introduce them to the more suitable climate, vegetation, fish, and wildlife of Isthmusi!''

''The coastal plains and the rain forests!'' exclaimed Retruance. ''A perfect solution! And somewhat closer from here in sea miles than Mantura Bay, I estimate.''

''Isthmusi isn't a part of Carolna,'' Manda explained to Byron Boldface. ''It has a few scattered peoples like the Lofters. We've had only a little contact with those tribesmen in the higher mountains.''

''The Lofters, yes!'' Retruance remembered. ''They're quite a sociable bunch. They'd be a great help getting the islanders settled.''

Just then Furbetrance, himself, arrived a-wing, bearing the wildly excited and shouting Clemssons on his head. As he was greeting his brother and the rest, a winded servant returned from the village at the foot of the mountain, followed more slowly by Samoy the Sage.

''We await your storm orders, *tiki!*'' he said, once he'd recovered from the shock of seeing him unmasked for the first time.

''I'll go down and help you prepare for the typhoon,''

Byron Boldface told him. "No place to run, this time, and no time, either.

"Gather as much of the crops as we can. The storm will sweep all away before it, as it floods the fields and paddies. When that's done, we'll hold a tribal conference. Everyone must be there!"

"Yes, Lord *tiki!*" puffed Samoy, bowing double. "At once!"

"And I think we should perhaps dispense with the 'Lord *tiki*' business," added Byron with some regret. "I am, as you can see very plainly, just a sun-dried old prune, unworthy of the title."

"*Never!*" cried the Parvaiti elder in genuine consternation at the thought. "You will *always* be our guardian spirit, wrinkles and all! In fact," he added, "wrinkles and white eyebrows are sure signs of wisdom. How do you think I got my position as Sage? We beg you not to desert us, *tiki.*"

"If you so wish," said Byron, genuinely moved and near tears. "Well, we'll take it up at the tribe meeting, tonight. I really, honestly, truly wish to remain your friendly, helpful *tiki* and will attempt to repay your trust, if you think I should stay."

Happy with what he considered a firm commitment, the Parvaiti elder even accepted a fast Dragon ride on Furbetrance down the mountainside to the village.

It was a wild ride, although swift and short, as rain was beginning to fall even more heavily and the west wind was gusting over the shoulders of the volcano, whipping the bamboo and palms wildly against the dark sky.

IN the deep darkness Tom's and Manda's party walked down to the village, passing first through the lush fern forest, then past the *tiki*'s bamboo palace, then between neatly terraced fields of pineapple, taro, vegetables, and sugarcane. Rice was just ripe, ready to be harvested.

Men and women were at work by torchlight, gathering all available fruits and grain against the coming storm's destruction.

"We'll not lack for food," said the *tiki*. "There's rice and pineapple and, of course, coconuts. And the sea is filled with fishes."

"No, the problem is how to carry you and your supplies to your new home," Manda agreed. "That . . . and doing it in time."

"This storm coming, according to Retruance's new friend, the Sea Dragon," said her husband, "will delay the shipbuilding for only a couple of days, at worst. What can we expect in the way of storm, Byron?"

"You experienced one at sea," the *tiki* answered. "You must have some idea."

"I suspect a typhoon is worse at sea than on land," Clem put in.

He was walking hand in hand with Mornie, their two boys ranging at will before and behind, showing their father everything of interest . . . especially the village children who came running up the path to meet them.

"Not much to choose between," sighed Byron, shaking his head. "Here we'll have flooding and landslides, trees uprooted, terraces collapsed, and houses blown apart by terrible winds. Which is why they're built of tough but light materials like bamboo. Easily rebuilt once the storm passes. My people have survived typhoons a hundred times in the past."

"Stormy weather's a time to huddle together in a safe, dry place. Maybe in a cave," said the Librarian, "where we can do some serious planning for a long sea voyage."

•   •   •

THE Parvaiti tribal meeting was called to order by Samoy the Sage immediately after a cold midnight supper. Everyone was in an excited but surprisingly confident mood, filled with roast pork, cold fried rice, and steamed bamboo shoots left over from luncheon, long hours before.

"Lord *tiki*," began Samoy, holding up his hand for silence, "has asked us to decide whether we wish him to remain as our guide and mentor, now that all pretense of godhood is abandoned. How say you, elders, citizens, gentlemen and ladies?"

One of the men held up his hand to be recognized. He said, sounding very serious, "I know *I* was never really convinced of the *tiki*'s divinity. It seems to me it was, and is, a convenience a tribal chieftain can don or take off, as needed."

Some of the assembly objected. Obviously many had taken Byron's demigodhood quite seriously, while others agreed that it was only a matter of form, custom, and tradition.

All agreed that Byron Boldface should stay on as their *tiki* with full title, powers, and privileges.

"You truly are all my children!" the elderly Mage squeaked through a mixed veil of tears and smiles. "I will stay with you always, no matter what. To advise—not to rule! I'll never knowingly advise you wrongly. You deserve better, but no man will serve you more faithfully than I."

Everybody, including the Carolna folk, cheered his words and pounded him on the back and kissed him on the cheek, and dried his tears with soft tapa cloths printed with colorful geometric designs.

That decided, Byron took Samoy's place as presiding officer.

"Now, good people! Listen most carefully, my children," he intoned. "This matter is life or death to us all, as individual men and women and as the whole Parvaiti people.''

He took almost an hour to explain in great, awful detail the catastrophe that faced their beautiful island. He explained the need to flee to safety, not from the coming typhoon, but from the volcano when it erupted.

At first some found it hard to accept, but the ready confirmation of the awesome Dragons and their Companions convinced even the doubters, at last.

''But there's no way we can build any more war canoes before the Equinox,'' protested Maorai the Shipwright. ''It's taken us weeks to fashion the six we've already completed, and two more aren't even rigged yet.''

''I'm aware of this,'' said the *tiki*. ''But our friend Thomas of Overhall has some suggestions. Please listen to him carefully, for he speaks with my voice.''

The natives, seated cross-legged on patterned reed mats around the *tiki*'s chair, leaned forward to hear the stranger in their midst.

''I'm called Tom,'' the Librarian began. ''I set little value on mere titles except as they define who I am to those who first meet me.

''I serve a great Carolna gentleman, Lord Murdan of Overhall. If he were here, he'd lend all his strength to support you in your time of need and danger. The same goes for the King of Carolna, Eduard Ten, who is my dear friend and father-in-law. You've met his daughter, my wife Princess Alix Amanda Trusslo-Whitehead.''

The Parvaiti clapped and called out their greetings and acceptance. Manda rose and waved and bowed back to them.

''Now, I'm not a Shipwright,'' resumed Tom when they had settled down on their mats again. ''Just a man who takes care of books. I know little of sailing, of ships, and of canoe-building. But my friends and I can help you. Perhaps enough to allow you to finish the needed eight great canoes after the storm, and before the coming eruption.''

He paused, considering his words carefully, so they would understand he didn't mean to tell them their business.

''Tell me, Master Shipwright, what takes the longest in constructing a war canoe?''

Maorai answered at once. ''The carving out and shaping of the hull from a single ship-tree. It takes many days of hard work by men with sure eyes and sharp axes. If there is one slip by a tired workman, a hull is ruined!''

''Recently, as you've heard, my friend Clem and I were shipwrecked on one of the Coral Rings. We fashioned two hulls and constructed a sturdy, seaworthy *double canoe*, in a single night and a day,'' Tom said quietly.

''In a *day*! I must believe you, Dragon Companion, but will your magick work again for us?'' cried Samoy, shaking his head in bewilderment.

''Yes, because it was *not* magick,'' Tom assured him. ''I'm no Magician! Nor is Clem! Our twin hulls were hollowed out of great timbers from your own *Pelehoehoe* by the Dragon Retruance Constable. He blew his flaming breath; did the job quickly, carefully, and quite skillfully, I'd say. You'll see when our *Julia* arrives. . . .''

''We can send some of the younger boys to fetch her when the winds die down,'' said the Shipwright. ''We can certainly use her!''

''Very good!'' said Byron. ''Tell us about this *Julia*. Sail well, did she?''

Clem reported, ''The rigging was rather awkward but we managed it well enough. She's a strong, forgiving craft.''

Tom laughed. ''But now we have you to do the rigging, Parvaiti! And three Dragons, too! They can finish the remaining two hulls and have them ready in a day or so.''

The meeting at once became a babble of excited comments, further suggestions, and expressions of delight.

"You'll know best how to shape and rig," put in Retrance in a booming voice that silenced the uproar, "but I think the idea of the double hull is worth your consideration. I've examined your six finished hulls, and they would benefit in stability—*and double in capacity*—from lashing pairs of hulls together rather than using flimsy outriggers."

"We've talked of this among ourselves," admitted Maorai. "It seems to us two canoes fitted as a catamaran, as you call it, must be safer and swifter as well as carrying much more than two single canoes because of the greater deck space and wider beam."

"That's for you to decide," said Tom. "You'll have our *Julia*, with any luck, as a model to follow and improve upon. Manda and I and Clem and his family will fly by Dragon when we leave this beautiful place. We'll watch over you while at sea and guide you safely to your new home."

"Next problem! Where will we go?" asked a matronly women in red and black. "To the Coral Rings?"

The *tiki* rose to answer. "Much further!"

He explained about Isthmusi and what they could expect once they reached that distant shore.

"No volcanoes?" asked the woman suspiciously.

"If there are volcanoes in Isthmusi," Furbetrance answered, "I never noticed them. My brother and I searched for our lost father there, not long ago."

"Then I vote for Isthmusi," cried the woman, throwing up her hands.

A general discussion of the proposed new home followed. It only ended when the first full typhoon gusts arrived suddenly, fiercely rattling the dried fronds of the village roofs.

"Elders! Come to the Dragon's cave," Byron Boldface shouted over the howl of the wind. "For safety through the night and planning tomorrow. The rest of you, take shelter. Shipwrights! Attend to your hulls and make them fast, high on the beach! The Sea Dragon says it will not be calm again until tomorrow evening or early the following morning.''

The crowd began at once to scatter to find shelter from the wind and the warm, driving rain.

"When this typhoon passes,'' shouted Byron as they left, "we will resume work on the war canoes!''

"WELL , it's dry, at least!'' said Mornie.

They were standing in the mouth of a cave that ran back deep into the mountain flank. Beyond the overhang of the entrance, the rain was thundering down in terrible rage, lightning crashing close by every other minute. The last of the tribal elders were coming up the rain-slippery path, bent against the blast and bearing sleeping mats and packets of food to last them through the storm.

"And hot!'' Tom added.

There was a constant flow of heated air from deep within the cave. It reminded Tom of the hot air register in the middle of the living room floor back home in wintertime Iowa.

He, Manda, and Mornie stood near the cave's mouth watching the rainwater pour down the mountainside in gathering torrents, illuminated by sheets of blue-white lightning. Tom put his arm about his wife and gave her a gentle squeeze.

"Tighter,'' she requested, nuzzling against his shoulder. "I'm not all that fragile, you know.''

"I didn't know,'' he answered with a kiss. "But I should have known, shouldn't I?''

"How could you know?'' she teased. "You're as new to childbirth as am I, sweetheart.''

"Seriously,'' her husband said when they moved back

from the rain. "Where do you *want* to be when your time comes?"

"It doesn't matter. Well, yes it does! I *really* would like to be in our very own house on our lake in our canyon. I would like my father and stepmother nearby, and my Dragon, and my favorite uncle, too. But all I *really* need is you."

"*And* an experienced midwife," Tom grunted. "I've no experience at birthing babies!"

"You'd learn!" Manda chuckled softly. "But . . . well, fine! A good midwife, if you insist. Flabianus insisted he must be present, of course."

"A well-intended, fluffy, huffy, self-important old donkey," Tom laughed aloud. "But willing to learn. I'll say that for him."

"I wonder, speaking of home, whether anyone bothers to water my 'maters?" Manda asked, lifting her head from his shoulder.

"I reminded Julia about it before we left. She'll see it gets done."

"Oh, my!" snorted Retruance, inserting his vast head and ears into the cave's mouth to grin at them. "Tomatoes! Sounds good. I'm a little tired of fish and coconuts and bamboo shoots, myself."

LATER Tom tried to describe to Murdan and the King the typhoon that hit Eversmoke Island.

He remembered it as a wild melange of very loud noises . . . roar of rain; howling, insane shrieking of wind; crash and clatter of tree limbs and palm fronds ripped from their trunks and converted into deadly airborne missiles.

There was the distant rumbling of high surf crashing against the western cliffs, as regular as an enormous heartbeat, beating, beating, shaking the very rock beneath them.

"But what I remember best is going to sleep in Furbetrance's cave, listening to the uneven drumbeat from deep inside the mountain!'' he told them. ''I felt surrounded by a terrifying menace of mortal danger.''

''And the fumes,'' he added. ''The awful hot smells of the fire in the mountain's belly!''

✷ 14 ✷
. . . There's Fire!

"IT'LL be a close-run thing," predicted Retruance.

He and Furbetrance had just returned from a visit with the Sea Dragon. They found Tom, Clem, and the *tiki* standing hip-deep in the lagoon below the ravaged village, watching the watertight and balance tests of the double canoe called *Seventy-eight*, the fourth and final double hull.

"We need to set her in braces," Tom estimated, his face reflecting the huge beast's worried frown. "Then we must step the mast and rig her, load supplies, and load the Parvaiti. It'll take days—maybe even a week."

"We may not have that long," Furbetrance warned. "Flo says it feels like any moment the eruption may begin. The heavy rain didn't do the volcano any good, he figures."

"The quakes are coming more often and ever stronger," agreed Clem. "That big one at daybreak knocked down the *tiki*'s palace."

"It was fortunate we moved down to the shore after the storm," said Byron with a somber nod. "It was the most pleasant home I ever knew, but . . ."

He waved to Maorai. The Shipwright came wading wearily through the uneasy chop, now whipped by short, frequent tremors when the island's skirts of coral and sand shifted uneasily.

"How long to get the masts stepped on *Seventy-eight*?" Byron asked Maorai without preamble. "The Sea Dragon says the mountain could blow any hour!"

"Late tonight . . . early tomorrow . . . if we work all night, *tiki*."

"But the hull is sound, tight-lashed, and well balanced?"

"As near perfect as Dragon and Shipwright can make her," answered the shipbuilder, grinning despite his exhaustion.

"If I may make a landlubberly suggestion," Retruance began.

"Of course, Dragon!"

The builders had come to admire and appreciate the great, scaly beasts who could serve as powerful, rock-steady lifting cranes at one moment, and bring weather reports and temblor warnings from the other side of the island a few minutes later.

"Load the sails and masts in the unrigged hull. Put everybody aboard, *now*! Furbie, Flo, and I will take *Seventy-eight* in tow. Once safely asea, we can put ashore somewhere and finish rigging."

The builders stood looking at each other, speculating.

"We can do that," decided Samoy, taking a quick vote with his eyes. "I'll order the people aboard the canoes at once . . . if I may, *tiki*."

"Do it!" ordered the Mage. "I'll come along and help. I've got the passenger lists right here."

"LASH *Seventy-eight*'s boom and masts down extra secure," Maorai ordered his assistants. "If we lose 'em, we may have to abandon the hulls. No island close enough to matter grows tall mast-timber like we'd need."

The men and older boys splashed back to their tasks, rushing to make sure needed paddles, ropes, sails, spars—everything—was properly stowed and firmly tied down.

"Flo suggests a volcano watch," said Retruance to Tom.

"A what? Oh, I see. Flo thinks we should keep a close eye on the caldera?"

"Right-o, Companion! He'll advise us of any changes undersea. He has a good vantage there, but beyond a certain time it'd be fatal for him to remain on the bottom. Poisonous gases and superheated steam are already jetting up from vents in the seafloor. Even a Dragon can take just so much!''

Tom waited for a sharp temblor to subside, then turned to Clem.

"We'll take turns on watch, you and I. I'll go first with Retruance. Borrow Furbetrance from Manda for the evening watch. Don't let Manda talk you into letting her go instead. She'll try. Two hours on and two off, watch and work. Right?''

"Agreed! That'll always leave one or two Dragons here for last-minute hoisting. What signal should we use, if something happens?''

"If the thing suddenly just *blows*," Tom said gravely, "no signal will be necessary! We have to pray the mountain gives us some minutes' grace before it *really* pops. If it does. we'll come warn you.''

"Flo says," put in Furbetrance, "we'll know when the darned thing is about to go off by the way the whole mountaintop swells. Like a red, angry boil on somebody's nose, fit to burst.''

"Quite graphic," Tom commented with a shiver. "Here we go! Tell Manda where I've gone.''

He glanced at the sun behind the dun clouds and estimated the time: close on four in the afternoon.

THE Parvaiti numbered seven hundred twenty-five souls . . . three hundred men and boys, three hundred girls and women, and a hundred and twenty-five small children.

They had four great war canoes—*Twelve, Thirty-four, Fifty-six,* and the unrigged *Seventy-eight*—plus the smaller *Julia*, which had been fetched from the western side by a crew of five young boys.

A hundred seventy crew and passengers could fit in each double-hull, with a dozen or so aboard *Julia*.

Tight quarters, Tom estimated, but just barely enough.

The villagers fell in line along the winding path from the village down to the beach, leaving empty, forlorn, tumbled-down houses behind, badly torn by the typhoon or shaken apart by quakes, that had been their homes for centuries. There were tears and many wistful backward glances.

But no panic.

Samoy and Byron stumped wearily up and down the line, making sure each matron knew to which of the five canoes she should lead her family.

"Your menfolk will join you, in most cases," the *tiki* assured them yet again. "A few of them are assigned special duties and have to be on *Twelve* with us. You understand?"

"Mabatai is nearing her time," one matron reminded him quietly. "I didn't know if you were told, *tiki*."

"I have her on my list," replied Byron Boldface. "The midwife is assigned to *Twelve*, I assure you, my dear, as well as Princess Manda."

"But her man, Salmai, is steersman of *Fifty-six*," protested another woman. "And Mabatai is assigned to *Twelve*?"

"Salmai must man his post, of course, and *Twelve* is *her* post. We'll try to keep close enough to call back and forth," Samoy said sternly.

"I'll speak to Mabatai, if she fears," promised the *tiki*.

"Oh, no, *tiki*!" cried the matron. "She's said nothing. Her friends are concerned for her and her husband. It's their first, you know."

"I know. Tell her I'll watch over her and she may name her son Byron after me, if the child is a boy."

"Thank you, *tiki*!" the woman exclaimed, beaming with pleasure, more immediate problems and dangers forgotten for a moment.

·   ·   ·

RETRUANCE decided they shouldn't risk touching down on the crumbling crater rim.

The caldera within looked like an enormous smelter's pot, pulsing vivid pink with heat, bubbling, boiling, fuming, roiling, and heaving like a living thing. It ejected huge bubbles and bursts of flaming gasses and globs of white-hot, half-molten lava which cooled as they hissed through the air, turning nearly solid before they splashed into the ocean or crashed through the breadfruit and palms on the lower slopes.

Everywhere grass and trees on the higher slopes were ablaze, torched by the incandescent lava from side fissures. Blue-and-purple flames shot from Furbetrance's cave, setting fire to the compound where Manda and Clem's family had been living until a few hours before.

Much worse was the shimmering column of nearly invisible superheated gas, fretted by jagged lightning bolts, roaring up from the caldera. The tremendous heat, fortunately for Dragon and Dragon rider, rose straight up with a high-pitched, frenzied screech.

A scant quarter-mile to one side of the rim the air remained fairly cool, but it was filled with flying debris, blazing palms, and bits of native huts, sucked aloft by the rising gas.

"In fact," yelled Retruance uneasily, "I'm having to fly *downward* just to keep place. Otherwise, this updraft'll toss me straight up a mile or more."

"Good thing to keep in mind, when Eversmoke decides to blow itself to pieces," Tom shouted into the Dragon's near-side forward ear.

The Dragon started to nod, rather than try to make himself heard over the awful din, but stopped before his action could send Tom flying from his head.

"We need a clear view of the inside of the crater," Tom reminded him. "Let's try when a gust blows the smoke aside for a moment, maybe? We'll have to move in and out again fast.''

Again the Dragon almost nodded, concentrating on keeping level and upright. The updrafts were turbulent and tricky.

"Now!" cried the Librarian.

Retruance drove forward almost to the edge of the rim, dodging a house-size chunk of glowing mountainside torn loose by the blast of rising gases.

Tom clung to the Dragon's harness and gritted his teeth until they ached, and was rewarded with a few seconds of clear view down the volcano's throat.

The lake of lava, so incredibly hot it had the consistency of boiling water, almost filled the basin. On the glowing surface, black islands of solid stone rose suddenly and sank again, rolling about like chunks of meat in a stew.

The lava-lake level was just thirty feet below the rim.

As Retruance veered up and away to return to clearer, cooler, calmer air, Tom saw a vast slice of the thinning rimrock suddenly crack loose and slide down the mountainside, allowing lava to flow out and down.

"I never thought to see or feel anything too hot even for a Dragon," remarked Retruance, once they'd returned to the less distressed air beyond the crater. "What do you think, Companion?"

"I've got an idea where it stands . . . at the moment. We'll take a look again in a few minutes and see if it's about to overflow . . . or to solidify and form a solid plug, as Flo fears.''

"Speaking of the Sea Dragon," roared Retruance, coasting away from the glowing summit, "here comes Flo."

The vast sea creature was a Dragon almost as huge as Retruance, but lighter of build and longer of neck and wings. His color was deep blue above and yellow-green beneath. Flo's powerful wings were not black, like the Constables' pinions, but were almost transparent. His claws were black onyx.

"Hail and greetings," Flo called as he approached. "Glad to see you, Dragon Companion."

"Pleasure's mutual," Tom yelled back. "Sorry it had to be under such circumstances."

"Yes, I would have preferred to have met you at sea level . . . or better, in my coral cavern under the reef. It's collapsed now, however."

"Were you able to remove your possessions?" Retruance asked politely.

"Hours ago," the Sea Dragon answered, nodding sadly. "I travel lightly. I'm ready to depart now, since there's nothing more I can do below. Shall I go down and present myself to the *tiki*? Are the islanders ready to sail?"

"As ready as they'll ever be," Retruance said as he sneezed at an errant cloud of hot rock-dust. "We'll be down in an hour or so, unless something happens before then."

"Ah, you're the volcano watch," the Sea Dragon said with an understanding nod. "Let me know if I can assist in any way."

"You can help most by volunteering to help tow the unrigged *Seventy-eight*," Tom called. "When everyone's loaded, we must move out to sea quickly, and as far as possible."

"See you shortly, then. And please be *very* careful," Flo trumpeted back over the din of a new series of explosions.

Doing a graceful wingover, he dove straight down, skimming the mountain's heaving side with only yards to spare, to avoid the worst of the updraft winds.

AT six that evening Furbetrance and Clem appeared, flung aloft by the updrafts like a great kite.

"How are things coming down there?" Tom shouted when they came close enough to hear.

"Not many minutes longer," Clem estimated. "Does the volcano overflow?"

Retruance showed the oncoming watch how to catch a quick, relatively safe glimpse of the inside of the caldera.

"The lava's been cooling and darkening, I'm afraid," observed Retruance, pointing his right foreclaw downward. "A bad sign, according to Flo. If it cools enough to form a solid crust, the pressure will mount from below and a tremendous explosion will be imminent . . . and inevitable."

"See? It's freezing . . . no longer swelling," Tom pointed out to Clem.

"No way to . . . judge how . . . much longer," Clem said, coughing from a whiff of hydrogen sulfide. "We'll just have to pray it doesn't go off before we're ready."

"If it does . . . get out of here, super-quick," Tom yelled back.

Retruance was already flaring away from the mountain-top.

Clem waved.

The green-and-gold Constable Dragon folded his leathery black wings against the sides of his body and plummeted like a dropped stone for the lagoon a thousand feet below.

"IF it'll just give us two or three more hours," Byron moaned, "we'll be ready. This Sea Dragon—quite a nice beast, actually—is already at sea with the unrigged *Seventy-eight* in tow, waiting for the rest of us. I sent *Julia* off with her crew, also. She's bound to be slower and harder to handle in this wind. The winds and tide are going to be against us at first, you realize."

Remembering the uprush of air along the volcano's

flanks, Tom was not surprised by this unusual condition of inrushing wind and water.

"Hurry! Well, it's all I can say to you, my friend," he coughed.

A dense cloud of smoke shot skyward as the Parvaiti village burst into flame. A rain of glowing cinders had smashed into the thatched roofs torn apart by the typhoon winds.

Dust and smoke obscured the sunset.

TOM found Manda, Mornie, and the boys aboard *Twelve*, wedged among rolled-up sleeping mats, bundles of sugarcane, and baskets of household goods.

"I wish you'd let me help," complained Manda. "I feel so useless."

"There isn't that much left to do, darling, unless you'd care to join the passing-chain bringing the last of the baggage out from the shore," Tom said. "Better to stay out of the way and let them do their work, I think."

"*Phew.*" Manda made a sour face when he settled down beside her. "You truly stink."

"Try flying over a volcano about to blow its top and see how *you* smell," Tom retorted good-naturedly.

To show she was just teasing, Manda happily snuggled against his shoulder, despite the stench of burning sulfur, burned wood, scorched cloth, singed hair, and sweat. They said little, anxiously watching the last of the villagers embark.

"There goes *Thirty-four*," called Mornie softly, so as not to waken her exhausted sons. "We'll go last, as soon as Byron Boldface boards."

"What's to do about Byron, when this is over?" wondered the Librarian.

"This is not the place nor the time to decide," Manda sounded a trifle irritable. "He's not a bad sort. He did what he thought he *had* to do in the way he thought it *had* to be done.''

"Misguided? I guess I'd agree.'' Tom's eyes were gritty with dust and heavy with sleep. "Wake me when it's time to relieve Clem up top . . . or time to set the sail.''

Manda gently combed his tangled hair with her fingers. It was caked with wet ash and powdered with fine grey pumice.

The baby moved within her . . . not uneasily nor urgently, but gently, as if he . . . she . . . too, was settling for needed sleep.

FURBETRANCE screamed down the near flank of Eversmoke. It sounded to Tom, jolted suddenly awake, like a runaway truck careening out of control down a long, steep hill, air-horns blasting.

"Drop everything. Into the boats. Get under way. *Flo*. Start pulling. *Retruance*. Tag onto that tow. We're coming.''

The Parvaiti, who had slowed near the end of their weary task of loading themselves and their baggage, were galvanized into final, furious action.

The water of the harbor leapt six feet in the air, straight up, soaking the passengers in the remaining canoes.

"Drop everything and run!'' shouted Byron in a terrible, loud shriek. "Hurry. *Everybody*.''

He came last, scrambling up the side of *Twelve*, fell back into the water, and was dragged unceremoniously aboard by Samoy the Sage.

Furbetrance, with Clem still clinging to his head harness, plunged into the deep water beyond the lagoon at full tilt. A moment later they emerged, shaking off a ton of water, and the Dragon shrugged into *Seventy-eight*'s multiple tow harness.

With Retruance and Flo also beating wings and paddling

strongly with all four feet, the heavy cables snapped out of the water and the mastless canoe began to plow ponderously toward the open ocean.

"Look!" screamed Manda, clutching Tom's arm.

She pointed back at the volcano.

A strange pinkish glow suffused the entire summit, as if it were being heated red-hot in a gigantic blast furnace.

Someone had slashed *Twelve*'s mooring lines. Forty-eight paddlers, twenty-four to a side, tumbled into their places and snatched up the leaf-bladed paddles. They dipped and drew in time to Maorai's urgent cadence.

"No burning rivers this time," Tom screamed above the tumult. "She'll burst like a boil."

"*Paddlers*. On my count. *Ready? Dip. Pull.* One . . . two. One . . . two . . ." Maorai's voice shrilled.

Twelve struggled to make the narrow pass from lagoon to open sea, trailing behind *Thirty-four* and *Fifty-six*. The inrushing winds were nearing gale force. Towering rollers charged the reef and shattered the stonelike coral and themselves with insane fury.

"Pull. *Pull*. One. *Two*. One. *Two*," came the ship-builder's hoarse voice.

A wave crest foamed over their bow, washing across the crowded deck, flooding the double bottoms, and soaking the crew and passengers. Scrambling men and women, including Manda, Tom, and Mornie, frantically bailed the water back over the sides with empty coconut shells, bamboo buckets, and bare hands.

Once *Twelve* was clear of the lagoon entrance, Maorai and his two husky steersmen forced the long, heavy tiller hard to starboard. The Sage shouted for the topmen to hoist the huge triangular mainsail.

The double-thick tapa snapped and boomed angrily as the wind caught at it.

Tom tailed onto a line and ran aft with the more expe-

rienced native seamen, hauling the heavy sail over to catch
the wild wind which heeled the canoe to starboard until its
whole fabric roared like a kettledrum and the lee rail dipped
under the foaming surface.

"Passengers to win'ard," shouted Samoy. "Over to
win'ard."

The women knew what to do. Manda, Mornie, even the
Clemsson boys, now fully awake, followed their lead,
perching on the high-side gun'l to lend their weight and
keep the canoe from plowing her starboard rail completely
under and causing the double canoe to broach-to in the
howling gale, perhaps to capsize, be smashed apart, and
founder in the crossing sea.

When he had time to look, Tom saw that the other four
craft, well ahead of them, were running swiftly southward
across the wind, sails on three of them hard as boards and
their rigging straining very near to parting.

The unrigged hull *Seventy-eight* was well in the fore,
moving steadily under triple Dragon-power that resisted the
wind which was attempting to blow her on the reef.

Wind rushed toward the volcano from all compass points
at once. Samoy ordered his sail-handlers to make a tack to
port and, shortly after, to starboard once again. *Twelve* and
her three sister-ships moved desperately, painfully, slowly,
clawing desperately for headway.

The three great Dragons in harness pulled against the
terrific opposition of wind and water, and *Seventy-eight*
made slow headway at last.

THE terrible fight went on for what seemed hours . . . or
minutes, depending on what you were doing, working
against time or trying to stay out of the way. Tom and the
crew of *Twelve* were soon hazy with fatigue.

At last the wind steadied from the south. *Twelve,* with
Samoy and his helmsmen clinging to the long steering

sweep, finally found a steady course that sped her on her way east.

The exhausted crew, men and women, boys and girls, collapsed to the crowded deck. Tom crawled wearily forward to find Manda slumped, bailer in hand, panting and groaning by turns. Mornie lay prone by her side.

"Are you right?" Tom gasped, crouching over his wife and clutching her hand.

"What an awful, awful place and time to birth a baby," Manda gasped, pressing her stomach with both hands. "Can you find that midwife anywhere about?"

Tom was too stunned by this new turn of events to move at first. Then Gregor and young Thomas appeared, leading a stout, smiling island woman by either hand.

"Well," the woman cried cheerfully, taking in the situation with comforting speed. "Another little one following the new baby boy born just now to young Mabatai. Mother and baby are fine. They say a baby born at sea will be fortunate all through life."

Manda gasped in sudden pain and Tom squeezed her hand.

"Wish I had some 'maters," the Princess of Carolna tried to joke.

"I'll see if I can find some," Tom promised.

"No. Stay nearby," the midwife ordered. "Her time draws very close, I can tell you."

✦ 15 ✦
Child of the Storm

TOM anxiously watched the cheerful midwife make Manda as comfortable and dry as possible. Everything aboard *Twelve* was soaked.

He tried to recall the woman's name.

"Garrai, Sir Thomas," the midwife grinned, guessing his thought. "No chance of a fire to warm some clean water? I thought not. Well, we'll have to make do with cool seawater, which isn't all that bad. Salt water cures many ills. It'll cleanse a baby and the mother quite well, you'll see."

She chattered on to Manda, encouraging her to relax between the spasms that came at shorter and shorter intervals, telling her what to expect and what to do.

"Deep breathing helps, young mother," murmured Garrai. "That's the way, sweet flower. Somebody find my scrip. It's up there in the bow. Red and white tied up with a fresh green bamboo withes. That's it. Bring it close and open it up for me, won't you, Mistress Mornie? *Good!* Soft old tapas, clean and dry. Best for a birthing anywhere."

Tom sat behind Manda, cradling her shoulders, head, and arms, gripping her hands tightly and feeling totally helpless, speaking softly to her in the intervals between contractions while the plump midwife moved surely about her preparations.

"A sip of this to ease the wait," Garrai recommended, offering Tom a stone cup of clear liquid. "Not for you, little mother. For the father. Fathers can be the biggest

problem at such times as these. But never fear . . . I've lost
very few fathers in my time.''

The watching women cackled at her timeworn joke.
Tom, realizing he was burning with thirst, drank deeply of
the elixir. It felt cool and comforting going down.

''Some sort of tranquilizer, I suppose?''

Yet he remained alert and attentive, but calmer after the
draught. Garrai gave Manda a tiny sip of the elixir now,
and she, too, seemed to relax. The unaccustomed fear Tom
had seen in her face smoothed away, and she smiled.

''Garrai, is it?'' Manda asked.

''Yes. She knows what to do, I can see,'' Tom whispered.

''She seems convinced it's to be a boy,'' Manda remarked, sounding almost normal.

''We'll know very shortly,'' the midwife cackled. ''Going very well, father. Princess, when I tell you 'now,' bear
down and push hard. It'll help us, all four.''

Garrai made no attempt to screen Manda from sight of
the crew or the passengers. After a protest he never spoke
aloud, Tom accepted the public nature of their child's birthing.

Manda didn't seem to care.

Garrai squatted between Manda's knees, watching her
contractions carefully, gently massaging her patient's ab-
domen and murmuring instructions, it seemed, to the
child.

The great canoe was cutting briskly through the waves,
rising and falling with comforting regularity, almost as if it
were doing deep-breathing exercises too.

''Hold your course a bit now,'' Garrai called sharply to
the helmsmen. ''No course changes until I've made my
catch.''

Samoy and Byron nodded agreement. Seeing them maintain their course to the southeast, the rest of the fleet followed suit, with the Dragon-towed hull well out in front.

TOM rose to his knees and glanced back at Eversmoke Island, now obscured by a thick yellowish-black haze. There were flickers of fire here and there as bamboo, banyan, and palms burst into flame from the intense heat.

"How long?" called Samoy. "We must tack before much longer, Garrai, or risk running on Sea Urchin Shoal."

"I'll tell you when to tack," snapped Garrai gruffly, concentrating on her task. "Not yet."

The contractions seemed to subside, and Manda drifted into a light sleep. Tom released her hands and stood to stretch his legs, which were cramping with the long time kneeling on the hard deck.

The red eye of the moon, about to dip into the cloud surrounding the doomed island, showed it was nearly midnight.

"We've *got* to tack," said a worried voice at his elbow. "There's white water ahead."

Maorai had turned the steering oar over to his quartermasters and come forward to see how the birthing was going.

"If you have to tack, do it," Tom decided. "Gently, if possible."

Garrai nodded, and the Shipwright glanced for a moment at Manda's placid face before he returned to stand with Byron Boldface and the Sage in the stern.

"*Tiki*," the Sage said softly. "Signal the fleet. Prepare to go about on the port tack as we move."

A number of things happened in the space of a single breath.

At the Sage's signal, the helmsmen put the steering oar hard to starboard. The long main boom swung overhead.

The canoe whipped past the eye of the howling wind, hesitated a moment, then dipped easily to her new course.

The great sail rustled and boomed like cannon.

With an absolutely stupefying roar, Eversmoke blew itself into fine, white-hot dust, clouds of incandescent steam, glowing blobs of molten stone, and spinning, screaming lava bombs.

A split second later, just as the canoe was surging onto her new heading, a blast of heated air struck her, driving her forward at breathtaking speed, every peg, lashing, line, and binding strained to the utmost.

The crewmen yelled excitedly. The women and children shouted in surprise more than fright.

Tom shook his head to clear the ringing from his ears.

"Manda?" he cried.

"Tom." He heard her answering gasp.

"Ah, *very* good," laughed Garrai, leaning forward, reaching for something pink-red, wet, naked, keening, and furiously squirming. "As good as a clap on the bottom, that was."

Tom watched, still stunned, as she deftly cut and tied the baby's umbilical cord. The baby wailed lustily, turning from side to side and waving little arms about, protesting this loud and frightening beginning to life.

"It's an 'it' no longer," announced the midwife, holding the wailing child aloft for all to see.

Tom, Mornie, the islanders, and Manda, opening her eyes wide, cried out in relief and joy while Byron, Samoy, and the crew cheered.

"A very neat, new, beautiful, little . . . *girl*," announced Garrai, placing the child in Manda's left arm-crook, near her swollen breasts. "A new little Princess for Carolna."

"A little Lady of Hidden Lake," Manda corrected her happily. "Isn't she pretty?"

"Almost as beautiful as her mother," Tom found breath to say.

He leaned over to kiss Manda's wet brow and drew to the side to look more closely at their girl-child, already beginning to suckle eagerly, the commotion of her arrival already forgotten.

"Her name?" asked someone.

It was Mornie.

Tom remembered she'd been crouching on Manda's right side ever since labor had begun. Behind her, the two small Clemsson boys gazed in awe on the scene.

"I had a nice, ordinary royal family name all picked out," Manda whispered so as not to disturb the eagerly nursing baby. "But I think we should call her Gale instead. Do you agree, Papa?"

"*Gale*," Tom said, trying it out. "A beautiful name. Very appropriate, and'll sound really fine at Court, too."

"Welcome, little Gale Thomassdotter," cried Mornie softly. "Princess Gale."

"Not if we're lucky," Manda objected. "For that would mean I had become Queen myself, and I'd rather not have that honor, thank you. Lady Gale, rather say."

"Better dress it up a bit for formal occasions," Tom suggested. "How about Lady Gale Amanda Thomassdotter Trusslo-Whitehead of Hidden Lake Canyon?"

Princess Alix Amanda Trusslo-Whitehead of Carolna laughed in pure delight.

Lady Gale herself, having satisfied her immediate hunger, turned her head to snuggle into her mother's warm, soft bosom and went to sleep.

THE unfinished double canoe had been caught in mid-swing by the blast of the explosion and had capsized, despite all the Dragons could do. The other four boats were quickly on the scene to rescue her passengers—all of whom could swim like dolphins, Clem reported to Tom later.

Once the floating baggage was rounded up and hoisted aboard the rescuing canoes, the capsized craft was easily and quickly righted by the powerful Dragons and her passengers and crew returned aboard. Her mast and rigging were still safe, and her sail was still lashed down, too. She could quickly become a full-rigged war canoe once they reached an anchorage.

"Course?" asked Samoy of Byron Boldface.

"Due east for now, if you can manage that, Samoy, my old friend," the *tiki* answered. "Signal the others to take station on us. Tom?"

"Yes, *tiki*?" Tom replied, giving the little man the title given to him by his people.

"A word to your Dragons, please, and discover from them how much longer they can continue to tow without rest. There's a small island two days' sail east, and the wind's favorable."

Samoy agreed. "We can put in at Milksap to make repairs and rig *Seventy-eight* and other things sure to be needed."

"Aye, aye, sir," said the Librarian.

He called to Retruance, who shrugged from his harness and came knifing through the water like a strange sort of green-and-gold whale, the past-full moon glinting off his scales.

"We can pull all night and all tomorrow," said he. "Further than that, if necessary."

He took a long minute to admire his new goddaughter. Gale was content to nap, ignoring the enormous beast bending over her making soft gurgling, clucking noises and puffing small pink clouds of celebration.

Manda dozed in the soft, warm night, letting the rolling of the double canoe soothe her strains and pains.

"A very easy, sweet, quick birthing," reported Garrai

proudly as she gathered her equipment together. "Most lucky. Despite the loud salute the old mountain gave the poor little thing!"

Retruance touched the little girl on her blonde curly head with a very gentle green claw.

"She'll be a Dragon Companion herself, one day," he predicted, mostly to himself. "Well, I'd better go relieve my brother, so he can come see her, too. And Flo and Clem'll want to visit, when it's proper."

"Anytime. Anytime at all," Tom told him, flinging his arms affectionately about the Dragon's muzzle.

One by one, each of the four catamarans was brought alongside so the Parvaiti could call good wishes to the mothers and fathers of the two newborns and admire their babies. Women sang for happiness, and men called to Tom with advice on raising a child—most of it humorous, some of it quite sensible, and all of it well-intended.

TOM looked for Retruance, who was resting on the wide beach of the shallow Milksap Island lagoon with Furbetrance and Flo.

The fleet had reached the island the second morning at dawn. Maorai and his shipwrights were already busy repairing storm damage and Furbetrance had helped them install the mast, boom, and spars on *Seventy-eight*.

The only sign of the volcano, now, was an inky smudge on the western horizon, reaching for the afternoon sun and spreading southwestward at high altitude. All night long the seafarers had listened to a constant rumble of explosions, and the helmsmen had guided on the bright glow in the sky behind them.

The women and children clustered about Manda and Mabatai and their babies in the shade of tall, smooth-barked trees, talking, preparing lunch, mending clothes torn in the confusion of escape, and sharing experiences of their own babies' arrivals.

"If you feel up to it," Tom called to his Dragon, "Clem and I'd like to see what, if anything, remains of Eversmoke."

"It's worth a fast flight," agreed Retruance, ever ready for a new adventure. "Let's go."

Mornie came along also; her boys had long since made friends among the island children and they all were off, eagerly exploring Milksap. She rode beside Clem on the younger Constable's head. It took them only an hour and a fraction at top Dragon-speed to reach the spot where the thousand-foot volcanic island had stood the day before.

"It *really* blew itself to flinders," gasped Mornie. "We were *really* lucky."

"Luck helped," agreed Retruance, solemnly viewing the still-boiling sea where the peak was no more. "We were also lucky the prevailing winds were from the northeast. Else we'd have sailed in total darkness, smothered in hot ash and choking dust."

Tom looked around the scene with a deep sense of sadness. Samoy, the little *tiki*, and even the Sea Dragon had refused to return to view the remains of their homeland and familiar waters.

Perhaps, Tom thought, *they were wisest.*

"Never look back," he told himself aloud.

"Someone might be sneaking up on you," said his Dragon, wheeling about to return to Milksap.

"You sound just like good ol' Satchel Paige," Tom chuckled.

"When you have time, you might explain that," muttered Retruance sarcastically, putting his massive shoulders into swift winging. "It made no sense to me at all."

Tom laughed, throwing his head back and gasping in

pent-up laughter until Furbetrance came alongside and Clem and Mornie called to learn the joke.

"Too complicated to explain," Tom coughed. "You had to be there to appreciate it."

"MILKSAP," Maorai explained, showing Tom a pail of grey-white, jellylike liquid. "Very handy for coating cloth. Makes it waterproof."

"Latex!" Tom cried in surprise. "These must be rubber trees."

"We often came here to gather it," the Sage explained, "when we needed it. Our sails will draw better, once we've painted them with the milksap. We'll coat our cargo covers with it, too, to keep out the salt spray."

"Bring cuttings or seeds of the trees with us to Isthmusi," Tom suggested thoughtfully. "I don't know if rubber trees'll grow there, but if they will, you can sell the milksap to Lexor merchants. There are lots of other useful things can be done with it, as I recall."

"We've completed the repairs, so we can leave anytime you want," Samoy said to the *tiki*.

"Morning would be best. A time to rest is a good idea. Do you have an estimate of the length of this voyage, Sage?"

"Only a very cloudy guess," Samoy admitted. "And any confidence that dry land is there, at all, comes from the assurances of the Dragons."

"The Dragons can fly ahead, if you like," Tom suggested. "That way we might avoid dangerous waters and have advance warning of new storms, if there are any."

"The trade winds blow from west to east, which favors a fast passage," Maorai figured. "We've plenty of stores, even without those lost overboard when *Seventy-eight* capsized. It seems weeks ago, doesn't it?"

"These be unknown and uncharted waters," Byron

Boldface cautioned. "We'll need the Dragons to keep watch beyond the horizon. Thank you, Librarian."

"Don't thank *me*," Tom said modestly. "I want to get there in one dry piece, too."

Shortly after dawn, with a hundred rubber tree cuttings in one of the bottoms carefully wrapped in moist tapa cloth and sand, the Parvaiti fleet set sail again, quartering a brisk northwest breeze to hold a course slightly north of due east.

Long Voyage

MANDA strolled up and down the platform deck, reveling in the fresh breeze, the hot sun in an intensely blue sky, and the friendly islanders who smiled at her on every hand.

She carried Gale on one arm, feeling already very much at home with the child. Gale ate furiously, slept soundly, and was already beginning to take notice of her surroundings.

"Which are rather spectacular, as such things go," Manda said to her husband.

Tom had just come from teaching a class. The Parvaiti had no writing, and had never needed any, it seemed. As a Librarian, this made Tom uncomfortable.

Hence, the daily class . . . even though its numbers were small and there were no books to teach from, not even a ship's log. Records were traditionally kept in the islander's memories and songs.

In fact, when the sun went down each night, the singers and musicians sat on the cooling decks, making music and recording the history of *The Great Escape* or *The End of Eversmoke*, back and forth between the great war canoes.

Tom said to the children, "Watch me form the letters. By this time next week, you'll be able to *read* what I'm writing, even if you've never heard the words direct from someone's mouth."

The boys and girls giggled at this impossible claim, but Gregor and even young Thomas gleefully demonstrated the truth of Tom's claims.

Tom divided the children into teams, with Gregor as afterguard leader and Thomas Clemsson in charge forward.

The Librarian would write a one-line note to Gregor. Gregor would show it to his teammates, carefully explaining each letter and written word and how it was sounded from the combination of letters.

Then Gregor would carefully print the same information but in slightly different words and send it forward to Thomas's group in the bows.

Thomas would read the note aloud, explain as best he could the lettering and sounds. Then his team would draft a message to the Librarian, reparaphrasing Gregor's words.

With the circuit complete, Tom called them all together and read the three messages aloud, in sequence. The differences, the mistakes, and some unintended humor, sent the children into gales of delighted laughter.

"*The sun rises each morning*," Tom had written to Gregor and his crew.

Gregor explained the written words to his fellows, then wrote:

"*Every morning the sun climbs into the sky.*"

A runner carried his slate forward to his brother's team in the bow, but left the original with Tom. The foreguard tittered and chattered and Thomas jotted, rather laboriously, for he was still a bit rusty in his lettering:

"*The sun comes up at dawn and the stars and the moon disappear.*"

The runner brought the foreguard's note to the Librarian, and the opposing crews gathered about the Librarian to hear the results.

"All three notes say *almost* the same thing, you see," Tom pointed out. "But each uses different words."

The class nodded solemnly, understanding dawning in their eager faces.

"Now, we can use the same words and make them mean something quite different. Shall I show you how that would work?"

"Yes! Yes! Show us!" shouted the children, and the game went on.

Older siblings, parents, aunts, uncles, and even Samoy the Sage watched and listened in amazement.

And they learned, also.

TIME might have dragged, but the Parvaiti naturally fell into the habits of a lifetime of sailing.

There were, of course, the maintenance tasks always needed aboard a ship of any size, such as coating the sails with milksap, or bailing the seawater or rain that collected in the bilges—the bottoms of the twin hulls—for comfort and health.

Ropes and lines had to be spliced or rigged anew. Rips in the tapa-cloth sails constantly demanded needle-and-thread work. From materials brought with them, the sailors and their women stitched spare sails, in case the originals were damaged beyond repair.

Manda sat with this group, amazing them with her needlework skills, whether with a five-inch ironwood bodkin used to stitch a sail, or a delicate, inch-long steel embroidery needle she'd brought with her from home, used to make, repair, or decorate clothing.

She explained how the very best thread was spun from tough flax leaves and the thread woven into fine cloth. The Parvaiti women told how tapa was soaked, chewed, and woven into traditional patterns and symbols of their families, clans, and the tribe.

"Now . . . see? This is our rune for 'Dragon,'" explained one of their new friends. "A wriggly line with two hooks on top, for wings. Anyone would recognize it as a Dragon, even without the stream of smoke coming from its nose."

Manda exclaimed with delight. What had at first appeared to be a childish squiggle suddenly took on a definitely Dragonish look.

"How would you draw a *specific* Dragon?" she wondered. "A name . . . like Furbetrance, for example?"

The seamstress shook her head. "Only if he had selected a symbol for himself, or we had agreed upon one *for* him. It could be almost any sort of line or loop or circle or . . ."

Manda lectured the ladies on the value of a written alphabetic language.

"Don't give up your beautiful, meaningful symbols, of course," she encouraged them. "But it's nice to recognize the name 'Furbetrance' when you see it written, from common sense, not fallible memory."

The women . . . and some of the men also . . . nodded doubtfully, for their simple lives demanded few ways to communicate other than by word of mouth.

"Do you always remember your grandmother's favorite recipes, word for word, ingredient for ingredient?" Mornie asked, seeing their lack of conviction.

"I remember not remembering ground ginger root," laughed a young mother cradling a tiny baby boy she proudly called Byron. "I couldn't think what was missing, and my stew was just *terrible*."

"See what I mean about trusting only to memory?" asked Mornie, and the others nodded thoughtfully.

Before the voyage was a fortnight old, they all saw their children writing notes to each other and deciding how to spell their names phonetically. Everyone, children, mothers, and fathers as well, became more and more interested and some quite expert.

"A marvelous thing you have done," Byron told Tom one evening.

"Marvelous? No, just passing the time usefully, *tiki*."

"But, no. Teaching them to read and write. How wonderful!" the little Mage insisted.

"Well, remember ... I'm a Librarian. Without readers and writers, where would a Librarian be?" Tom said earnestly.

SAMOY was a born teacher, too. He named and described the working parts of the great war canoes to Clem and Tom, explaining how wind and sails interacted to drive the ship through the water.

" 'Tacking,' as you call it," he lectured, "is merely a sensible way to turn the force of the wind to your own purposes. Not magic at all."

"Anything we can't understand we call 'magic,' " Clem said. "Now, to me, the ways of critters in the forest have no mystery."

The strange animals he described, and the odd necessity for warm clothing also, intrigued the Parvaiti, who had never experienced real cold in their entire lives and, in fact, had no words to describe it.

The Parvaiti, all strong swimmers from childhood, thought nothing of leaping into the sea and cavorting merrily in the water, even crossing to the other canoes to visit with friends or deliver orders and messages to the captains. There were always, in daylight hours, visitors aboard *Twelve* to exchange information and return social visits.

A week after Gale Thomassdotter was born, even Manda went swimming, closely guarded by Furbetrance and Mornie, lest she become overtired. The island women insisted it would do her no harm and, in fact, would be quite good for a new mother.

Manda's constitution was robust from a lifetime of active outdoor living. Tom's fears for her quickly disappeared. She went over the side carrying her wriggling daughter to bathe her in the warm salt sea and let her splash joyously, encouraged by the Parvaiti children who swam about mother and child like a school of brown fish.

Their own mothers had taught them to swim this way at just such an early age.

THEIR eastward course didn't pass close to many landfalls. On the thirteenth day they approached a towering, rugged island and hove to in its lee waiting for a heavy rainstorm to pass.

Retruance and his fellow Dragons circled the steep-sided island and returned to report no suitable anchorages anywhere, not even shelving beaches at the feet of the cliffs.

They'd spotted a population of wild pigs, however. At the *tiki*'s request the Dragons ferried a hunting party ashore, armed with light spears and sharp knives. Their original supply of salted and smoked pork was beginning to run low.

The wild hogs turned out to be lean, tough, and stringy, but quite tasty after they were roasted over slow fires, which gave them a sweet, smoky flavor much prized by the islanders.

Tall Island, as they dubbed their discovery, also provided in clear streams and pools all they could carry of fresh water. Their baked clay water-jars were scrubbed with coarse sand and refilled to overflowing. The three Dragons flew ashore parties of men, women, and children for their first freshwater baths in two weeks.

Tom took the holiday to interview Samoy and the other canoe captains on their estimates of speed and direction. He carefully transferred their memorized logs, which were surprisingly consistent, each with the others, to his notebook.

"A cartographer can use this information to map this part of the Quietness," he explained to the *tiki*. "You, of all people, should realize the value of accurate charts. You were a seaman for a long time, as I recall."

"You remind me of something I have long considered,"

said Byron Boldface. "Many seafarers publish accounts of their travels, in the hope that they will help others avoid dangers and find profitable ports of call."

Unfortunately, there wasn't enough paper in the whole fleet for him to attempt the whole of his life's story. He made brief notes, however, now that he had time to do so, which would one day be expanded into useful *Sailing Instructions*, as he termed them. Tom promised to have them printed and bound by the new Overhall printer when they reached Carolna.

"There's always interest in strange places and foreign lands," he said. "And new things to learn."

"By the same token, you must tell me about Carolna," insisted the Mage. "We know very little about it."

ALL was not idyllic, of course.

For three days and four nights they huddled together on the open decks while a heavy sea-storm roared over them. The foul weather was unwelcome, undoubtedly dangerous, and very uncomfortable. Everything above decks and not carefully protected became cold and wet.

For one long week the fleet lay becalmed on a flat sea. Samoy ordered water to be rationed and freshwater bathing stopped, even for the babies. Oil was laboriously pressed from their coconut supply, and substituted for washing dry, salty skin, to avoid painful rashes and sunburn.

The Parvaiti, however, took even the bad weather cheerfully. Storm and calm were just things that happened, they said, when you went to sea.

BABY Gale was so entirely spoiled she rarely found occasion to fuss. There was always someone, Mornie, or Tom, or one of the younger girls, or one of the matrons, to take her from Manda when the child or her mother became tired or chilled by the rain.

The children adopted the little Lady of Hidden Lake Canyon as their own. They sang to her, rocked her, played games with her toes, and made faces for her to giggle at, wide-eyed and filled with joy.

"I wish *I'd* been brought up in such surroundings," Manda told Tom one beautiful starlit evening.

They were seated with the Woodsman and his wife on the forward edge of *Twelve*'s deck between the two sharp prows, watching the double bow-waves sparkle with sea-glow as they foamed and rushed between the hulls.

"I believe you'd be a happy and cheerful lass under almost any circumstances," Tom laughed happily. "But I know what you mean. Personally, I had much the same sort of childhood as Gale's. Lots of sisters, cousins, uncles, aunts, and playmates, not to mention animals, to play with."

"I wonder you didn't go to farming," Clem said. "Boyhood was pleasant enough, for us Herronsson. I learned about the woods and hunting and fishing from my older brothers and my pa."

"You've never told us much about your family," said Tom, turning to his friend.

"No reason why," Clem said, shrugging. "Never thought anyone'd be interested."

He thought about it for a moment, then began, "I was born not far from where I later built my winter cabin, the one Mornie and I call Home Place.

"Ma's a forest gal. Name's Lily. Best cook ever. She sews better even than Mornie . . . which is saying quite a bit. Ma's famous for her sharp yellow cheeses and roast woodland turkey. She bakes wonderful breads and makes churned sweet butter and raised five sons and two daughters to be healthy, honest, useful people.

"Pa was named Herron, a Woodsman," Clem added proudly.

"My folks now live aside this very sea. Pa decided he was getting too old to trap and tramp about longer, so he built a sawmill on a creek above a deep anchorage. He cuts timber in the coastal forest and saws lumber for shipwrights and carpenters. He felled and sawed the redwood great-beams for Hidden Lake House for you, Tom."

"I never knew," Tom said in surprise.

"When did you see them last?" asked Mornie, for this was all new to her as well.

"Not too recent. I wrote 'em about our marriage, and when each of the lads was born. I know they got my letters because the great-beams arrived right on time. None of us are much as letter-writers, I'm afraid."

"We *must* visit them," declared Mornie. "I want to meet my in-laws."

Her own parents still lived at Morningside, where her father was chief farrier to Granger of Gantrell.

"Folk'll love you," exclaimed Clem. "Yes, we'll take the boys and go to Herron's Mill."

"And what is your lady mother like?" Manda wanted to know.

"Lily? She's hard-working, always pleasant and cheerful, and a poet, of sorts. She named all her babies for flowers, including me. There's Rose and there's Azalea, o' course . . . they're the girls. Both well married with families of their own, to good foresters."

He stroked his chin before he continued.

"Now, of the five boys there's Clematis, of course, and Cuss . . . Narcissus. He's the youngest. Cuss's unmarried, last I heard, and helps Pa at the sawmill.

"Next up is Portulaca . . . Port, we call him. And Columbine . . . Col, for short. Both're trappers and hunters, like me. Is that all?"

"I count four, so far," said Manda with a laugh. "Who else?"

"Oh, yes. Hy . . . Hibiscus . . . who nobody's seen nor heard from for years. He went to sea when I was first away in the forests and he was fourteen. We don't know where Hy is. As I said," he added, a touch sadly, "we're none of us much as letter-writers."

"I'd like to see the west coast, myself," said Tom, "and see where those magnificent beams came from. Redwoods, were they?"

"Millions of 'em," exclaimed Clem, regaining his good humor at the thought. "And 'magnificent' is truly the right word for 'em."

ONCE they were well on their way, Tom asked Retruance to fly home to report their doings and the birth of Gale to Murdan and the King.

"They must be quite worried about us by now," Manda agreed.

"Why not come with me?" asked the Dragon. "Everybody'll want to see the baby."

Manda shook her head. "We'll stay with the Parvaiti 'til they're safe ashore in Isthmusi. There may yet be troubles and dangers."

"I'll go fast and return at once," promised Retruance. "Furbetrance will fly with me as far as Obsydian Isle, to see his family. He should be back before me."

"I'll stay. I consider these *my* people now," declared Florenz Sea Dragon. "When they're all settled in their new home I shall resume my studies of ocean currents. I'll add my findings to Byron's *Sailing Instructions*. We've already decided upon that."

ON the evening of the forty-third day since fleeing the exploding volcano, the lookout at the masthead of *Twelve* electrified them all with a loud cry of "Land! Land there!"

It was all Samoy could do to keep his entire crew and

half his passengers from shinnying up the mast to see for themselves, threatening to turn the ship turtle.

"If we've reckoned correctly, we've hit Isthmusi right in the middle reaches," Tom told Manda, hugging her gleefully.

"We'll all see it clearly tomorrow," the Sage was shouting. "Stay on deck, you boys! You want to turn us over?"

But for three full days they had only distant glimpses of tall, blue mountains and a thin line of lush tropical greenery. Offshore winds and churning green shallows kept the fleet well out to sea.

"*Tiki?*" asked the Sage wearily, on the third evening. "Have you no spells or incantations to make the wind blow in a better direction?"

"Unfortunately, no," Byron Boldface sighed. "But look on the brighter side. With such strong seasonals, our future fishing and trading ships will always make easy and quick offing when leaving port."

On the fourth morning the wind turned completely around.

Twelve led the five canoes north along the sandy beach until they reached an estuary, located by Flo some days before, which offered sheltered anchorage.

It was a shore of golden sand, a rumpled brown river, and in the distance tall forest dotted with wide, grassy flats, then an upswept mountain range the likes of which the Parvaiti had never imagined . . . a mile tall and capped with strange snow. The mountains stretched from the far north, and out of sight to the south.

They declared aloud and often that it was wondrously splendid.

"Almost anywhere would look beautiful after two months at sea," sighed Manda, lifting Gale so she could see her first dry land. "Not that I didn't enjoy it, after the first few days and nights. But I think I'd rather be a scullery-maid at Hidden Lake House than admiral of all the oceans.''

"Look!" cried Tom. "There's Retruance. And he has a welcoming party waiting for us, too.''

The huge green-and-gold Constable Dragon couldn't be missed, even at that distance, but the tiny figures he had aboard, now seen waving and, presumably, shouting, might easily have been overlooked.

The Dragon's passengers proved to be important: King Eduard Ten himself, his Queen Beatrix, and their young twins, accompanied by the Royal Historian, Murdan of Overhall.

Retruance spread his great black wings and coasted over the calm sea to splash beside *Twelve*, cheerfully nodding and calling to everybody.

Manda held her daughter high so her father and step-mother could get a good first glimpse of her.

"Look! There's your Grampa Eduard, darling. Wave to good Queen Bea, my pet.''

"How did you know where to meet us?" Tom asked Retruance soon after they'd landed. The last of the great war canoes was just touching the strand to shouts of joy from all sides.

"We saw you from the Lofters' village yesterday evening," Retruance explained. "I'd already picked this as a good landing place, but you came right this way without my guidance, after all.''

"Perfect!" cried the wildly excited *tiki*, pounding Tom and Clem on their backs and pumping vigorously at the Dragon's right foreclaw. "A perfect spot. Obviously a rich, rich land. Will we be welcomed by those fierce-looking warriors coming from the forest, do y'think? They would be forgiven if they wanted to drive us away.''

"Not so," Retruance laughed aloud with a celebratory

swoosh of green fire. "Lofters prefer mountaintops to sea-shores. They're pleased to have friendly neighbors, for this's a lonely wilderness for the most part."

He went off to warn the Parvaiti children not to swim in the river, just yet, for it was home to great, long, green, sharp-toothed, grinning crocodiles who, unused to strangers, might take the swimmers for between-meal snacks.

"SPEAKING of food," said Quillan, Chief of the Lofters, after he'd been introduced to everybody and had shepherded the newcomers under the shade of the forest. "Our womenfolk have prepared what yonder green Dragon calls a 'picnic,' over there in the deeper shade. It's hot down here on the flats! Hope you like spiced goat with chunky guava-and-red-pepper sauce."

"Sounds delicious," exclaimed Manda. "We've been eating salt pork for days and fresh fish for weeks. Oh, dear! *Oh, my!* How the land rocks and rolls. Is there a volcano underfoot?"

"It's your sea legs," laughed Maorai. "It'll pass quickly once you're used to walking solid ground again."

"No fiery mountains here," cheered the Parvaiti women. "No thundering volcanoes nor awful fires nor showers of burning stones and choking ash raining down."

"Showers of rain we will have shortly, however," warned the Chief of the Lofters. "Baths for everyone. Then come under the trees and have the picnic. Everybody'll get soaked anyway, although it might be," he added in an aside to Tom, "a welcome thing to all, including us mountain folk, after all your days and nights without bathing."

✦ 17 ✦
A Place of Their Own

"THEY consider fish of any kind a marvelous delicacy . . . fried, broiled, boiled, grilled, baked, even marinated in lemon juice and eaten raw," the *tiki* chuckled, his wrinkled little face beaming as he spoke of the Lofters. "Well, fish is one thing we can give aplenty. Have a fillet of whatever fish this is, my dear Historian. Delicious, I guarantee."

Murdan politely accepted one of the large, flat leaves that served the picnickers as plates and nibbled a tiny bite of the flaky, white flesh steaming hot from the grill.

"*Ummm*," he cried in surprise. "Never tasted anything better."

Byron's lined face shone even more brightly as he watched the Historian finish off the tuna steak and lick his fingers clean of the savory pineapple condiment.

"You tempt me to stay and gorge myself," Murdan said, refusing a second helping. "I came but to bid you come talk to our King. Over there by the beached canoes, you see?"

"Gladly," cried the *tiki*, jumping to his feet. "I'll bring a platter of *pupu* deep-fried in coconut oil. Our King must be hungry after a day of flying."

Eduard was indeed hungry, and between them the royal party made short work of the huge *pupu* tray.

"Speak with us for a while, *tiki*," Tom requested. "We need to discuss a certain matter. You may be able to assist us."

His mouth full of deep-fried shrimp, the former Mage could only nod enthusiastically.

• • •

MANDA smiled proudly at her father, seated on the sand
dandling his first grandchild on his knee. Tiny Gale burbled
happily.

"You've forgiven this person for kidnapping you?" Eduard asked Manda, nodding toward Byron Boldface.

"We've talked it all over," Manda replied. "Byron did
what he thought needful, I'm convinced, with no really
wicked intention."

The King handed Gale to her mother. " 'Twas difficult
for you and Tom to forgive, surely. I know how it is to
have a child stolen away."

The party strolled by moonlight on the soft sand beach.
The air was soft, too, and filled with the heady perfumes
of flowering trees in the jungle.

They heard the calls of night birds and the occasional
booming of the crocodiles . . . who'd been sternly warned
by Retruance to let the newcomers bathe in their river, to
wash away the salt dried on their skins and in their hair.
The islanders had never seen so much fresh water at one
time in all their lives.

"You have no shortage for baby care," Eduard said to
his elder daughter.

"Gale has more nannies than you would care to shake
your scepter at," Manda told him with a comfortable
chuckle.

"We need to talk about Byron Boldface. What's his
story?" The Historian recalled them to the subject at hand.

Tom launched into a detailed account of the *tiki*'s past,
deeds, and circumstances. It took quite a long time, for
Murdan was curious about many points along the way.
They walked and talked and ended sitting on the deserted
deck of *Twelve*, swinging their bare feet over the murmuring river.

The Parvaiti had already named it Wonderful Stream.
They'd never seen a river before.

"You think he should go unpunished?" asked the King bluntly.

"We would rather see him encouraged in his role as leader of these kind, honest, cheerful, wonderful people. They are a very real and valuable addition to your realm, Sire," Manda murmured solemnly.

"I won't gainsay you, Princess. But there are still quite a few people in Carolna, you must know, who criticize me . . . and you . . . and Tom and Murdan, too . . . for being too lenient to your Uncle Peter, considering the really terrible things he did to us."

"There's that, I admit," the Princess considered. "But circumstances alter cases, as it says in the Trusslo Royal Code."

" 'Justice should be tempered with mercy,' " Tom quoted.

Eduard exchanged glances with his good friend and half-brother, his Royal Historian.

"Well, then . . . a token punishment? We can't have people saying, 'I can do *this*, for the King once allowed *that*.' You know how people think and react, my dear."

"Too well, but on this . . ."

"I suggest," Tom interrupted quickly to stop an argument before it started, "that we require Byron Boldface and the Parvaiti to take a solemn oath of allegiance to the Crown of Carolna, first. No one, not even the Lofters, claims sovereignty over Isthmusi, I'm told. It will peacefully add considerable territory to your domain, sir."

"Our southern borders have always been our weakest," Eduard admitted. "If the Lofters don't object, I'll demand this of the good islanders, yes. They'd become officially our colonists, then, I should think."

"I also suggest that we fine the *tiki* for his wicked acts," Tom went on.

"What sort of fine?" Murdan demanded, somewhat mollified, for he respected Tom's common sense.

"A yearly tribute . . . ?" Tom suggested.

"A yearly payment toward the upkeep of Lady Gale Thomassdotter," exclaimed the King. "It'll sound reasonable to the carpers and detractors, and help you and Manda defray the costs of raising my granddaughter, Tom. I imagine it'll be some years before you're in any way wealthy from your desert Achievement."

Tom and Manda thought about this for a while.

The house at Hidden Lake had been expensive to build. Manda had brought some wealth to the marriage, and Murdan had advanced them some of the needed money. Retruance wished to supplement that from his Dragon's hoard, secreted away somewhere, but they had so far refused his offer.

And the Achievement would be expensive to maintain. Travel to and from the capital for spring and fall Sessions, alone, would be very costly, not to mention suitable clothing, equipment, decorations, attendants to outfit, and riverboats and the lake carriers to be chartered.

Wages had to be paid and fees rendered. Cash was short for most of Carolna. Most legacies and fortunes consisted of land and rents paid in kind.

"I like it," said Manda at last. "Let's do that."

The *tiki*, who had listened to all this silently, nodded his grey head, and said, "I see no problem with that for me, nor for my people."

"And publish it at home," agreed Tom, "so our critics will know that justice has been served."

"They don't have to know how much or how willingly," conceded Murdan.

"I . . . *we*, rather . . . will pay gladly," said the *tiki*. "The little Lady Gale is officially and by birth a Parvaiti. We'll soon be active seagoing traders and may even become rather wealthy, I predict. I've a bit of experience in merchant shipping. And there's the matter of the milksap.''

"What's that, for goodness' sake?'' asked the King.

"Sap from a certain tree used to make cloth waterproof, and soften the iron tires of wains, wagons, carriages, carts, and coaches, so they won't jolt passengers and cargo nearly so much,'' Tom explained. "Once the many uses of milk-sap, brought to market by the Parvaiti in their own fast ships, are known, it'll be in great demand.''

"I've already learned to use it to make pantaloons for the baby,'' Manda said. "They keep her nursemaids dry, in case of an accident.''

"Now *there's* something Carolnans really could use,'' cried Beatrix. "The Parvaiti should certainly prosper and pay their bills.''

They returned to the campfire on the beach where the Parvaiti were teaching their Lofter hosts the music of the islands, including the long epic chants about the exploding mountain and their long voyage to the east.

Eduard drew Byron aside and talked to him, so that by midnight, when they all retired to the palm-frond pavilions prepared for them under the trees, the matter was settled.

"Now,'' Tom said to Murdan the next noontime. "There's another matter I didn't mention, so as not to worry the King or Manda. At least not just yet.''

"Trouble?'' sighed the Historian.

He deftly impaled a fat worm on a fishhook and dropped his line into the amber water of Wonderful Stream. They were alone in midstream, aboard *Julia*.

"I haven't told you all Byron overheard when he hid in Ahmedek's palace in Rajal, years back, after he had returned from exile in the far west.''

"When he was going to confront the old thief and get his Jewel of Displacement back? Brave, but perhaps more than a bit foolish, I'd say.''

"In many ways our *tiki* is rather naive, even now," Tom agreed.

He described the scene between Ahmedek and the unknown Mage who demanded the blue stone.

Tom ticked off items on his fingers.

"First, this stranger knew of the stone. Byron and Ahmedek had kept it secret for years.

"Second, he transported Ahmedek to a 'far distant place' but only sent Byron a relatively short way, where he perhaps would look to Carolna for assistance. And . . ."

"Some assistance," muttered Murdan, watching his cork bobber dip below the surface of the water. He pulled his line up only to find that his bait had been stolen.

"Smart damn fishes," he swore happily.

He reached for the bait box.

". . . and third," Tom continued, "what about Plume?"

Murdan almost dropped his fishing pole in the river.

"Plume? Is there a connection between that rascal and this mysterious eastern business?"

"It just came to me—a hunch. A Mage possessing a powerful magic tool by which people can be whisked from place to place over great distances? Maybe there's no connection at all. But it's a possibility, and one I think we should explore."

"Lets go ashore and find this *tiki* person. I may not learn to like or trust him, but I'll be eternally grateful to him if he can provide the least clue in the matter of who or what sent Plume against us . . . and the sudden and unexplained appearance of a certain young Human in the middle of Elvish Carolna."

THEY found Byron Boldface with Samoy, Maorai, Clem, and a half-dozen Parvaiti elders, pacing out a plan for a new village under the towering trees near where the river emerged from the shadows of the forest.

"A moment of your time, good sir," said Murdan to the *tiki*. "If you can be spared."

"Of course, Lord Historian. The elders and Master Clem are better at this than am I. I'm the student here."

Murdan and Tom led him off to a quiet spot on the edge of the grove where they could talk undisturbed.

"About your cruel handling by the man named Ahmedek," began Murdan. "It interests me greatly. Can you tell us more exactly what the stranger said, before he sent you to Eversmoke Island?"

Byron thought about it for a while, drawing circles and lines in the soft sand with a stick. Looking down, Tom saw he had written the words "Eastern Scholar."

"May I assume that you are interested in this strange name he mentioned?" asked the *tiki* at last. "For there wasn't much else, except this name or title, mentioned only in passing."

"We have long been seeking a certain Accountant we knew as Plume," Murdan explained. "He's a spy and a traitor and perhaps a good deal more than that. Could he be this 'Eastern Scholar,' do you think?"

The Historian told the story of the Accountant's years of treachery, his discovery, and subsequent escape from justice.

"We've been looking for him ever since. Not just to avenge ourselves for his perfidy," Murdan concluded, "but also to discover for whom he acted. There's been a lot of powerful magick practiced against our Carolna and we'd like to know by whom . . . and why."

"I see," said the wizened *tiki* with a slow nod. "Well, Historian. As far as I recall . . . and I was quite filled with terror at the time, you must understand . . . the unknown Wizard demanded Ahmedek sell him the blue stone . . . ."

"Demanded he *sell* it?" Tom asked, interrupting. "Not that he give it to him?"

"No, I distinctly remember the Mage offering to buy the gem. He named a very handsome price, in fact. One that would have made Ahmedek one of the richest men in the Hintoo Empire."

"Did they haggle over the price?" Tom asked.

"Ahmadek refused to bargain, and the stranger grew impatient. He reminded Ahmedek that Ahmedek had embezzled the stone in the first place. From me. Ahmedek still refused to sell. The stranger threatened to reveal Ahmedek's means of gaining leadership of the Mages' Guild, which would have ruined Ahmedek for once and all, and probably gotten him beheaded."

The *tiki* paused, thinking hard, frowning.

"Ahmedek refused the offer a third time. At last the stranger shouted, 'Enough,' and plucked the stone from its hiding place.

" 'You should have accepted my honest offer, thief,' " he hissed at Ahmedek. And he recited the proper spell, saying, 'Go to a distant place where your petty magicks won't work.' "

"And," Murdan murmured, "where do you think that might be, Byron Boldface?"

"I've no idea, M'Lord. I never heard of such a place. Where magick won't work? What a terrible place to be, especially if one is a Mage. Can you imagine?"

Tom stared out over the sea and said softly, "I can imagine," but the *tiki* was continuing his account and didn't hear.

"He tore down the arras behind which I hid," he was saying. "And said, 'Ah, there you are. You're a bold one, aren't you? Good. I'll send you off, too, for your own protection.'

"And with that he spoke the spell-words again, even more quickly, and I was plopped down in the mangrove

swamp of southern Eversmoke Island in the middle of a
minor eruption.''

''So . . . we at least begin to understand *who* if not yet
why,'' Murdan told the King.

''We must return home,'' said Eduard Ten with a sigh.
''Fall Session, you know. This would be a really wonderful
place to spend a week or a month. Well, perhaps later? It's
to be, after all, our southern frontier. The mountainmen
have agreed to our proposal.''

''Meanwhile,'' Murdan told him, ''Tom and I will pur-
sue this other matter. The Dragons will help.''

''I'm sure they will,'' Tom said, laying his hand on the
Historian's arm. ''They've said as much, you see.''

✦ 18 ✦
Bad Penny

THE three Constables formed a quickly vanishing *vee* over Isthmusi with Papa Arbitrance at point. In a very short time they'd disappeared to the north, heading for Carolna proper and Overhall Castle.

"Children," the *tiki* spoke earnestly to the Parvaiti, "we've been most fortunate. We've escaped certain and terrible death and complete destruction. We've safely sailed across the whole wide Quietness, guarded by three Dragons. We've made many fast and powerful friends. Now we must make a new home in this wilderness. It's early in the day yet. Time we got to work!"

One of the women—midwife Garrai, in fact—brought to him a banner she'd made of a single large rectangle of sun-bleached tapa cloth with fine stitchery of blue and yellow, red and green, showing a great, curling blue ocean wave over which, wings spread wide, flew a grand green-and-gold Dragon breathing red fire and black smoke.

"Raise our banner here in the middle of Eduardland," cried Byron, weeping unashamedly. "Pick up your saws, your adzes, your hammers and shovels. Let us build a new home."

MANDA and Mornie, with their children and husbands, were shouted for, exclaimed about, and wept over when they arrived at Overhall Castle.

People came from miles around to see Manda's baby princess and learn her name. Rosemary's pretty young daughters offered at once to be Maids-in-Waiting to the little Lady of Hidden Lake Canyon, while their younger brother Eddie stoutly declared himself Lady Gale's at-once-and-forever Knight Champion. He flourished a fine wooden sword and round leather-bound buckler with which he was determined to guard and protect the beautiful infant.

Gale, of course, peacefully consumed her mother's milk . . . plus well-pureed carrots, peas, and an occasional bit of stewed tomato from Ffallmar Farm's kitchen garden, smiled brilliantly at everyone, no matter who, slept when she was tired, kicked her heels and waved her chubby arms for exercise, and crowed happily.

HER father and his employer gathered a few trusted friends in Murdan's study atop Foretower, around a great oval table. To it they summoned Peter Gantrell, Manda's uncle, from Lexor where he now made his home.

Peter was indeed a changed man since his rescue from freezing to death on an ice island floating . . . and rapidly melting away . . . in the northern Blue. He was as handsome as ever, if a bit grey at the temples, but not nearly so proud nor pompous to all he met.

"How do you pass your days?" Tom asked him as they waited for the conference to begin.

"I'm compiling a history of the Gantrells," Peter replied. "I'm determined to include both the good and the ill. And Eduard, bless him, allows me a house and garden inside the walls of Lexor. I find surprising pleasure in helping things to grow. My candy-striped carnations won first prize at the Queen's Summer Fair, did you hear? I'd entered them under a fictitious name, so they'd be judged on their merits alone."

He was genuinely pleased by his gardening and the gold medal.

"I admit that I sometimes miss the more active life, the horseback rides, the journeys from Achievement to Achievement, but Murdan advises those will have to wait yet a while. I've always had a desire to explore the north-west coast above Wall.''

''When the time comes,'' Clem offered generously, ''I'll be happy to act as your guide, Peter.''

''Kindly offered and gratefully accepted, Woodsman,'' said Peter, bowing to the Broken Land trapper. ''Perhaps between us we can open up some of that land for settlement.''

''Hadn't thought o' that,'' admitted Clem. ''I'm not at all sure it's a good idea. Forests and lakes and such places are really quite fragile.''

''Perhaps,'' nodded the former Lord of Gantrell . . . technically he was just a private citizen, now, his lands and titles stripped away by King and Session. ''Yet, Carolna needs wide room for our young people who seek their own Achievements. And they can't *all* be furtrappers and huntsmen.''

Clem nodded, still unconvinced, but just then Murdan and Manda took their places at the head and foot of the table respectively.

''Can you tell us anything we don't already know about this man Plume?'' Murdan asked Peter without ado.

''I don't really think so,'' answered Peter slowly, shaking his head. ''He came to me at Overtide House one evening . . . twelve years ago . . . bearing a recommendation from an old acquaintance and seeking to enter my service.''

''Who was this old friend?'' Tom wondered.

''His name was Pepperdane, and he was an officer in my father's service. He'd been dead for some months when Plume came to me, actually. I never checked his references.''

''The sort of trick old Plume would play,'' commented Retruance, who was standing in the forecourt below with his head thrust through the open doors of Murdan's private balcony.

"A slippery eel, I agree. Never really liked him, if you can believe me," Peter nodded, "and I won't blame you if you did not. But at the time, under those circumstances . . . well, you know what I mean."

"We should," growled Murdan testily, remembering the trouble this powerful Lord had caused him in those days.

Peter had the grace to blush and merely cleared his throat.

"Do go on, Uncle Peter," Manda urged him, making a face at the Historian. "We need to know more about this wretched Elf and we know so very little to begin with. Anything you can remember would help."

"He presented himself as a trained scribe and account-keeper. Every Achievement needs a skilled number-juggler, and good ones are scarce. I hired him on the spot."

After a year or two he'd became aware of his new Accountant's considerable abilities and had sent him to manage the Gantrell commercial enterprises in Lexor.

"He wrote to me saying Royal Historian Murdan of Overhall had offered him a position," Peter went on. "He suggested that he accept it, not mentioning his association with the House of Gantrell. He could then provide me with useful information about your businesses and household, Murdan. I was to pay for his services by deposits into a merchant's bank in Lexor."

"Has he ever withdrawn any of that money . . . since he fled, I mean?" asked Clem.

"I don't know. I remember telling you about it, Murdan. I assume you checked."

"The banker said the account was cleared out by Plume, personally, every year, from the very first. No record or trace of where he put it, after that," Murdan told them. "You say Plume claimed *I* approached him about working for me, eh?"

"So his letter said. A copy is in my files. Files that you hold, I believe."

"We do," confirmed Tom, who, as Librarian of Over-hall, was responsible for keeping safe all such documents.

"He approached *me*, actually. And he told me nothing of serving you," continued the Historian. "Not that it would have made any difference. I probably would have hired him, anyway. I was in hot fiscal waters at the time."

"After the matter of the Mercenary Knights," Tom pressed Peter, "Plume narrowly escaped discovery. Did you urge him to stay here, or did he offer to stay of his own accord?"

"We really never discussed it," Peter admitted with an apologetic shrug. "I always assumed he'd sense enough to flee if things got too dangerous."

"Back up a moment, Uncle," interrupted Manda. "Whose idea, honestly now that it's over, was it to let those Incendiary Knights . . ."

"*Mercenary* Knights," her husband corrected her softly.

"Whatever . . . *Mercenary* Knights into Overhall in the first place?"

"It was Plume's idea. He wrote me you had run away from my brother's house and placed yourself under Mur-dan's protection. Plume proposed I send an armed party to snatch you from Overhall when Murdan went to Lexor for spring Session."

"The purpose of taking Overhall was simply to recover me?" asked the Princess.

"That . . . and to reduce Murdan's ability to interfere with my plans. Relief of Overhall would have been very expensive if your husband hadn't appeared and done things to the plumbing." Peter smiled pleasantly at Tom. "A clever action, if I may say so."

•   •   •

WHEN it was obvious that Peter could tell them nothing more about his spy, they sent him back to his books and his garden.

There was a long, thoughtful silence . . . punctuated by the sounds of children playing in the forecourt and cows lowing in the castle byre, waiting to be milked.

"We must hire ourselves a very good Seer," decided Murdan at last, "and trace this absconding Accountant by magick."

"We've tried that," Manda protested. "He charged you and me and Father the cost of a good-sized Achievement and he found no trace."

"But what *else* is there to do?" demanded the Historian, throwing up his hands. "We're quite stumped."

Tom raised his hand.

"Any good ideas, m'boy?"

"We've exhausted magick but not logic, I think. Common sense, I really mean."

"You're the expert in that department, love." Manda smiled fondly at him. "What does your common sense have to say in this tangled mess?"

"It's occurred to me while we were talking to Byron Boldface on the beach in Isthmusi," Tom replied, "that we've expended our efforts in the belief that Plume, when he escaped Overhall, fled south into the jungles and is hiding there yet."

"He was seen running that way," Retruance reminded his Companion.

"But you and Arbitrance, and Furbetrance, as well as half a dozen prides of mountain lions and herds of elephants, too . . . not to forget the Lofters . . . never've been able to find the least sign of him."

"Plume is nothing if not clever at sneaking about," Murdan insisted disgustedly. "He could be there yet. A big and empty land is Isthmusi."

"Clever," Tom agreed, "but from all *I* know of him, not the sort for the open spaces, for jungles, or mountain wildernesses. Do you agree, Woodsman?"

Clem nodded slowly. "Not the type to live on roots and broil snake cutlets for dinner, no."

Manda and Murdan exchanged glances.

"What about it, Librarian?" the Historian asked.

"Well, perhaps we're not looking in the right places," Tom replied. "Where *would* a fox like Plume go to ground? Where *could* he fade into the background, if you understand what I mean."

"You mean, what's his natural covert?" asked Clem. "I understand you well, Tom. Like a deer in the forest. Big as it is, as long as it stands still, it's practically invisible."

"Precisely." Tom nodded. "Where would you guess?"

Clem leaned forward and stared at his large, capable hands folded before him on the polished tabletop.

"Like the deer in the forest, he'd need a settling-place where he could and would fit in. An Accountant? Ink stains and paper cuts? Where do a whole lot of clerks work and live and buzz about like a hive full of bees?"

"Lexor!" exclaimed both Manda and Murdan at once.

"He could change his appearance a bit. Maybe grow a beard or shave his head. Wear spectacles. Walk with a stoop. . . . No, he already did that. Speak with a different accent?" Clem counted on his fingers. "Maybe Plume hides among the money-grubbers in the city. Who'd ever notice?"

"How to find him, though, if you're right?" Manda asked eagerly.

"Call upon Murdan's factor, Grindley. I'd think he knows every factor's clerk and cost-accountant in town," Tom suggested.

"Grindley'll know how to find out without tipping our

game,'' exclaimed Murdan softly. ''It's certainly worth a try. A *careful* try.''

''I must go to Lexor shortly. Tom and Gale will go with me. Our visit will cause no surprise.'' Manda took up the idea. ''If you went now, Murdan, everyone would wonder why, and Plume, if he's there, would slink deeper into cover. Tom and I are expected to take Gale to my father's house and show her off to the magnates and earls who live in the east. Hidden Lake Canyon House is at a stage when we need to hire servants. That'll give us an excuse to make inquiries about Accountants as well as gardeners and cooks.''

It was decided that Clem and Mornie would go to Hidden Lake Canyon and take up the tasks of preparing it for the return of its Lord and Lady after Session. Murdan would stay at Overhall Castle, acting as a clearing house for information and preparing for fall Session.

''We'll fly to Lexor on Thursday morning,'' Tom decided, patting his Dragon affectionately on the nose. ''It's always nice to have a Dragon around when there's a bandit or a pirate or a sneaky number-fumbler to sniff out.''

Retruance grinned happily. ''I look forward to fumbling Master Plume quite a bit, once we find him.''

''But not before we have a chance to ask him some questions,'' Murdan warned. ''Such as . . . was he the strange mage in Hintoo? . . . And who plucked Tom from his Human world? That's the mystery I really want to fathom.''

''WHY a *Human*?'' Manda asked Tom. ''And why *you* in particular?''

They were seated on their favorite perch on Overhall's lofty outer battlements, overlooking the wide, green valley of Overhall River, the rising downs to the north, the distant, snow-capped mountains, and the pleasant farmlands and woodlots to either side.

''Maybe I can guess,'' answered Tom. ''What have I done to make a difference, since I arrived?''

''Easy. You saved me from the Incendi . . . *Mercenary* Knights. You recovered Overhall Castle for Murdan. You tracked down that nasty bully Brevory and rescued Rosemary and her children when Uncle Peter had them stolen away.''

She bent fingers down to keep track of Tom's adventures, one by one.

''Who was it who dug Retruance out of a hollow mountain when he fell in and got stuck? Who found little Crown Prince Ednol when Arbitrance carried him off? And who crossed an ocean to save me and our baby from a volcano's blast . . . and the Parvaiti and Byron Boldface, too? Don't blush, silly. It's all a matter of hysterical record.''

Tom had to nod in agreement.

''Historical,'' he said, grinning broadly.

''Whatever.'' His wife grinned back.

''You didn't mention the lady pirates of Lakeheart,'' Retruance chuckled.

''Them too! Who can figure which of these things changed Carolna's history the most? It's obvious to me. Whoever brought you here, brought you to *bump* history in the right direction.''

''It might have been as simple a thing as falling in love with a Princess and marrying her . . . and getting her with child,'' Tom added.

''Establishing a new blood line mixing Human with Elfish gems . . . or whatever you called 'em last winter when I first told you I was pregnant.''

''*Genes*,'' Tom laughed. ''Not gems.''

''I'll *never* understand *that* business,'' Manda muttered under her breath.

She leaned back against him, and they sat in silence for a long while as the sun set and a cool, wet breeze promised an early autumn shower. Amid the clamor of the castle courtyards below, they heard a clash of arms where Graham's guardsmen practiced, much to the delight of little Eddie Ffallmar and a dozen of his Overhall friends.

Retruance called to Arbitrance, who appeared in the courtyard just then. Constable father and son flew over the foregate and slid down the steep grassy slope to the edge of the woods locally known as Murdan's Bivouac. Here Murdan and his men had pitched their tents when they had laid siege to the Historian's own castle, years before.

The Constables sank down in the tall grass, waiting for the rain to start, chatting amiably together, sending up into the still evening air, when they laughed, pastel rings and balls and streamers of Dragon's fire and smoke.

Murdan came from the wide front door of Foretower, striding purposefully off to talk to Graham about the night guards' duties.

A chattering flock of farmwives, leaving late after delivering their day's produce, new-churned butter, fresh eggs, and chickens to the castle kitchen, rode off in a hurried bustle on their placid donkeys or in one-horse traps, clucking like a flock of their own chickens. They hastened to reach home and hearth before rain and darkness fell.

"What's the *main* question, though?" Tom wondered aloud. "Not what I've done, but who benefited from my doings. Oh, I don't mean any of us, my sweet. But somewhere, someone we haven't figured into the puzzle went to a great deal of trouble and no small magick, too, with all its time and expense, to bring me here. Who might that be?"

"My father . . . or his hired Wizards and Seers. But he says no, and I believe him. Why deny it? Murdan, of course, but he couldn't have afforded the fees. Me . . . but that's foolish! I would have moved sky and earth to bring you, had I but known about you. But I didn't. Oh, it's a tangled web woven of invisible goals and cross purposes!''

"What do you mean?"

"Well, if there's some unknown person who brought you for the good of the Kingdom . . . or whatever . . . there *had* to be someone else seeking to do us ill. Who wanted to help us? Who was his adversary? I just don't understand the matter.''

"Nor I. Not yet. Maybe Plume can help us when we track him down.'' Tom didn't sound too sure of it. "You think there's *one* party who wanted to harm or destroy Carolna, or your father, or you . . . and *another* who wished to protect and guard you against the first party?''

Deep within Middle tower a sous-chef enthusiastically struck the great bronze dinner gong six times. In the courtyards and baileys people stopped work or left their late afternoon leisure, turning quickly to the Great Hall and dinner.

"I'm starved,'' cried Manda, popping to her feet. "We'll think better, perhaps, on full stomachs.''

"More likely sleep better,'' grinned her husband. "Puzzles and mysteries always make me hungry, too. I wonder what's for supper.''

It would not have surprised them that, about the castle, other conversations were on the same topic from different viewpoints.

Retruance and his father spread their wings to fly over the walls together, settling at the door to the Great Hall to watch Murdan's household and guests assemble for their evening meal.

"It's the kind of thing a couple of great Mages might do, if they were involved in a battle of wits and powers,'' Altruance was saying. "But I, for one, fail to put a name to 'em.''

"I counsel patience . . . and some gratitude, too,'' Retruance advised, folding his wings carefully so as not to sweep

an approaching squad of off-duty archers off their feet.
"Whoever it was, we've come out ahead of everything.
Carolna's safe and happy."

"For the moment," Arbitrance muttered.

He tied a huge linen napkin, the size of the catamaran
Julia's mainsail, under his chin and reached for his
monster-sized knife and fork.

✦ 19 ✦
Finding the Accountant

MASTER Grindley bowed deeply before the King, and bowed again to the Queen, then the young Prince and Princess playing on the floor beside the throne.

He respectfully bobbed his head also to Princess Manda, the Royal Historian, the Royal Librarian, and grinned broadly as he saluted the two enormous Dragons.

Retruance and Arbitrance lay along either side of Eduard's throne room, their tails stretching all the way to the elaborately carved doors at the far end.

"It's no great wonder so many of your courtiers are on the slim side, Sire," the Lexor merchant puffed, straightening up at last. "All this bending at the waist and bobbing about. How may I serve Your Majesty?"

Eduard laughed and led the plump merchant to a seat among the cozy group in a wide, deep window alcove behind the throne.

"Maybe that's why a monarch requires so much bowing and scraping," he suggested. "To keep his subjects in good trim."

"Maybe you should require more of it," Grindley replied with a wink.

The King chuckled and beckoned everyone close so they could hear better.

"We're seeking a man named Plume . . . an Accountant, late of the Lord Historian's household, placed there as a spy by Peter of Gantrell."

"I've heard the tale, Sire," Grindley said with a grim nod. "What can I do to help your search?"

"Remain perfectly silent about what we say here, first

of all," suggested the King gravely. "We don't want to flush our game before our bow is even bent."

"Agreed," responded the factor, who'd never drawn a bow in his life but well understood the metaphor.

"Our Royal Librarian, here, Sir Thomas . . . you've met?"

"I've had that pleasure, and the additional joy of doing business with him and the Princess Alix Amanda."

"Tom has an idea . . . you might say a hunch . . . a guess . . . that Plume the spy is hiding right here in Lexor, disguised perhaps, working as a clerk or a penman," Eduard explained carefully. "Do you think this's possible?"

"Entirely possible." The merchant nodded. "It wouldn't surprise me a bit, Sire. I hear he's the dry, sly, slippery, sharp-nosed ink-blotter who managed the Gantrell family businesses here in Lexor, some years back. There were always whispers of underhanded dealings, skimmings, kickbacks from favored suppliers, under-the-table discounts in return for . . . ah . . . *favors* would be the gentlemanly way to term them."

"How," Tom asked, "would *you* go about finding such a man, if he hid himself in the maze of counting houses, banks, and business offices in Lexor?"

Grindley considered this for a long while as the King and his advisors waited in silence. At last he brightened and snapped his fingers.

"Several years ago your Majesty decreed all persons handling both public and private funds must be examined and licensed yearly. If this Plume person is working as a lowly clerk or as a full Accountant, he must be examined, certified, and bonded, by the honorable Minister of Commerce."

"Very true," exclaimed Eduard, leaning forward. "How does that help us?"

"Each autumn before Sessions your Minister of Commerce audits, or causes to be audited, all current licensees, to ensure they're performing their duties honorably and in accordance with royal laws. Each certificate-holder must appear *in person* before a Royal Examiner to swear to his records, explain any anomalies, take an oath of clear conscience, and renew his bond for the coming year.''

''A large bond?'' asked Manda, interested always in the workings of her father's government.

''No, Princess, only the equivalent of a month's salary. It's placed in an interest-bearing escrow account, to be returned to each clerk upon his leaving ranks or reaching retirement age. This serves, among other things, to keep them honest, you see. They'll all have a nest egg awaiting them when they can or will no longer practice their profession, so they're less prone to steal . . . or embezzle, as is the legal term.''

''And there will be such an examination this fall?'' Tom asked.

''To work even as a very minor subclerk, Plume'd have had to post his bond and register when he first went to work. It's not something that can be easily avoided, Sir Librarian. If the man works in Lexor or anywhere runs the royal writ, he must have been bonded and registered, as I've said. To do anything else would bring imprisonment and a large fine to the culprit *and* his employer.''

''When will the Examination occur this year?'' asked the King.

''No one knows,'' replied the merchant with a shrug. ''It's called for by the Minister of Commerce each year at some date prior to preparing his report to the fall Session in October. Last year it was just a fortnight before Session began. Some years it's been as much as a month or six weeks before. At Your Majesty's convenience and pleasure, of course.''

''Ah, then . . . I'll have a word privately with Lord Wrig-

gles," decided the King. " 'Twere sooner the better, but
not so soon as to warn our quarry."

When Grindley had bowed to all once again and departed, puffing slightly, promising to wait upon Manda and
Tom later in the week to discuss additional purchases for
Hidden Lake House, the King sent for Lord Wriggles, a
lifelong public servant whose only claims to fame were his
enthusiastic dancing at Session Balls each spring and fall,
and his undoubted honesty.

While they waited, Eduard said, "You're appointed Special Auditor, Murdan. As is Manda. And Tom, too."

"What are you planning, Father?" Manda asked.

"Actually, it's Tom's idea. As I recall, there are two
hundred forty-three Master Accountants in the city. And six
thousand fifty-two Registered Fiscal Clerks. It's a long-
drawn affair to audit them all, I'm afraid. Lord Wriggles
has his work cut out for him, as he has only two or three
underministers and a small number of clerks. He'll welcome assistance in this matter, I should think."

"You will sit as Royal Auditors and catch Plume when
and if he appears?" asked Retruance. "But won't he recognize Tom, or Manda, or the Historian, when he comes?"

"Of course," said Eduard with a grin. "But that'll be
too late. If he suspects a trap . . . well, you Dragons'll be
watching who runs away. Ah, my dear Minister! Thank you
for coming so quickly."

Lord Wriggles glided gracefully from the far door,
stepped carefully around Princess Amelia's large family of
dolls, and bowed gracefully to the King and Queen.

"Your Majesties. My pleasure, entirely. Ah, Lord Murdan. It's been some time since we last met. Princess Manda,
you've grown and become even more beautiful than you
were as a child, my dear. And married and a mother, now,
to boot."

Eduard patiently allowed him time to greet everyone

present, whether he knew their names or not, even the two Constable Dragons. At last the King waved him to a seat in the window niche and Queen Beatrix called for tea and cakes.

Eduard explained that he wished to set the date for the audition of clerks and accountants. The Minister made no objection. The King picked a day a week hence. The Minister agreed.

"Can you prepare for it in that time?" Murdan asked.

"No doubt about it . . . none at all, Lord Historian. With your kind permission I will begin at once, Majesty."

"Just keep to yourself the fact that I and members of my household will participate as auditors. For reasons of state. I'll send you a list of Special Examiners I will appoint this evening. The names will, of course, be highly confidential."

Wriggles promised all and, bowing and gliding out, he rushed off importantly to set bureaucratic wheels in motion.

"Sire, we Constables will arrange a cordon on the ground and in the air about the capital and the harbor, once the audition is announced," Retruance declared, unwinding himself from a curving line of alabaster columns. "In case our quarry gets word somehow and tries to slip away."

"Very good!" Eduard approved. "Let me know what you'll need to set it up. Your own regiment is currently on duty here in Lexor, as you know. Meanwhile, we'll get our net ready, and see if we can catch a slippery eel."

Six mornings later, twelve magnificently accoutered Royal Heralds appeared in the Great Square before Princess Alix Amanda Alone Palace.

Forming a long, brilliant arc, they winded long-belled golden trumpets and proclaimed officially the Fifth Annual Audition of Accountants and Fiscal Clerks, to be conducted by the Most Honorable Minister of Commerce, Lord Filigrod of Wriggles and his Deputies as prescribed by royal law of Code Trusslo, as amended, on the following Saturday, beginning at seven o'clock in the morning and proceeding until the last clerk or Accountant was duly examined and certified and had renewed his bond.

All wishing to become or to remain registered and bonded as required by royal law for said fiscal positions in the Kingdom of Carolna were herewith summonsed to the Hall of Justice at the appointed times, said times to be published immediately, arranged by seniority, senior Accountants first.

This announcement was followed by a printed broadside which was posted all about the city, including the audit locations and schedule of fees required.

Clem, who'd been fetched from Hidden Lake Canyon by Retruance for the audition, and Tom made the rounds of taverns and public houses frequented by the financial and business community in the city.

News of the audition was on everyone's lips.

A few grumbled, recalling the old days when such government interference with business was unheard of in Lexor. Others admitted it kept unscrupulous coin-nippers and disreputable account-twisters from stealing from private and public purses while pretending to be honest men.

"Nobody really minds," Clem, rather surprised, told King Eduard later that night. "They agree, generally, it's a good idea. Besides, I think they like the attention."

"Good," cried the King. "I'm thinking of announcing a gold medal for *Best Accountant in the Kingdom*. That should calm the carpers a bit."

"The strongest impression I got," Tom added to the Woodsman's report, "was the Accountants and their fiscal clerks all welcome audition as a holiday."

"I counted on that," the King said, throwing back his head in a great laugh. "And it won't do any harm for the crown to reward some important business figures, either.''

Owing to the number of applicants involved, Tom, Manda, Clem (by special appointment from the King, for he held no patent of nobility), Murdan, Granger Gantrell of Morningside, and Ffallmar of Ffallmar Farm and his wife Rosemary, who all knew Plume very well by sight, were assigned hearing rooms in the Hall of Justice in which to conduct auditions.

With that many auditors, Tom figured for Manda, the one thousand four-hundred-odd candidates could be examined in a single day.

"We thought of appointing Peter," Murdan told Queen Beatrix. "But it seemed like too much of a temptation for him. Reformed or not, my dear Queen, it's still better to watch our Peter carefully, I say."

"And I heartily agree," cried the diminutive Queen. "Manda's sure he's turned over a new leaf, but I'll never quite trust Peter Gantrell."

"TELL me again," begged Manda of Tom the next morning as they dressed. "What will I do if Plume appears at *my* court?"

"Look right through him and write down his assumed name and where he's employed. Nothing else. If he bolts at the sight of you? Send the guards to chase him down and arrest him. But knowing Plume . . . well, he's a cool cucumber and I don't think he'll bolt."

"And if he gets away from the policemen when they try to arrest him," Clem added, "trust the Dragons to catch him and take him firmly in claw."

"There's no doubt about that," said Manda rather grimly. "Well, we'd better get started, hadn't we?"

TOM'S courtroom was a low, square, ground-level room paneled in dark, old oak and smelling faintly and not unpleasantly of horse sweat, manure, oiled leather, and strong disinfectants. It was, in normal course of business, a court of small claims specializing in contract disputes involving horse dealers . . . notoriously sharp operators.

Tom was assisted by two civil servants who would know the answers to difficult questions and points of law . . . he hoped.

He promptly forgot their names. In his mind he referred to them, respectively, as the Horse and the Mouse. The first whinnied and snorted a lot, while the Mouse very diffidently made quiet suggestions and shuffled his papers nervously.

The procedure was quite simple. Applicants were called in order of seniority and came, one at a time, before the bench.

Tom confirmed their names according to the list he'd been given. The Mouse riffled through his records to find previous licensing information on each. Most of them were renewals; only a few, late in the day, were new applicants.

The Horse asked the required questions in a loud nasal voice and the Mouse verified personal information, including name of current employer, and home and office addresses.

If they recommended granting or extending the license and accepted the fee, the Mouse merely nodded to Tom who applied the King's privy seal to the man's new certificate, then dated and signed it "Thomas of Hidden Lake Canyon, in the name of Eduard Ten, King of Carolna."

Most cases went smoothly and quickly, taking no more than two or three minutes.

New applicants presented references and employment records, and vouched for their accuracy under oath, administered by the Horse.

Tom did what he could to put these poor novices at ease, welcoming them to their new profession and reminding them to perform diligently and honestly for their employers, who stood near the back of the room looking gloomy and nervous.

At half-past ten o'clock Tom used his prerogative as Deputy Minister *Pro Tempore* to call a short break. He sipped hot tea, nibbled a walnut muffin, and used the quarter-hour break to check over a new batch of applicants presenting their credentials at the door.

There were old, stooped clerks and young, bright Accountants, all squinting from reading cramped and faded entries in vast ledgers. The handful of young hopefuls sprinkled through the throng, applicants for the first time, were quite nervous and very anxious.

He didn't see Plume's name, of course, nor his face in the waiting crowd. Nor anyone there who might be the missing Accountant in disguise.

The greatest number of renewals were middle-aged Elves ... with a sprinkling of ladies ... obviously middle-class, comfortably off, well fed, sure of themselves and their skills. They dressed conservatively and behaved gravely, taking themselves and their work quite seriously.

A few were obviously well-to-do businessmen who owned their own counting houses or banks and considered it rather a nuisance to be relicensed by the King's young son-in-law. They had sense enough to keep silent about it in Tom's presence, however.

The Librarian greeted them all, rich and poor, young and old, gravely and politely, and warmly congratulated them on their successful auditions.

NOONTIME recess came at last.

Tom went off to find Manda in a larger courtroom on the second floor. They walked slowly across the square to luncheon in the private suite they maintained in Alix Amanda Palace.

"No sign of the bloody rascal," groused Clem, who joined them there. "I will say that I've gained respect for these money-counters . . . more than I ever thought I would. One knew as much about the fur trade as I do."

"Gain is the purpose of most enterprises, even furtrapping," Manda laughed. "And Princessing. Several have tried to get me to invite them to Hidden Lake House to keep our books."

"What did you answer?" her husband asked around a minced ham sandwich. "We'll need an Accountant shortly. It takes me more and more time to handle business details, I find."

"I took names and made notes," Manda assured him. "Another cup of tea? It'll keep you awake this long afternoon. Oh, my. When I was a little Princess, I never knew being a Royal Minister was such ardent . . . I mean *arduous* . . . work."

She went off to see how sunny Gale was doing in the next room.

"She loves it," chuckled Clem. "I detest it, but *she* was born to do things like this, I vow."

"Not me," groaned Tom. "I wish we were off fishing or riding down to Greenlevel. It's a beautiful fall day for outdoor things."

"Actually it's raining, in case you didn't notice," snorted Murdan, just arrived under a large, red umbrella with a gold handle. "Give me tea. I got halfway across the square and it came down like a waterfall."

King Eduard and Queen Beatrix came in, having stopped to see their own children at their lunch, and to look in on their granddaughter, blissfully being nursed by Manda in a wide window overlooking the rain-slicked square.

"I need tea also," sighed Beatrix, accepting a cup. "I was so wearied by noon that I was sure if Plume stepped up to the bench and announced himself, I wouldn't have known what he said.''

"Buck up, my dear," cried her royal husband. "Obligations and all that. I had trouble keeping my eyes open myself. I must be getting old."

Tom walked Manda back across the wet square to the court a few minutes before two, holding her hand and talking about odds and ends, of babies, business, and about Hidden Lake House. Then he returned to his own horsey courtroom to resume hearings.

At a quarter of six, with ten more applicants still to process, Tom wearily called a halt for a stretch of legs and breath of fresh air.

As he stepped into the corridor, a panting page handed him a folded note, bowed quickly, and skipped away, several other notes clutched in hand.

The note was in the King's neat, controlled script.

> *Tom:*
> *Beatrix has spotted our man. She is positive. Retruance and the other Dragons have been alerted, but the Queen doesn't think Plume knew he was recognized. He's only seen her once or twice, as you know. We are in luck. See me in the Cabinet Room after you finish your auditions, please.*
> > *Eduard*

The Librarian gulped in excitement and started off down the hall, but drew up after three steps.

He had to finish his auditions.

"Well, I don't think old Plume'll be able to slip out of Retruance's net," he muttered to himself, wishing he felt more confident than he sounded.

He called the Audit Commission to order five minutes

early and clamped a tight control on his impatience through the final hour.

"Court is adjourned, having completed its task as assigned by our gracious King, Eduard Ten Trusslo," intoned the Horse. "Honorable Sir Thomas Librarian of Overhall and . . . er . . . Hidden Lake Canyon Achievement presiding."

"Pop the gavel, please, sir," whispered the Mouse in Tom's ear. "And we can go home to good meals and loving families."

Tom rapped once with the gavel, hard enough to crack the handle in two, and was out of the room a few hour-long minutes later, after shaking hands with everybody who'd remained, hoping to talk to him about a position at his new Achievement.

"Later, I'm afraid," Tom said several times. "Call on us. I'm not quite ready to hire yet. You understand? Thank you, thank you."

He sprinted up the wide stair to collect his Princess. They walked quickly together across the square in heavy rain, nodding and smiling to the good Lexor burghers hurrying on their way home.

"Where *is* he?" cried Manda when they entered the Royal Cabinet. "Where's that thieving, lying, cheating, miserable little pip-squawk of an Accountant?"

End Game

"WE got ourselves tied down by our own bureaucracy," Tom complained, half-humorously. "We all had to finish business before we could take up the chase."

"No problem, actually," Murdan said soothingly. "The Constables are perfectly capable . . ."

"Of course," sighed the weary young Librarian, plunking himself into a plush armchair. "But I'd rather be *in* the chase than sitting here in comfort, waiting for news."

"Have some cold chicken and a salad," urged Beatrix, laying a comforting hand on her son-in-law's arm. "The Dragons'll need us to help them, sooner than later, I imagine."

"I certainly hope so," sighed Eduard. "Listen, everybody . . ."

Family and close friends gathered about the King.

"Everybody here? Well, then . . . we're going to sit down quietly, eat a good supper, maybe play whist or a game or two of hearts. My wife and my daughter must see to their children, of course. The rest of us will await news from the Constables. It's all we *can* do at the moment."

"That . . . and worry," muttered Tom, shaking his head.

"Eat something and relax," Manda advised them all. "We may be here all night."

Tom, Clem, Manda, and Mornie found a comfortable corner and began a game of double cribbage to pass the time. The King lay down on a couch and closed his eyes, more to set an example to the others than to sleep.

Queen Beatrix took up a bit of needlepoint and chatted

quietly with the Historian about printing books and lessons for her children, once they were old enough for formal schooling.

Several hours passed.

Very slowly.

CAPTAIN Graham of Overhall, fully armed and rattling with sword, dagger, chain mail, and loosened helmet visor, entered the King's sitting room well after midnight.

Tom glanced up at him and pointed at the far corner, where Murdan was asleep on a settee much too short for his length, snoring softly. He awoke at a touch, however.

"What news?"

Graham gestured his sleepy employer out into the hall so they could speak. Tom went out at once, with Clem, Mornie, and Manda trailing behind.

"Pigeon mail from the Constables?" Manda asked the old soldier.

"Indirectly, Princess," the Overhall captain said, handing Murdan a piece of folded parchment. "From the Bailiff of Lakehead."

The Historian read the scrawled note, reread it, and passed it on to Tom and Manda.

Tom read it aloud to the rest, who were still rubbing sleep from their eyes.

From Kedry, Bailiff of Lakehead County:
Retruance Constable stopped to speak to Lord
Mayor Fellows briefly but an hour since. He asked
me to tell you that his quarry seems to be headed
to either Ffallmar Farm or Overhall . . . or points
beyond.
    Retruance said the Dragons will send for their

Companions as soon as the quarry's course is con-
firmed. He predicts a long chase.

                                    Your Ob'd'nt Servant
                                    ... Kedry

Murdan nodded, his forehead furrowed in worry.

"Old Plume's moving fast. Lakehead, already. And why
Overhall, I wonder?"

"The garrison's on alert," insisted Graham to his liege.
"They'll defend Overhall to the death, M'Lord."

"I'm sure of it, old friend," the Historian said softly.
"But I would rather be there than here, if that's where the
action is."

"So would we all," exclaimed Manda.

"I suggest we Dragon Companions prepare to leave as
soon as Furbetrance or Hetabelle come," Tom urged.

"The best preparation would be some more sleep," Murdan said. "I'll wake the King—and wake you all when the
Dragons come."

He thanked Graham warmly, recommending to him a
few hours of sleep also.

"You'll go with us, of course," Murdan told the Overhall Guards Captain. "Set the rest of your men with you
here on fast horses and start them for Overhall, at once!"

"Aye, Historian. Get some sleep, too, if you can."

But for most of them, sleep came very slowly, if at all.

"I rule out Ffallmar Farm," Retruance Constable had said to
his younger brother some hours before. "He may have reason to go to Overhall, even if he knows the garrison is on
wakeful guard. But not Ffallmar Farm. Nobody's there."

Furbetrance had nodded wordlessly, concentrating on
keeping up with his older brother. Arbitrance and Hetabelle
had turned back after the brief pause at Lakehead, to bring
up the Companions as quickly as possible.

The fleeing Accountant was making use of some sort of

Flying Spell. He traveled fast . . . fast, that is, for anything except a Dragon in a hurry.

The Dragon brothers circled down to silent Overhall in the first light of a wet dawn.

IN a heavy drizzle of early fall, the Historian and his party, including Tom, Manda, and Clem, arrived nine hours later aboard Hetabelle and her father-in-law. They were all exhausted, windblown, and concerned.

"Not a sign beyond here," Retruance reported, once they were ensconced in front of the fireplace in the Great Hall. "The trace completely disappears."

Tom poked a log, raising a torrent of sparks that shot up the chimney.

"Magick, is it?" he asked.

"Probably," replied the Historian. "What say you, Arcolas?"

"If it was magick, it'd be easy to trace, Liege Lord. Very strong magic leaves strong traces," the Physician-Magician told them. "He was in and out before I even detected his presence."

"He came in the middle of the night, and showed not a light at all," said Captain Graham after talking to his guardsmen. "I've checked and double-checked the duty men . . . and those off duty, as well. No sign nor sound. Nothing!"

"No one blames you or your men, Graham," said Murdan.

"Actually, I *was* aware of someone approaching last evening," the Overhall Physician admitted. "I couldn't tell *who* or from *where*, but *someone* was approaching. I thought it might be you, Lord Historian. Or Sir Thomas."

"Did you detect us Dragons coming?" asked Retruance. "With two of us, Arcolas, it would seem . . ."

"I knew it was you almost at once, of course," Arcolas

insisted. "Very clearly. Plume's magick is *strong* magicking, I vow, Sirs. I'm the first to admit it's beyond my learning."

The company sat in silence for a time, each preoccupied with his own thoughts.

Finally, Tom sat up straighter and said, "Murdan? We're wasting our time like this."

"What do you recommend? Aside from sending one of the Dragons for a professional Wizard like Shuttledock or Longbeam, I'm stumped completely."

"We still have a very good tracker here," Tom said, pointing at Clem. "If Plume touched ground anywhere nearby, Clem should be able to tell us where and when, within reason."

"Perhaps," said Clem. "It'll take time. We should search the castle from bottom to top, very closely, first."

"Start at the Accountant's old haunts . . . his apartment, his office, and so on. Work outward from there," Retruance suggested from the window.

"He came here either to hide . . . or to fetch something, I suppose," said Tom, sounding thoughtful. "Yes, if he came to get something secreted away here, it'd most likely be close to his working and living areas, where he could get at it easily. Money, perhaps? I'll go with you, Clem. My tired eyes may help with your searching."

Murdan nodded his agreement.

Tom and Clem went off to Middle Tower and the Historian dashed off a note to King Eduard, who had stayed at his post in Lexor, along with the queen and Manda. He handed it to Graham to dispatch by mail pigeon. "After you've done that, I think it best we make our own inspection of the premises. We've lived here longer than anybody."

"At your service, Historian," the soldier said, saluting. "I'll be back in ten minutes."

• • •

"MISTRESS Plume is off a-visiting her sister down at Sprend," said a chambermaid. "She left three weeks ago, after the Lord Historian departed for the south, Sirs."

"Very well," decided Clem. "We'll have to pick or smash our way inside."

He drew a thin skinning blade from his boot sheath and began probing the heavy iron lock on Mistress Plume's door.

It swung open at his first soft touch.

"Unlocked," Tom cried.

"He's been here, then," decided the Woodsman. "Mistress Plume woulda locked up tight before she left."

They entered the suite of three small rooms deep within Middletower and began searching it carefully for signs of the Accountant's last visit. Clem's sharp eyes covered every inch of the floor, walls, and ceiling, as well as the furniture.

Mistress Plume, a local lady, had married the Accountant shortly after he'd come to Overhall. With her husband gone for several years, the apartment was largely her own with few signs of her missing husband.

"Oh-*ho*," cried Clem at last. "A bit of mortar dust here behind the bed. There must be a secret compartment here in this wall."

He showed Tom where a square of stone in the wall behind an old arras was loose. With the point of his knife he pried it away from its fellows, disclosing a deep, square cavity.

An empty cavity.

"Whatever he came for, he found."

"Most likely," agreed Clem. "Up to this point the Dragons could follow his tracings. Beyond here . . . he disappeared. Stands to reason whatever he picked out of this hiding hole helped him disappear, wouldn't you guess?"

"Must be," Tom sighed.

He sat on the neatly made bed, thinking. Clem ranged about the apartment, poking under things, examining the poor lady's underclothing and some rather sad souvenirs of her failed marriage.

After a quarter-hour the Librarian rose, gestured to his friend, and they left the Accountant's rooms to go out into Middle Courtyard. The friends sat side by side on the well curbing, listening to the Overhall children at play in new rain puddles and to the faint murmuring of Gugglerun.

Shortly the Historian and Retruance found them there.

"Not a single sign, dammit," Murdan swore, sounding both angry and weary. "There may be hidden corners even *I* don't know of. I think we'd better dig out old plans and search more carefully, m'boy."

"No, he's not here," Tom said flatly. "He's flown off where we won't easily find him."

"To the deepest jungles of Isthmusi? Or the cold Northern Wastes?" asked Retruance. He'd been searching the surrounding area from the air, with no luck at all.

"No, if I'm right, he's fled west, back to his own real Master. He's failed here at whatever he was supposed to accomplish."

"That's a relief . . . if true," Murdan puffed, seating himself on the curbing also. "How do you know it, son?"

"No one can know for sure, but I *think* he came here to recover something called the Blue Stone. . . ."

"The stone old Boldface found? *Ah*. I begin to see." Retruance snorted fire. "That unknown mage in Byron's story . . . the one who sent him to Eversmoke. Across the sea in . . . whatever he called that far place."

"Hintoo. My *guess*," said Tom. "Also my hope. But it leaves our mystery unsolved, Sir. Who brought me here? Who sent Plume to unseat Eduard by encouraging and abetting Gantrell? And then stirred up the Rellings to invade Carolna?''

''Whoever it was hoped to destroy the very fabric of Carolna, and leave it powerless. Why? Conquest? Revenge?'' Retruance shook his head, mystified.

''Conquest,'' Murdan muttered. ''With Peter on the throne . . . or the real power behind a helpless Queen Alix Amanda Two? We could have been conquered easily enough.''

''But as you've said once or twice before,'' the Dragon smiled, ''my Companion was the foreign flavor that spoiled their stew.''

Tom sighed. ''We may never know for sure.''

''We might send old Byron to this Rajal place, and give him some cash to spread around. He could do a few useful spells, maybe? And then he could look for answers,'' suggested the Historian. ''Quietly, of course. Hintoo's a large and powerful Empire.''

''Totally lacking in Dragons, according to Byron,'' said Retruance. ''There used to be Dragons in the west, I know. It's been something of a mystery why they disappeared. A conundrum of sorts, among Dragon-folk. I wonder . . .''

''The Dragon-folk disappeared . . . and I appeared. Maybe some day we'll know why,'' Tom said. ''Goodness knows I'm not looking forward to another foreign adventure. But, as Murdan evidently believes, we may still be in some danger, here in Carolna. Revenge, if nothing else.''

Murdan rose, stretched his arms wide, and groaned.

''I think I'll go take a nice, long, hot bath. It's beyond me! I feel strongly that danger has passed—at least for a while. You can go back to furnishing your house and bringing water to your desert, Librarian. After the fall Session, at any rate.''

''And I want to talk to Byron Boldface,'' said the great

green-and-gold Dragon. "Will you go with me, Dragon Companion?"

Tom stood, thinking hard and silently for several moments.

"Not until things are well in hand in the Canyon, Retruance, my very dear friend. And Manda and the child safe, and the winter crops sown in the Canyon. And the desert irrigation begun. So much to do and so many people depending on me and you!"

"There'll be time to find a villain, later," agreed the Dragon.

"No story ever *really* ends, of course," said Princess Alix Amanda Trusslo-Whitehead of Hidden Lake Canyon Achievement.

Her husband nodded. "We'll find out more of the story later, perhaps. For now, precious Princess, we've a house to finish and a home to furnish, a daughter to raise, and a desert to tame . . . *somewhat*, at least."

Lady Gale of Hidden Lake Canyon waved her plump, pink arms gleefully at her father. Tom took her on his lap and counted her toes, much to the child's unending delight.

And, if truth be told, to the delight and contentment of her papa and mama also.